First Case of Beers

Also by P.M. LaRose

Beers on Ice
Bayou Beers
Beers Tapped Out
Beers Abroad
Beers Ahead
Bet on Beers

First Case of Beers

A Chilling Mystery

P.M. LaRose

liquid
rabbit
publishing

Cover design and illustration by P.M. LaRose

Liquid Rabbit Publishing
2010 Glasgow Ave.
Baton Rouge, LA 70808

pmlarose.com
email: BeersAhead@gmail.com
Facebook: PM LaRose
Facebook: Beers Detective Agency

ISBN 978-1-7324951-6-6

Second Edition: September 2022
10 9 8 7 6 5 4 3 2

For Gigi

FOREWORD

BACK IN THE DAY, shopping at a big department store used to be glamorous. It was one of those simple pleasures in life.

Mom and Dad would get dressed up in fine clothes: Mom in a smart dress, high heels, a hat and gloves, and Dad in a suit. The kids also would need to be somewhat presentable: clean underwear, socks and shoes, mud washed off the face. Then they would load in the station wagon on a Saturday afternoon and visit the world of commerce at a fine store such as Saks or Macy's or Bergdorf Goodman. Here in the Deep South, it was I.H. Rubenstein's, D.H. Holmes or Goudchaux's. It was like going into someone's mansion.

This is how I envisioned it as a kid, and how I thought it would be when I joined the ranks of La Scala employees. La Scala was one of those fine, old department stores, nattily attired in the splendors of Italian art, history and architecture. You entered another world, separate from the mundane existence of everyday life.

Of course, it didn't play out that way. My idealized vision of a grander environment was constantly marred by the trials and tribulations of human survival. I'm mainly talking about the crime and murder. My background, sportswriting, didn't set me up for it.

Sure, Mom had some experience in retail. For a while, after quitting her elementary schoolteacher job, she worked at Woolworth. But that was a totally different experience.

Woolworth sold stuff you *needed* but didn't necessarily want: toothpaste, pencils, iron-on patches, Scotch tape and bubblegum. OK, so I wanted *and* needed bubblegum. Try being a 10-year-old without it.

On the other hand, La Scala sold things people *wanted* but didn't necessarily need: Gucci handbags, Cardin suits, high-end food processors, cologne, etched glassware and chocolate candy shaped like hearts. Well, maybe the chocolate was needed.

For folks who perhaps couldn't afford to live like they were rich, escaping into this fantasy land for a short time was a welcome respite.

I equate it to the airlines of years ago, when flying was likewise glamorous. The stewardesses were all babes, they treated you like royalty, brought you a hot meal and supplied a deck of cards if requested. They pinned wings on the kids, while Mom and

Dad coolly smoked and sent clouds of burnt tobacco through the fuselage. It was glorious.

Perhaps not the smoking part. In the station wagon, we could roll down the windows. Not so much in the friendly skies.

But we all need a bit of glamor, elegance in our lives. If sojourning to a classy department store rocks your world, I'm happy for you.

My experience at La Scala taught me otherwise. There is no escape from the travail of your own life. It will follow you, waiting to pounce when you least anticipate it. You can't get away or outrun it or hope it bypasses you.

In some ways, I miss La Scala, looking back on it through the veil of years. My short tenure shaped me into the person I am today. I would say "man," but that implies growing up, maturing. I'm still waiting for that to happen. In my head, I'm eternally a kid.

Simpler times, for sure. Someone else made the decisions for me, whereas now I am charged with that duty as CEO of Beers Detective Agency. Having Lena and Tina beside me makes it a joy some days, a raging headache others. They are dear friends and exasperating partners at the same time. But I wouldn't have it any other way.

Our agency wasn't established back then, but this case is what I consider our first foray into joint detecting work, the roots of the establishment of our business.

I still occasionally hear from La Scala cohorts and the big boss, but can view that world from a distance, like watching a scene inside a snow globe. It's better that way.

A word about the codes: La Scala developed a system of alerting store personnel to any situations that might arise. In this case, it was a situation involving a customer. But there are many codes that can be announced. For example, Code 81—truck breakdown at the loading dock.

In the early days, the system used a series of flashing red and green lights to indicate the number. Clerks would punch in a code on a panel under the counter.

For instance, a green, a red, two greens, two reds would equal a Code 12—dead horse on a delivery cart. The reds were the stop signals, signifying a break between numbers, with two reds indicating the end of the code. One green, one red, seven greens and two reds would report a Code 17—a jam in the pneumatic tube system.

These codes were transmitted to the business office, where a clerk would interpret and alert the necessary staff to solve the problem.

Some of the codes, obviously, are obsolete, since tubes and horses are rarely used nowadays. And the current transmission method is simpler, via phone. Solutions, however, can be time consuming and frustrating.

Also, an explanation of my note-taking system. I developed it over my years in the newspaper business, as a necessary adjunct to interviews with sometimes hard-to-understand subjects. To me it is a secret language, and I have yet to discover anyone who can decipher my arcane scribblings without my assistance.

Without a notepad, I wouldn't be able to reconstruct this case or the ones that follow. It is absolutely vital, and I refer to it constantly for prompts to my leaky memory. One day, my notepads will be studied by archaeologists, who might conclude they are an indication that aliens did live among humankind.

After reading back through my first case, I decided it might be helpful to provide a rudimentary schematic of the store, so you see the playing field I was on. It's a rough sketch. The bedding department, for example, also encompassed bedroom furniture, oriental rugs and, somewhat incongruously, trendy plumbing fixtures. But it shows the main departments I dealt with on a daily basis.

So join me on this walk down memory lane. For me, it's always a bit painful. I trust it will be instructive and entertaining for you.

Jim Biersovich
August 2020

Oh, the weather outside is frightful...
—"Let It Snow" by Sammy Cahn & Jule Styne

La Scala Minneapolis

9 Executive Offices

8 Bedding · Men's Shoes · Luggage

7 Break Room · Kitchenware

6 Men's Dept. · Seasonal Gifts · Candy Counter

5 Purses · Jewelry · Watches

4 Electronics · Appliances · Returns

3 Casual Wear · Women's Foundations

2 Women's Shoes · Fashion Wear

1 Sportswear · Cosmetics

B Deli · Sporting Goods · Maint.

1

Tuesday morning, Dec. 14, 1999
11 shopping days till Christmas
Temperature: 29, light snow; wind chill, 24

I looked down from my throne at the North Pole to the line of youngsters stretching down the aisle, around the corner and into sportswear, letting out an audible groan. It was going to be a long lunch hour.

Why, I asked the gods of whimsy, did parents and their drooling hordes have to launch their attacks at noon, right when my belly was eager for satiation? Such is the life of a department store Santa, I thought. Oh well, it's only temporary.

To top it off, I couldn't shake the melody of "Jingle Bell Rock," which had been playing continuously in my head since I caught snatches of it from a passing car on the way in this morning. That's the problem with a brain—it latches onto something trivial and won't let go.

The little squirt on my lap was beginning to wriggle like a large-mouth bass in the bottom of a bateau, wiping his still wet snow boots on my red pants, so I knew it was time to wrap up his session of "gimme, gimme." Not certain what he had asked for, I assured the scamp his Christmas wishes would certainly come true.

"Ho ho ho! Santa likes good little boys, and if you're a good little boy, on Christmas morning, you'll find a lot of joy under your tree." I added for emphasis: "Just be a good little boy." Hah! Fat chance of that, I thought.

It's not that I resented being Santa, if only to fill in for a couple of days until La Scala hired a new jolly olde elf. But these were trying times for someone in my position. Piling the awesome duties

1

of St. Nick on top of store security during the holiday shopping season was a real headache.

And the line of runny-nosed little snots, bound up in their eighteen layers of polar fleece, mittens and knit caps, was interminable.

"Beers. Psst, hey, Beers." It was my elf assistant, Bambi Schroeder, jolting me out of my reverie. I glanced to my left and saw her holding a cell phone out toward me.

"What's up, Bambi?" I whispered.

"Call. Trouble in front-of-store display."

"I can't," I said. "I'm supposed to be Santa." *Jingle bell, jingle bell, jingle bell rock...*

"You gotta. Big trouble. Boss is pissed."

I sighed. "All right. But can Santa's little helper do something with this line?"

"You bet." Bambi turned cheerfully toward the line of little faces, held in place by rope barricades, as I scooted the wiggly tyke off my lap. "Attention, kids. Santa's taking a break now," she announced. "He'll be back in a little bit. Have your Mommy take a number, and Santa will be back shortly."

There were lots of moans and some crying following this tragic announcement, and the kids seemed pretty upset themselves. But a job had to be done, one only Santa could do. That is, Jimmy Biersovich, part-time temporary fill-in Santa.

On the line was my boss, Jane Mertin, who informed me there was a situation developing and I'd better check it out.

She sounded concerned.

As I walked toward the front-of-store display area, I summoned other Christmas tunes to try to rid my thoughts of the dreaded notes currently plaguing me. I also pondered my delicate situation as chief of security for La Scala's flagship location, right in the heart of downtown Minneapolis.

The owner, Johnny Scalabrino, lives in a mansion along the parkway to the south. His other La Scala locations are in Las Vegas, Chicago and San Francisco, but this is home base.

With 10 floors and more than 350 employees, it was a fairly large business in which I was a small cog.

Stuck halfway between upper management and the rank-and-file, I walked a precarious line each day, careful not to get on the wrong side of either group. No one wanted trouble, but in my 10 short months here, I always seemed to be in the middle of it.

I wondered if the security chiefs at the other locations had any more clout, but I suspected they were peons as well. One day we might all get together and compare notes.

"Jingle Bell Rock" was making me mental. I tried to force the needle into a new groove...*Please allow me to introduce myself, I'm a man of wealth and taste...*

MY NAME IS James Alfred Biersovich. I like my initials—JAB. Always wanted to be called Jab, but you can't pick your nickname.

I tried for a long time: "Just call me Jab." But everyone calls me Beers. Always have, always will.

Fourth-generation American of very mixed lineage. There's Italian, Slav, Irish, Armenian and French in my background, although if you ask me a question in one of those tongues, the reply is always "Huh?"

One brother, Tom, one sister, Jean. Mom and Dad retired in South Florida until Mom died. Now Dad lives here in the Twin Cities. He came out of retirement recently and works part time at La Scala. I can't figure out whether that's good or bad.

We moved around a lot when we were kids. Technically, born in Butte, Montana, but that's because we were on vacation. Family camping trip. Yeah, I was a little early. Surprised my folks almost as much as my big brother, who was a worldly five-year-old at the time. Sis came along later. She had the sense not to ruin a vacation.

Grew up in Cicero, Illinois, New Orleans, Phoenix, Blacksburg, Virginia, and Laurel, Vermont, so I consider myself a man of the world. Or at least the American world.

When I was in grammar school, I grew up fast. By eighth grade, I was the biggest kid in the class, center on the basketball team and a decent inside linebacker. Then came high school, when late bloomers started passing me by almost daily. I stopped growing at six feet—actually five-eleven and three-quarters, to be accurate. Average weight, but any current growth is from the belly out, unfortunately.

I live in a high-rise apartment overlooking the Walker museum and sculpture garden in the heart of Minneapolis. Don't ask what it costs—it's almost criminal. But I have my standards, and a bit of inheritance from Mom certainly helps.

Looks? Well, I like to think I look like Tom Selleck, just without the moustache. My friends don't see it, however. A couple think I look more like Tom Hanks. But what do they know?

Despite the Mick Jagger lyric playing in my head and my current place of employ, I'm not exactly a fashion plate. My typical getup: black high-top sneakers, frayed-at-the-cuffs black jeans, black Devo sweatshirt, black English driving cap pulled low on my head. I guess I'm Johnny Cash. Today, of course, I'm Santa.

Forgot to mention the black mark against my work history.

I'm a shamus. That's fancy lingo for store security. My job is to keep merchandise from walking out the store, and everything else my boss decides I should do.

Jane Mertin, vice president of facilities and my immediate supervisor, is a nice lady. She's a few balls short of a full rack, but I like her. Besides, she took a chance on me and gave me a job when I thought I might have to really learn a skill to get gainful employment.

You see, I used to be a sportswriter.

That's another story. For now, I had to see what new crisis was threatening the viability of the good ship La Scala.

LA SCALA IS SOMEWHAT OF AN ODDITY in downtown Minneapolis.

Old man Scalabrino, whose parents immigrated from Italy, started the store in the 1940s in a converted office building on Minneapolis' main thoroughfare, Hennepin Avenue. He had the facade renovated to resemble the famous Milan opera house of the same name, with fake columns and arched windows.

Inside, tributes to that heritage predominate, with the Italian flag flying above the checkout counter in every department and murals of landmarks throughout: the Leaning Tower of Pisa, Vatican City, the canals of Venice, the Ponte Vecchio, the Colosseum. On Italian holidays, you can hear "La Traviata" or "Rigoletto" wafting through the store's speaker system.

Walkways of Italian marble and terra cotta walls present a veneer of class and charm missing in most modern department stores. This is perhaps lost on practical Minnesotans, who are renowned for their frugality and simplicity. Just give them a bargain and they'll be happy.

When Johnny Scalabrino took over his old man's business, he maintained those testimonials to Italian culture, replicating them in stores in three more cities.

And now the usual decor was festooned with the trappings of Christmas—lights, garlands, holly, tinsel and fake snow. In addition, there was a theme to the current sale that tied in with the end of the year: "Millennium Mania."

The marketing folks went round and round on that one. At first, they came up with "The End Is Near!" That seemed too dire; some of the veeps thought it would scare away customers. So they tried "Don't Panic!" Again, a little too strident for the Christmas season.

After a few more misguided efforts ("Don't Worry About Crashing Your Computer—Crash a Party!"), they settled on the simplest slogan, because they really had no clue whether the world was coming to an end.

Gerald Difansa, our artiste window dresser, stated outright that he had no way of possibly depicting "the end of the year, decade, century or millennium" in his displays, and he was just going to stick with a Christmas theme.

So the marketing brainiacs settled for Millennium Mania sale signs on every rack of merchandise. Most folks, I imagine, were more interested in the discount percentage listed on the sign than the theme.

Christmas fits the La Scala decor nicely. After all, the Italian flag's colors are green, white and red. But the marketing gurus decided the sale needed its own color scheme, to make it more noticeable. They opted for purple and gold, the Vikings' colors. It helped that the football season was still in progress, and the team had hopes of making the playoffs.

The clashing color schemes grated on my sensibilities, making me wish for a rapid conclusion to the season. Not to mention that dreaded North Pole.

Arriving at FOS, as we call it in the biz, I spotted Tina McEntire, cosmetician extraordinaire and surreptitious security staffer, along with Gerald, who was obviously upset. Tina—short, sturdy, the girl-next-door-with-an-attitude. Gerald—tall but muscular, effeminate, dramatic—all the symptoms of a raging queen, and several piercings to boot.

He was a hard guy to figure out. He looked like an athlete, used to be one, so I've heard. But his mannerisms screamed something else. In my short time at La Scala, I hadn't had many dealings with him, but they always seemed to be histrionic.

Gerald was wound a little too tight.

"I just don't understand who would do something like this," Gerald was saying. "It's just horrible!" He was fanning himself as he said this, despite the frigid atmosphere of the store, which was maintained at a constant 66 degrees to keep customers moving and in a frame of mind to purchase high-priced winter outerwear.

Tina, for her part, was carefully surveying the scene while trying to calm Gerald. Thank God for Tina, I thought. Her relaxed demeanor always made me happy with my choice for first security assistant—unofficial, of course.

"So what's the matter?" I asked, reaching into my costume and pulling out my reporter's notepad. Tina nodded over to Gerald and said, "Steroid-boy here is a bit miffed that his mannequins have been messed with. Look."

She pointed toward the opened panels of the main window, where a Christmas scene had been transformed into something lewd. The pilgrim-looking mother, in bonnet and petticoat, was bent over the kitchen table, her skirt hiked up and pantaloons touching the floor. The last thing customers want to see is bare mannequin rump, I thought.

"It's ghastly! Who would do this?" Gerald said, alternately wringing his hands and fanning himself.

"Settle, Gerald. Just tell me from the beginning," I said, glancing over at Tina and winking. I looked out toward Hennepin Avenue and observed the small but growing crowd that was pointing and giggling at the scene.

"Well, I just went on midmorning break, a little later than usual because my doctor has advised that I space out my meals a bit mo— What's with the Santa getup?"

"Gerry," I said. "The mannequin?"

He glared at me. "My name is Gerald." He let that sink in a moment. "Right. Well, like I say, I was on my break, in the break room, y'know, and people started coming in and snickering. At me," he added, with a rise in his voice. He was still fanning himself. "So, I just tried to ignore them, because you know how nasty some people here can be, and I just don't—"

"Gerald! The mannequin!"

"Oh. OK. So I finish up my break—you know those breaks are all too short and management needs to consider something a little more…" He noticed my stern look and broke off his train of thought. "Anyway, I had to straighten up in the back and check the window design website, and got back out here to find this!" He gestured with both hands at the decidedly un-Puritanical scene before us.

"You have no idea how this got this way?" I asked, already certain of the answer.

"I should say not!" Gerald said. "This is an abomination!"

Tina nudged me, and I could hear her snicker lightly.

"Why didn't you notice this when you came in this morning?" I asked.

"The panel was closed, and I came in through the warehouse. I was setting up the Valentine's Day exhibit at my workbench," he explained, defensively.

"So I suggest you fix it ASAP. We'll find the culprit," I assured Gerald, who by now was in that lip-trembling-on-the-verge-of-tears state that I'd seen him in before. Sheesh, I thought. Why do we have to hire the overly sensitive?

While Gerald set to work fixing his tableau, Tina and I walked back toward the cosmetics counter, most surely thinking the same thing: This is a crisis? Par for the course, I say, in the zoo that is La Scala.

"You got any ideas about this?" I asked her.

"Some hunches. But it could be anyone—one of the new guys in sporting goods, maybe. It's just a prank, probably someone messing with Gerald's head," she added with a shrug. "No big deal."

"Bambi said the boss was on a rampage about it. Is that true?"

Tina smiled. "Maybe she got the wrong impression. You know how Bambi is." Tina waved and veered off toward the Lancome counter, already shifting gears to her smarmy, you're-my-best-friend customer greeting.

As I walked back toward my post, I peeked around a corner to see Bambi in the middle of a swarm of angry mothers. I decided it might be best to lay low a bit longer, give things time to cool down.

Heading up toward the break room on seven, I ran into Jane. She was wearing a frown and grumbling to herself about something.

"Hi, Jane," I said, breaking her concentration. I was hoping for confirmation that she was in the dark about the true nature of this latest episode of insanity.

"Oh, hi, Beers. Why aren't you at Santa station?" she asked.

"Had to answer a call," I explained. "Gerald had a minor situation."

"Oh, right." She nodded, thankfully uninterested in following up. Gerald was a talented window dresser but almost too high-strung to work in the stress-inducing world of retail.

Jane was well aware of his peculiarities. And she was obviously distracted about something else. "Well, let's keep in mind the season and the importance of keeping it all under control," she said in her best management voice.

"Got it. It's handled," I said, nodding to reassure her all was well.

"This is the most important selling season, you know. Also, see me later about the plans for the Christmas party."

"Will do."

"OK. Good," she said. "Well, I'll see you."

"Yes, ma'am," I said. "Have a good day."

As she walked down the aisle toward kitchenware, I let out a breath and again thanked my lucky stars that my boss wasn't the intense, snooping type. As a bonus, I had turned off the broken record of that bad Christmas ditty inhabiting my cranium.

But it was still going to be a long day.

2

Tuesday afternoon
Temperature: 33, overcast; wind chill, 24

I suppose it might be instructive to learn a bit about me and why I'm telling you all this. As with most things in life, the path of my journey into sleuthing was chosen for me by circumstance and the whims of fate. Although I pride myself on parsing and interpreting the course of everyday life through common sense, this adventure was a prime example of the power of serendipity.

Dissecting the logic of life isn't a fetish for me, although it seems to fit me like a wetsuit. It probably first found me at age 6, when the anticipation of Christmas goodies was abruptly replaced by the certainty that Santa couldn't possibly visit every home in the world in one night, and something was terribly wrong with the bedtime story my Mom was reading to me, about a mean giant who stole all the children's presents, but had a change of heart and gave them back. All in one night, of course.

My funk lasted well into puberty as I continued to peek behind the curtains at life's many aspects—religion, sports, politics, science, economics—determining that there was quite a bit more logic in some fields than others.

In sports, for example, I spent far more time examining record books of baseball, basketball and football than actual time participating or watching games. If you crunch the numbers, you can't help but come to the conclusion that for at least half the teams, it's not even worth showing up to play. They might as well disband those teams and use the stadiums for concerts or rummage sales.

Take the Cubs, for instance. Is it really worth it, year after year, to sit through a whole season with the certainty that there will be no title to celebrate at the end of the year?

This critical eye got me in big trouble in high school, naturally, where it battled constantly with the raging hormones of impending adulthood. Dates were disasters, and after a couple of dances and parties that ended with hurt feelings because I refused to play the game and lie about a girl's awful dress or snotty friends, I basically stopped worrying about girls and became an outstanding nerd.

Stints on the school paper and yearbook staffs firmly rooted me in my future, and I gleefully studied journalism in college as a means of cutting through to the truth and making sense of life.

If only common sense were that easy. Events and people conspire to thwart it at every turn, as I was to learn in the puzzling case about to confront me.

DRINKING A COLA in the far corner of the employee lounge, I pondered my fate, as I always did when situations seemed strange. Where had I gone wrong? How did I end up a glorified gofer for an undeservedly rich Mafioso bigwig?

OK, so Johnny Scalabrino wasn't officially in the Mafia—there were plenty of rumors, nothing substantiated—he was still the kind of boss you were scared to cross, if only for the name and the reputed family history. I mean, your first impression was here's a kook with too much money and not much above the eyebrows. He frequently sported a monocle and spats, and always carried a putter, even though he never played golf. He wore Armani and Cardin suits that cost as much as an SUV, but always accessorized with a bolo tie.

I watched how Jane and the other vice presidents tiptoed around him on his infrequent visits to the store, even though he looked to all concerned as harmless as your goofy uncle who always drinks a bit too much and tells too many off-color jokes. But he was spending more and more time at the Vegas branch, and in my understanding of math, one wop plus one sin city plus one boatload of money equals one made guy.

After all, I lived in Cicero, Illinois, for a time, a place once owned by probably the most famous mobster, Al Capone. I understood how that worked.

Of course, I had to thank my present position to my foresight in schmoozing a VP. It was my feature on Jane's over-40 soccer team that convinced her I was a talented guy, capable of serving as her security assistant, since the last guy had sealed his resignation by bringing a gun into the executive suite and threatening to shoot someone unless he got some time off.

Ah, Jane. She was a case. I admired and respected her, but I wasn't certain she was cut out to be a corporate vice president. However, she saw something in me that told her I was trustworthy, friendly, cheerful—in other words, a Boy Scout. I had told her I was thinking about getting out of the journalism racket but didn't really know what I wanted to do. She slipped me her card, said call her if I did want out. I did, and the rest is history.

Unfortunately, a degree in journalism doesn't quite prepare a person for the world of high-profit retail, much less provide an advanced understanding of financial principles. Sure, in retail, like journalism, you had to deal with the public on a daily basis, but that's where the similarities ended. In the print world, truth is the goal. In sales, lies aren't necessarily the goal, but they sure get you there faster.

I tried not to think about it too much. Besides, my link with the actual output of retail fabrications and embellishments was only tangential, seeing as I was mainly there to keep the sales trimmed and the ship of fools afloat.

And there were always pirates to contend with. Normally, the security job was little more than busy work: lining up a substitute guard when our normal First Sentinel temp was sick, calling the locksmith when a door jammed, following up fire marshal-mandated fixes (that took a month by itself).

Occasionally, I had to look into a case of shoplifting. This is what we in the business call "shrinkage," a tasteful euphemism for stealing. So far, I had failed to make a collar on my own, but I was always on alert. Very rarely, a customer went postal on a sales clerk, or a deli diner got ill and I had to hand out gift certificates as appeasement.

In short, I handled any strange occurrences that fell outside the jurisdictions of the other departments. That covered a lot of territory. But usually not sabotage. I thought business would be simpler without customers—or employees.

"Hey, Beers, what's with the red suit?"

It was Bibb Tokan, code monkey in the online department. He should talk—his getup was usually more outrageous than any trendy fashion La Scala could offer. Today he had a tie-dyed T-shirt with "LUCKY" stenciled on it, topping green cutoffs and high-heel sandals. His desk was the typical litter of paper, Star Wars figurines, code printouts and pizza-stained paper napkins. His slovenly appearance and pig-sty workspace made me shudder.

"Hi, Bibb," I said. "Santa. Filling in. We're between." We were between Santas because the last fake Jolly Fat Man always left the store a bit wobblier than when he arrived. With the Christmas rush in full swing, and a dearth of viable Santa candidates, I was elected to fill in for a few days.

"You're not fat enough," Bibb said.

But you are, I thought, holding my tongue while gauging the circumference of his midsection. "Yeah, I know," I replied. I considered his stomach and knew he could do the suit proud. Note to self: Send memo to Jane suggesting a more appropriate Santa. "Somebody's gotta do it, and, well, I'm expendable."

"You got that right," Bibb said, chuckling. " 'Hey, Santy, I want a chooo-chooooooo.' " He was snickering as he walked off. If I had had a BB gun, his rear end would have been Swiss cheese, because his parting comment wedged "Chattanooga Choo Choo" into my brainwaves. *Pardon me, boys…* Damnit.

I turned back to my soda and swore to myself that I would update my resume as soon as my shift ended.

I say "shift," but it's not really like I had set hours. I served at the whimsy of Jane and the other veeps who weekly set the agenda for middle management. For example, this week.

My normal early arrival for opening was pushed forward to fit nicely into the prime-time Santa-harassing time slot. The first day wasn't too bad. It was a novelty. Today was looking more like the nightmare before Christmas.

Besides the impatient line of whining kids and exasperated moms awaiting my return, as I walked back toward the throne, I saw Bambi again rushing toward me with the cell phone out in front.

"Beers! Another call!" she said, and let out a huff. I could see by her expression Santa's head elf wasn't exactly the most popular minor celebrity on the floor at the moment. She also looked like she was about to choke me.

"What now?" I asked, taking the phone. "Jim here."

"Mr. Byers, this is George Doone in ladies' foundations, third floor. I need you."

"It's Biersovich. Beers. What's up?" I asked.

"Trouble. Mannequin down. Damn kids!" he half-whispered.

Another mannequin, I thought. What the hell? Has someone got a vendetta against our mannequins all of a sudden, or maybe trying to drive Gerald the short distance to complete dementia? "Be there in a sec," I said, hanging up and tossing the phone back to Bambi. "Gotta check something on three. Be right back."

"Beers! What about the Santa line?" Bambi asked, a note of panic in her voice.

I looked at the waiting line of shuffling, snuffling, fidgeting children. And mothers. Grabbing Bambi by the arm, I pulled her over to the Santa throne and sat her down, then addressed the mob. "Santa's assistant will fill in for me while I attend to some urgent business with my elves." I threw in a ho-ho-ho to make it more authentic, but I could tell they weren't buying it.

Bambi was like a deer in headlights. "Just be a second," I called over my shoulder, hustling toward the elevator as the chorus of whining and moaning rose in pitch.

Mannequins. Real people were bad enough; now I had to contend with problematic fake people.

As I exited the elevator on three, I could see straight ahead a small group gathered near a register. To their left was a fallen mannequin, brazenly sporting a Wonderbra and the skimpiest of bikini panties in a swirling print. Approaching the group, I saw the agitated look on George Doone's face as he listened to an angry woman scold two young boys—perhaps the perpetrators of this and similar crimes? "Morning, ma'am. Doone. I'm Jim Biersovich, store security. Can I assist you?"

"I told these little ragamuffins I'm going to tan their hides when we get home!" the woman said heatedly. The sheepish boys mostly kept their eyes on the floor, occasionally stealing a glance at the mannequin.

"What happened?" I asked.

"I was helping a customer and I heard a crash—" Doone began. He was in his early 60s, balding, thin, actually looked like the prototype for a gentleman's gentleman. Even had the faux British accent.

"These two were playing tag!" the mother almost shouted, pointing at the guilty pair. "I told them to sit quiet for just two minutes. Two minutes! Can't they sit still for two minutes?"

I could tell she was put out about the situation, so I tried to decelerate the rhetoric. "OK, ma'am, no problem. We'll just set it back up and we'll just forget this happened. I'm sure they meant no harm. You know how boys are," I said, putting on a big smile to ease her anger. "No harm, no foul—"

"It's broken!" Doone interjected.

"What? The mannequin?" I asked.

"Yes. Arm. And at the base," he said, pointing.

I looked down and finally noticed that, yes, there was something unusual about this dummy—one arm was off, halfway peeking out from under a rack of teddies, and from the jagged look of the end, it wasn't going back on easily. Also, one foot and ankle remained attached to the metal base. Oh God, I groaned inwardly. Gerald will have a fit. Again.

"Did you alert Gerald?" I asked Doone.

"No," he said nervously, glancing between me and the downed model.

Why is it that people around here are afraid of Gerald, I wondered. He's a muscle-bound wuss. "OK, here's what we do. Ma'am, thank you. I'm sorry this happened,c but we'll take care of it." I ushered her away from the scene, hoping she would calm down, but from the rant that faded in the distance, I could tell the boys were in for more than a tongue-lashing.

"Something's not right," Doone said when I returned.

"What?"

"With the foot. It's not right," he said.

I squatted and took a closer look at the lone foot that remained on the stand, like a bad piece of conceptual art. The break was above the joint where the foot is normally attached to the leg. But the strange part was that most of the break was smooth, except for about a one-inch segment near the front that was jagged. I inched closer to look inside the foot and saw a fine powder. What's this? Someone must have sawn most of the way through the leg, maybe with a hacksaw.

"Did you move it?" I asked Doone, rising quickly.

"Move it? No," he said.

I went behind the counter and dialed the basement. After six rings (as usual), Don Anderson, head of the maintenance crew, picked up. "Yeah?"

"Hey, Don. Jim Biersovich here. I need a cart up on three."

"Big or little?"

"Big," I said. "Oh, and bring some gloves, wouldya?"

"Gloves?" he asked, hanging up the phone without waiting for an explanation.

"Are you going to tell Mr. Difansa?" Doone asked as I walked back out to the scene of devastation.

"Not yet," I told him. "Let's just keep this quiet for a bit, OK?"

"Riiiight." Doone eased back behind the register.

Turning toward the felled statue, I looked for other clues that might lead to a suspect. While the right foot was still stuck to the base, the left showed no signs of damage.

I made some notes. A few minutes later, a young worker from the maintenance group rolled up a bin that looked like an industrial laundry hamper, only color-coded to match the store's red-and-green logo. Trailing him were two other maintenance guys, even younger, looked like teen-agers.

"Is this underwear?" the kid asked. "Whoa! Nice outfit, dude!"

"Foundations," Doone answered indignantly.

The kid's puzzled look told me I needed to translate for him. "That's underwear. And you are...?"

"Bradley. Don said to ask for some beer...?"

"Beers. That's me, Jim Biersovich," I explained. "OK, Bradley, could you pick this mannequin up and bring the cart up to nine? With the gloves, please. You know where the security office is?"

"No. What floor is it on?" he asked, obviously not paying attention. "Whoa! Better outfit, dude!" he said, finally looking down at the mannequin.

"Nine. My office is on the ninth floor. Just roll it up there, ask someone where my office is and leave it outside the door, wouldya?"

"Sure." I looked at the two other guys, who were just standing there.

"It takes three of you to carry this?"

Bradley glanced behind him. "No, man, those are my interns. That's Sergei Strugatsky"—the one on the left nodded—"and that's Pete." The other one waved and said, "Pyotr Alexandrov.

For your serve." He nodded, then said something in a dialect that could have been Russian, Ukrainian, Estonian or any number of Eastern European tongues.

I turned back to Bradley. "And one other thing."

"Yeah?" he asked.

"You brought gloves?"

"Uh, yeah."

"Could you wear them when you pick this up?"

He looked down at the fallen idol, then back at me. "I won't cut myself, if that's what you're worried about."

"No, just wear them, OK?"

"Whatever." He pulled the work gloves from his back pocket, put them on and proceeded to load the broken display into the cart. After he rolled it away, trailed by his interns, I noticed a bit of residue on the floor. I bent down and pinched a bit, rubbing it between my thumb and finger. Powdery, slightly gritty. Hmmm.

Straightening up, I walked over to Doone and told him I'd send the maintenance guys back down to sweep up the floor.

I knew it was beneath his station to actually pick up a whisk broom and tidy up the 2-inch-square spot. There were probably union rules about that anyway.

It was already ten after one and I knew Bambi would be throwing a fit, but I had to secure the evidence. I walked back to the elevators and rode up to the ninth floor, where the executive offices were located. My tiny office was down a back corridor. I saw Bradley leaning against the wall, waiting for me, with the cart blocking the doorway.

"Need the cart back," he said.

"OK, let me just open the office and we can unload it." As I opened the door, I felt his eyes on me.

"You supposed to be Santa or something?" he asked.

"How'd you guess?"

He snickered. "It's not working for me, man."

I sighed. "We're between Santas, OK? I'm just filling in till they get a new one. Just a couple days."

"Whatever."

"Look, can you just put this in the corner over there—and use the gloves?"

"Yeah, yeah, whatever." He donned the gloves again and dropped the mannequin pieces on the floor.

"Thanks," I said, sitting in my worn but comfortable swivel chair as he rolled the cart away. The blinking light on the phone console flashed urgency at me, and the message light on my cell phone, sitting in my inbox, was also blinking. No time for that, I thought. I'll just rest a minute before getting back to the ho-ho-ho-ing routine.

No such luck. The phone started ringing, and after a short debate on whether to answer it, I picked up.

"Jim Biersovich here."

"Beers! Where are you!" Bambi's intense tone, and the voices in the background, told me the situation at the North Pole wasn't good.

"I'm on my way," I told her. "Just had to stop in my office for—"

"Just hurry!" she shouted, hanging up.

Sigh. I guessed I'd better get back there before a riot broke out. I actually hated to put Bambi on the spot like that. Like me, she was drafted for North Pole duty. She couldn't help it that she was stacked like a Playboy bunny and oozed sexuality from every square centimeter of skin surface. As I was closing the door to my office, the phone rang again. Against all common sense, I picked up.

"Jim here."

"Jim, this is Jane." It was my boss, and her tone of concern sent an instant flash of panic through me. "What's going on today? I thought you were Santa? And what's the story in FOS?"

"We had a little situation I had to attend to, nothing major," I tried to reassure her. "I'm just heading back to Santaland." I hoped she wouldn't mention the latest incident.

"Some customers have been complaining…"

"I'm sorry. Couldn't be helped. I was just rushing back there when you called."

"OK. Go on. But tell me later about this thing with the display."

"Don't worry, I will. Bye," I said, hanging up.

The trip back down to the first floor took under a minute, though it seemed like 15 as I juggled the possibilities of two mannequin-related acts of sabotage in one morning. Who could hate a mannequin?

"Santa!"

My concentration was broken by the screeches of several million kids who spotted me as I reapproached my assigned post. I could tell by the angry looks on the moms' faces that they were really put out. Bambi was nowhere around.

"Ho ho ho!" I exclaimed, reclaiming my perch. "Santa is back and ready to talk with all of you children. But Santa needs to try to talk with everyone, so I'm going to ask you to limit your requests to three toys. OK, kids?" I said with a jolly Santa tone. The first little tyke jumped in my lap and immediately began reciting an endless list of requests.

"I want a Ninja Turtle and a Transformer and a color set and a baseball glove and some blue jeans and drums and a Star Wars sword and some—"

"Whoa, whoa, whoa," I cut him off. "You want a lot, young man. OK, Santa wants you to be a good little boy and you'll get some nice things under the tree on Christmas morning." I gently lifted him off my lap, nudged him toward his mother and gestured for the next greedy youngster to ascend the throne.

There was jostling in the line as impatient mothers tried to elbow their way forward, and how a rumble didn't break out without Bambi to help with crowd control I'll never figure out.

But over the next hour I managed to whittle down the throng in assembly-line fashion. None of the children asked for the requested trio of items, but I noticed they started speeding up their wish lists to work more in before I ushered them on their way.

By the time three o'clock rolled around and the Santa shift ended, I was exhausted. In contrast to the laid-back first day, when no interruptions disturbed the smooth flow of supplicants, this was torture. I had a feeling I'd need to visit my old buddy Sam Skejeski at The Crater down the street.

Although I had done my duty and technically was free to leave early, I decided I'd better hang around a bit and make sure there wasn't any fallout from the day's incidents.

Returning to my office, I changed back into real-people clothes and put the Doobie Brothers in the cassette deck. One drawer of my filing cabinet was devoted to classic rock, sort of a satellite collection to my main music library in my apartment.

I sat down to check my messages. Sandwiched between calls from Jane outlining my schedule for the rest of the week and inquiring about the FOS incident were three frantic calls from

Bambi, each more intense than the last. I made a mental note to check on her before I left for the day.

She had also called my cell phone twice, hanging up without leaving a message the second time. My girlfriend, Rosie, had called to say she was tied up tonight and couldn't come over to cook me dinner.

I had known Rosie for several years after meeting her at a sportswriters convention in Buffalo. She was an information specialist for the University of Wisconsin Athletic Department, which means she put together the sports media guides. She got tired of cleaning up athletes' broken English (that was part of the entertainment of my sportswriting career) and transferred into college administration, where she bounced around a number of places before landing in the Twin Cities. And hooking up with me.

I think what turned the tide in my direction was my extensive music collection. Also, she thought I was offbeat, since I once mailed her a cracker in a letter to see if it would arrive intact. No, it didn't. The rest, as they say, is mundane.

So no good Rosie-cooked meal for me this evening. Rats. It looked like peanut butter and wings again, my staple backup meal plan.

Just as I was pondering a break from the diet routine, the phone rang yet again. Groan. Please let this not be another dummy assault, I prayed.

"Jim here."

"Beers, you better get down to three, like pronto," Tina said.

"What's going on?"

"Gerald just discovered the missing mannequin in foundations."

"How do you know about it?"

"Beers! I know it all. I have ears all over. Ain't a price tag falls that I don't hear about."

"So you know it was knocked over. It broke, so I took the pieces up here to my office."

"Yep. Gerald's pissed, big time."

"Did Doone tell him what happened? It was at his station."

"Doone played dumb," she said. "You know he's scared of Gerald, probably because of his size. Doone told him he went on break and when he got back, it had just disappeared."

"Figures," I said. "Well, I'll be down in a sec. You still on three?"

"No, had to get back to the counter. Emergency rouge job on some old biddy."

"OK. But when I finish on three, I want to ask you something. What time you get off today?"

"Doing the whole nine. Cindy's closing, so I can go at six."

"Later." I hung up, grabbed my cell phone and headed out the door, pausing only to glance in the corner at the heap of ... what? Plastic? Ceramic? Composite polymer? There was more to the day's episodes than mere coincidence, of that I was certain.

But I was going to need help figuring out what that was.

I scribbled a few more notes as I left.

3

Like I said, I wasn't always a security guru. When I left the South and headed out to the world of work, journalism was my profession, specifically sports reporting. A succession of beats in a succession of locations led me to the Twin Cities, where I dropped anchor at the Minnesota Herald and thought I was docked for the long haul.

Some might call it a mid-life crisis. I turned 40 and suddenly, talking to kids half my age and thousands of times richer seemed ludicrous. I didn't want to be a sportswriter anymore, but I didn't know what I wanted to do. Jane's offer seemed like a good idea at the time. Unfortunately, one criminal science course in college, an elective, didn't prepare me for the job.

Security is a world poles apart from reporting. I mean, I still have to deal with difficult people on a daily basis, and I'm not just talking about my bosses. The rank-and-file at this edifice to capitalism are every bit as diverse and temperamental as some of the pro stars I had to cover—although slightly less well paid.

The thing about the news business is that every day brings a new story, a new challenge, featuring a cast of wacky characters.

Wait—that also describes life at La Scala to a T.

Take my "assistants," for example. They don't get any wackier than my unofficial staff, the girls who assist me because of their keen interest in problem-solving. Tina and Lena had become more than just co-workers in the short time I had called La Scala my second home. Possibly because I spent so much time in cosmetics and jewelry, dealing with shoplifting incidents. The girls were especially good at chasing down light-fingered Lorettas who helped themselves to merchandise.

They were also fascinating once you got to know them, and pretty fun to hang out with after work.

Tina McEntire, a tiny, feisty 20-something cosmetician who looked like she would be more at home in a boxing ring, was surprisingly adept at connecting the dots between diverse bits of information. Maybe that was because she was so well plugged in to sources—everyone knew her, and she had a way of getting them to pony up facts, secrets and rumors without realizing they were being pumped for information.

It helped that she was a dark-haired cutie—guys couldn't keep their yaps shut around her, and ladies found her kewpie-like, unintimidating and so best-friendly and perky (all an act, I might add) that they also blabbed more than they should around her.

That's why she got the scoop on a certain vice president who was boinking a young associate in china (she worked in china, that is, wasn't boinked in china) and blew the lid off a kickback scheme in appliances. Having worked at La Scala for six years, she knew most of the players and all of the recent history.

Of course, Lena was a whole different matter. A bit older at 32 and book-smarter, but far less street savvy, Lena Fangeaux is a New Orleans yat through and through. To look at her, you'd think she just stepped off the beauty pageant runway—shoulder-length blond hair, killer figure and model height. She had that come-hither look. I didn't know where hither was, but everyone wanted to go there.

The minute she opened her mouth, though, her Crescent City roots were evident, and I knew we were going to be friends. A died-in-the-wool native of Chalmette, she was a real "chawmah," with beauty and brains, but heavily outweighed by Tina in the common sense and toughness departments.

So when my information quest called for research and technical detail, Lena was on the case. For reconnaissance and the word on the street, Tina was my trusted source. In the current situation, I needed both if I was going to figure out what was going on with the mannequins.

Although I gave up reporting, I did retain one habit from those years of putting pen to paper: I carried a reporter's notepad with me everywhere, and made notes about everything. It was the only way I could jog my memory, which was shorter-term than airport parking.

After leaving my office, I stopped on the fifth floor to chat with Lena. As I approached, I saw her adjusting a diamond-studded necklace on a large woman in a too-tight dress.

She saw me out of the corner of her eye, winked and told her customer, "There, Mrs. Alford, I think that's the one you're looking for. What do you think?" Lena said it in her best neutral accent. It was amazing to me that she never slipped into her native drawl around customers.

The woman twisted left and right while gazing in the counter mirror, frowned a couple of times and said, "I don't know…"

"I did tell you about the sale, right?" Lena said, trying to seal the deal. "Twenty percent, only through tomorrow."

"Well…"

"Of course, you could always wait till l the after-Christmas sale, and hope it's still here…"

The woman bit her lip. "Can you hold it for me? I just need to convince one person, and he's, you know, trying to impress some people, and, well, we're having a big party and this would certainly help, don't you think?"

"Absolutely!" Lena exclaimed. "I understand perfectly. I'll just put your name on it and hold it until noon tomorrow. Noon—is that OK?"

The woman nodded her big head, now reeled in and ready to be netted. "Yes, oh my, yes. I'll call you before noon. I certainly will." She removed the necklace, handed it to Lena and rushed off.

"Da whale dat got away," Lena said. She reverted quickly to yatism out of the earshot of customers.

"Oh, well," I commiserated, "maybe she'll call."

"Yeah, maybe, but I'm not countin' my commission before it's plucked."

"So, Lena, how you doing? You look great." I'd learned through painful experience that a little buttering up always made my unreasonable demands so much easier.

"Great, Beers. How's wit' you up dere in ya big awfiss?"

"Rough day. Did the Santa stint again," I said, shaking my head. "Too bad."

"Yeah. Had some strange events, though, and was wondering if you could help me with something."

"Sure, sugah. Shoot."

I explained that there had been two separate incidents with mannequins, one that seemed to be a harmless prank and one that resulted in damage. "I need to get a few things checked out, and you're so good at that ..."

"Well ...," she said, sucking up the compliment.

"I need you to find out what kind of substance our mannequins are made from, what kind of tool you'd need to cut one—and one more thing."

"Yeah, what?"

"Whether we can lift prints off it."

Her eyes got big. "Fingahprints?"

"And we need to be discreet on this." I gave her a serious look.

"Duh-skreet's my middle name, dawlin'," she said with a nod. "Fingahprints."

On my way back down to the first floor, I ran into Bambi as the elevator door opened.

"Bambi, you OK?" The red mark on her left cheek told me it had gotten a bit rougher than I thought.

"No. I hate this place!" She stormed into the elevator, punched a button and the doors closed. Whew, have to smooth that over before tomorrow or Santa's going to have a very long day again.

At the cosmetics counter, Tina was putting things away and whistling, although her boss had told her countless times to cut it out. I had learned to read that as her involuntary sign of nervousness. She had some information.

"Whatcha got, Tina?"

She looked around, then signaled me to lean over the counter.

"There was another incident you didn't hear about," she whispered.

"What?"

"Second floor, while you were finishing up in Santaland. Men's suits."

"Uh-oh."

"Mr. Hantack stuck a customer again. Lawyer."

I groaned. Hantack was our inheritance from old man Scalabrino, perhaps one of the original employees, for all I knew. He was well beyond retirement age, and until I got the scoop from Jane after the last incident, wouldn't have believed he was 82. The only giveaway was that his motor skills seemed to be deteriorating somewhat, resulting in more frequent cases of pin the tail on the customer.

"What's the damage? Is he suing?" I asked.

"He made a lot of noise but backed off when Hantack started crying," Tina said. "He's got the talent."

"You mean he can cry at will?"

"No, he was really upset," she explained. "He's a master tailor, really knows his stuff. It's just a shame he's so damn old."

Tina's sentimentality sometimes left me speechless. "So why didn't I hear about this? A lawyer—we could hear from him again."

"Naw, I don't think so. It was over in a just a few minutes. The guy actually started apologizing to Hantack for getting him upset. Bought the suit, to boot."

"Geez, I'll be glad when this day's over."

"Go home," Tina said. "You did your duty."

"I will. Have to figure out how to make it up to Bambi. She looked pretty upset."

"Oh, you didn't hear about that either?"

"What? Something else?"

"I'll let Bambi tell you. I'm sure it will be much more dramatic," Tina said. "Now, if you'll excuse me, I gotta go take a dump." She winked and headed off toward the ladies' room.

Sheesh. This is my "assistant." I loved Tina, but sometimes…she was just too much for a normal person.

4

Tuesday night
Temperature: 13, snow; wind chill, 4

I am a normal person. At least I thought I was. Sure, you have to be a little insane to be a sportswriter, but I gave that up, right? So now I'm sane? Don't even try to answer that.

By the time I got back up to the sixth floor, Bambi had already checked out for the day. Either it was so bad she had to leave early or...well, there was no second choice. Maybe I would need to draft a new elf for the rest of my stint as St. Nick, which I hoped would end tomorrow.

On the way back up to my office, I decided maybe I should just call it a day and get rested up for whatever onslaught of kids tomorrow would bring. If I can weasel out of this duty after one more day, I thought, the rest of the week would be easy.

Of course, there were messages waiting for me, one from Gerald, wondering where the hell his mannequin was, and one from Jane, wanting to know what happened in foundations.

Better take care of the boss first, I thought. That would be the easier call.

Her secretary answered. "Jane Mertin's office."

"Hi, Sandy, it's Jim. Jane called?"

"Hey, Jim. Just a minute. Let me see if she's available." She had me on hold for just a few seconds before Jane picked up. "Jim, what's this about a stolen mannequin?"

"Not stolen, Jane, I've got it. There was an accident—"

"Gerald Difansa said someone stole it."

"He was misinformed," I said calmly. "Some kids knocked it over, it was broken and I took it up to my office. That's all."

26

"Well, you know how Gerald is about his 'people,' " Jane said. "What do we need to do to take care of this?"

"He's got extras. He can replace it and we'll just order a new one after..." I paused, trying to figure out how to say this.

"After what? Jim?"

She had to know. "After I figure out who wanted it broken. There was a...the mannequin had a...well, it looked like someone had damaged it deliberately."

"Deliberately! Why? Who would want to do that?"

"I don't know. I'm looking into it," I assured her. "I'll try to tell you more tomorrow." Time to make my pitch. "Y'know, I don't mind playing Santa, but with the incidents today, it was kind of hard to take care of my primary duties..."

"I know, Jim, and I appreciate your efforts," she said. "Personnel assures me they'll have a new Santa by next week."

Next week! No, no, no, it's got to be this week, my brain was screaming. Thursday latest!

"So just hang in there, Jim. And Jim?"

"Yes?"

"If we need to call in some outside help with security..."

"No, no, I can handle it," I said. "Let me work on it. I've got it under control."

"OK. Bye, Jim."

"Bye."

Did I think the rest of the week would be easy? Wrong. I debated calling Gerald back for a few minutes but decided it had to be done sometime. Might as well get it over with.

"Display—this is Gerald Difansa."

"Hi, Gerald, this is Jim Biers—"

"Sonofabitch! What did you do with my mannequin??!!" Gerald screamed.

Oh God, another scene.

"Calm down, Gerald. It's broken beyond repair, so I just got it out of the way."

"Why didn't you bring it down here to the basement?"

"Well, I just didn't think you needed that in your way while you're working on other displays. Don't you have a spare you can plug in there?"

"Spare? There's no spare!" he shrieked. "That's a Cleopatra model. A stork. I don't have a spare!"

"Stork?" I asked, puzzled.

"Stork. One foot attached, one free," he explained. "Very rare nowadays. And a Cleopatra—you can't get them without a six-month wait!"

"Don't you have some other model you can put there for the time being?"

"What? A Marilyn or a Jayne? No, that won't do!"

"Well, this one is just broken. You can't use it," I explained. "I'll bring you the pieces tomorrow."

"Oh my Lord! What is this place coming to? I can't work under conditions like this. First the front window, now this!" His voice was trembling, on the brink of tears again. Time to break this off before it got messier.

"Gotta go now, Gerald. I'll talk to you tomorrow." I hung up over his protests, grabbed my jacket and headed out the door.

On my way down, I dialed Freddie, my bud in the sports department at the paper. Freddie is probably my closest friend in the Twin Cities. We used to hang out after hours when I was at the paper, shooting pool and downing way too many brews. He's what we call a utility infielder. When the regular beat writer is on vacation, Freddie gets assigned to cover the Gophers or the Twins. He's pushing for a first-team gig but hasn't landed one yet.

"Sports. This is Fred Skelton."

"Hey, Freddie, Jim. You up for a brew?"

"Just wrapping up. Crater?"

"On my way there."

"See you in about ten," he said.

Stopping off at two, I passed by women's shoes to say so long to Dad. He was busy with a customer, so I waved and headed on out through the skyway, across Hennepin to The Crater.

It was still hard to believe my own father was working in the same city as me, much less the same building. But two years of sitting around as a retired widower without a hobby was enough to convince him to start a second career. It wasn't such a huge jump from selling plumbing supplies to selling shoes, I guess.

THE CRATER IS THE TYPE OF BAR that was trendy a decade ago, but had aged to the point that it catered to old-time regulars, while the terminally trendy had moved on to newer pastures.

It was the perfect hangout for sportswriters. With pumice-looking walls the color of a dirty fireplace, it had a cavernous feel, except for the heat. For some reason, Sam the proprietor kept the heat pumping, winter and summer. I guess on the theory that it was more conducive to selling cold drinks. He's the consummate bartender—he knows when to listen and when to interject an opinion, which isn't often. He also can judge my mood and offer the appropriate quaff.

"Sam," I called, plopping down at the end of the bar. He looked up from the register and walked over.

"Beers, the king of beers!" Sam greeted me with his usual corny line. He was the kind of guy I looked up to—literally, since he had a good eight inches on me. He could have been a power forward in an earlier life, or maybe an astronaut. I had no clue. He never talked about himself. He was a listener, not a talker.

"You out early today?" he asked.

"Yeah, I'm on special duty. Know any out-of-work Santas?"

Sam squinted at me. "Don't tell me. They got you playing Santa?" He started laughing. "That's a good one."

"Well, if you can stop laughing long enough, can you get me a Summit?"

"Sure." He continued laughing as he pulled a frosty mug out of the chiller and drew the winter ale. "Here ya go," he said between chuckles.

I took a big swig and Sam kept laughing. He couldn't control himself and started laughing even harder.

"It's not that funny, Sam. Get a grip," I told him.

By this time he was laughing so hard he was crying, and as he pulled out a towel to muffle his guffaws, I didn't even notice Freddie slipping onto the stool beside me.

"Beers! What's so funny?" he asked.

"I told Sam a good one. Funniest joke he's heard in months."

"Must be good," Freddie said. "So tell me."

"Maybe later."

"You hanging with me tonight instead of Rosie?"

"For a while. Got to get home and rest up. Long day."

"So what gives?" I drained the rest of my beer and signaled Sam for a second round.

"So what gives is there were a couple of incidents today that are going to keep me real busy for the next few days, trying to figure out what's going on."

"Can you give me a clue?"

"Mannequins."

"Mannequins?" Freddie snickered. "What, you got a crush on the hot number in the push-up bra?"

Sam plopped a new beer in front of me and said, "Who's in a push-up bra? She here now?"

"No, Sam. It's…I…I can't talk about it yet. Could be a sensitive inside situation."

"Humph. You ask me over here, then you clam up." Freddie put on his best hurt look. I glanced at Sam and he mimicked Freddie's pout.

"Look, it's probably nothing," I said. "The only reason I can't say any more is my Santa duties didn't give me time—"

"Whoa, whoa, whoa. Santa duties?" Freddie asked.

"Dick Tracy here is the new jolly fat man at the store," Sam informed Freddie. He started chuckling again.

Freddie had nothing to say. He just stared with his mouth open. I could see the unasked questions forming in his predictable brain. Finally, he asked. "What happened to the last fat man?"

"He didn't pan out."

"Don't tell me—overweight. And since you're the new St. Nick, the store is obviously appealing to the low-carb crowd."

"Wrong, beer-breath. The last Santa was ideal in the obesity department," I said.

"So why didn't he last? Not jolly enough?"

"Oh, he was plenty jolly. But—and I'm just gonna go out on a limb here—it might, just maybe have been because he came back from lunch last Friday plastered out of his mind, then proceeded to throw up on little Katy, her mother and several other doe-eyed kiddies clutching their wish lists."

"Whoa. Blowing chunks on the clientele," Freddie said. "A definite no-no."

"Yeah, also the fact that he felt entitled to the five-finger discount a little too frequently. So it won't take much for me to be an improvement in the Santa department, scrawny physique or no."

"Don't they screen these guys before they hire them?"

I took another big swig. "Freddie, think about it. Santa applicants don't look like that because they're eccentric CEOs. It's not the look you want to cultivate unless you live at the North Pole."

"I don't know—I can see you growing into that role," Freddie chuckled.

"Funny. I don't think I can take much more of this. I mean, when Bambi got beat up by—"

"Bambi?"

"Bambi Schroeder. She's the elf," I explained.

"Bambi?" Freddie laughed. "Didya Thumper?" Sam started his uncontrollable guffawing again, joined by Freddie this time.

"I don't think Seinfeld is gonna like this," Freddie said.

"Sinfield. It's Rosie Sinfield," I said. "Like the guy who wrote the lyrics for the first King Crimson album."

"Whatever. She know about Bambi?"

"There's nothing to 'know,' " I told him. "She's a co-worker."

"Bambi. Oh deer!" Freddie said, and the laughing started all over again.

I figured it was time to drink up, call it a night and get home early. Peanut butter and wings was sounding better all the time.

5

Wednesday morning, Dec. 15
10 shopping days till Christmas
Temperature: 36, cloudy; wind chill, 33

Normally, incidents like Tuesday's events wouldn't freak me out. Usually the security beat was pretty straightforward— minor episodes of shoplifting, broken locks and glass displays to get fixed, irate customers to placate. I would file a simple report for Jane that would put a case to bed.

Now I had an open case, two actually, that needed more investigation and no time to devote to them since I was assigned to the greedy urchins beat.

My crack investigation team, Lena and Tina, had agreed to meet me for breakfast to discuss the events. Martin's Mocha Java three blocks from the store was the rendezvous spot. Armed with tall cups of overpriced coffee and blueberry scones, we grabbed a table near the window and dove into strategy.

"OK, here's what I know," I said. "Someone gets into the front-of-store display and creates a scandalous tableau to shock passers-by and embarrass the store, or maybe specifically Gerald Difansa."

"Check," Tina said.

"Later, another mannequin, different floor, is broken when it's knocked over by rowdy kids."

"Could be coincidence?" Lena said.

"What I didn't tell you is that the dummy was damaged on purpose."

"How?" Lena asked.

"It was cut. Someone sawed through the leg to the point that it would break if it was pushed over."

"Gawd, no!" Lena said. "So dat's why you wanted ta know how ta cut one. And dat's why you wanted info on fingahprintin'. Maybe da criminal's prints are on dere."

"I'm not saying it's a criminal. Could just be a prankster. Or someone trying to sabotage a certain display technician," I said, raising an eyebrow.

"So you think we got us a sabba-toor?" Lena asked. "Someone who doesn't like mannequins…"

"Who would want to have a vendetta against mannequins?" Tina asked. "Doesn't make sense. Now a grudge against Gerald I can understand."

"Maybe. So we've got to figure out who and why."

"Simple enough," Lena said. "If we can get a look at da security tapes…"

"No security tapes," I said.

"No cameras in da store?" Lena asked.

"Nope. The boss man likes his privacy. That's one of the first things Jane told me about my job. Apparently, he's never had cameras and doesn't want them. Something about an incident where he was caught on film. Lena, what about fingerprinting?"

"So ya think dey's some prints on da sawed leg?" Lena shook her head. "Well, lemme tell ya, ya can't just go down ta da hawdweah store and pick up a fingahprintin' kit, y'know. It's not a ovah-da-countah type deal. I looked around a bit, and it seems like ya gotta be in law enfawcement ta get dat stuff."

"Hmm. So we're at a dead end, unless we turn this over to the cops, and they do the fingerprinting," Tina said.

"Not necessarily." Lena smiled and blinked a couple of times, then pulled a piece of paper out of her handbag. "Evah hearda 3M?"

"No, never heard of it," I said in my most sarcastic tone. "Duh. They're like the biggest company around here."

"Well, I was readin' some tech reports on da web yestahday."

"And?"

"Dey might have what we need. Lissen here. Dey got a scientist name of Teshley, he 'parently made dis new adhesive spray? Somethin' like SunTite or TiteGrip or such. Y'know, dey make lotsa glues 'n stuff."

"Yeah, I'm well aware, Lena," I said, growing impatient. "What has this got to do with our investigation?"

"Hang onta ya Joe Boxahs, wouldya?" she said. "I'm getting' ta da good part. Dis new stuff has some strange chemical propahties, y'know, like bonding. It's peelable."

"Peelable?" Tina asked.

"Yeah, so dey think it's got lotsa other applications, and one dis report mentioned was fingahprintin'."

"This stuff for sale?" Tina asked.

"Not yet. But maybe we can convince dis guy ta give us a sample."

I looked at Lena, trying to figure out her thought process, which I knew going in was a losing battle.

"Are you nuts?" Tina asked. "They're not gonna let us have that! If it's not on the shelves, how are we going to get it?"

"Just call and ask?"

"One of us is crazy, Lena. I'll let you figure out which," Tina said. "Wouldn't it be simpler just to ask a cop for a kit? I know a guy at the downtown precinct. He probably owes me a favor." She gave us a smug look.

I checked my watch. "Look, I have to get dressed and get to my post. Can you meet me after work at 6 o'clock? I want to go over a few more possibilities."

"Sure, honey."

"Tina?"

"I got a date at 7. With a cop," Tina said. Lena snickered.

"It won't take that long," I said.

"OK."

We trekked to La Scala and went our separate ways. Heading up to my office, I decided there were two paths laid out before me— do a half-ass job as Santa while trying to figure out a pair of puzzling cases, or let Jane call in some outside security help and deal with only the one jolly headache. Of course, the police were out of the question; they would just laugh at this major crime wave, instigated by a mannequin hater.

Or more likely it was a campaign against the mannequins' keeper. I could understand why someone might not want to take on Gerald directly. At 6-5, 240 pounds and pumped up like an Arnold wannabe, Gerald was an imposing presence to his co-workers and any member of the public that happened to encounter him. How he got to be a window dresser was beyond me.

I knew he wasn't gay because he was constantly being spotted at restaurants and nightclubs with the fox du jour. Tina somehow always knew about his latest fling. But maybe he was bi, since his mannerisms suggested he didn't always bat from the left side of the plate.

Could be a jealous boyfriend. Or girlfriend. Or both? Somewhere I heard that he once played pro football, but that didn't sound like the Gerald I knew. I made a note to call Freddie and see if he could find out anything that might help.

Reaching my office, I decided what the hell, I'll give this 3M guy a call and see if there was some way he could help us.

I rang the jewelry counter and got Lena on the line.

"What was that 3M guy's name again?"

"Teshley," she said. "Rod, I think."

"And his invention…?"

"SunTite, GripTite, somethin' like dat. Tite fa sure."

"OK, thanks." The phonebook yielded only the main number at 3M. Working through the voice-mail system, I finally got a receptionist.

"3M. How may I direct your call?"

"Could I speak with Mr. Teshley?"

"Dr. Rodrick Teshley? May I ask who's calling?"

"Uh, this is James Biersovich. Assistant to the vice president for facilities for La Scala." She hesitated a few seconds, then said, "One moment please." This is too easy, I thought while listening to 3M's version of Muzak, a series of promotions for Scotchgard. Finally, someone picked up.

"Hello. This is Mike Barker. Can I help you?"

"Hi, Mr. Barker. Trying to get in touch with Dr. Teshley."

"I'm sorry, he's not available. May I ask who's calling?"

"This is Jim Biersovich. I'm assistant to the facilities vice president at La Scala—the department store?"

"What can I do for you, Mr. Biersovich?"

"Well, I wanted to talk to Mr. Tesh—Dr. Teshley about his new formula…"

There was dead silence for a few seconds. Then he said, "I'm not sure what you're talking about."

"Uh, the new adhesive, named SunTite or something like that."

"How do you know about that?" Barker asked, a definite edge to his voice. Uh-oh.

"A colleague saw the report on the web—"

"That wasn't an official report, if you saw such a thing. 3M does not announce products under development on the web."

Wow, I thought, I've really stepped into one here. "Could you just leave a message with him that I'd like to chat with him…"

"I'm afraid Dr. Teshley is rather busy. If there's anything else I could help you with?" He gave me that dismissive you're-not-getting-past-me-so-give-up tone. So I gave up.

"No, thanks. Goodbye."

I glanced at the still skimpily clad mannequin lying in the corner. It stared back with a blank look that taunted me: What are you staring at? As I was climbing into my red suit, the phone rang.

"Jim Biersovich."

"Hi, Jim. It's Jack Rogers in the luggage department. We need you down here right away."

"What's the problem?" I asked.

"Code 54," he said, the dreaded store lingo for a serious situation involving a customer.

"On my way," I said, hanging up and leaving the Santa coat behind.

I took the back stairway down to the eighth floor and came upon a scene that sends chills through store managers. A woman was lying on the floor screaming, with about a dozen people gathered around her talking at once—and loudly.

Locating the most obvious candidate to be the luggage department clerk, I touched his arm and he pulled me to the side.

"Mr. Rogers? What happened?" I whispered.

"Snake," he whispered back.

"What?!"

"Woman opened a suitcase. There was a snake in it," he said, exhaling nervously. "It bit her."

"Oh my God!" I said. "Did you call an ambulance?"

"Not yet. I called you first."

"OK, go call an ambulance. Let's get her to the hospital. I'll take care of the crowd."

As Rogers made the call, I shooed the crowd away and managed to calm the woman down just enough to get her to stop howling, and found out her name and that she had been bitten on the forearm.

"Mrs. Dallon, we've got an ambulance coming. We're going to get you to a doctor and get everything taken care of. I just need you to be calm and it's going to be OK. OK?"

With tears of fright streaming down her cheeks, she managed to nod her head and I helped her into a chair. I recited the La Scala pledge that I had come to memorize whenever a delicate situation with the buying public arose: La Scala is a family owned company that adheres to the highest standards in both our merchandise and our employees. La Scala values you as a customer blah blah blah. By the time I finished, she had calmed down a bit more.

"Ma'am, can you show me where it bit you?" I asked.

"On the arm," she said, thrusting it toward me. Examining it, I saw no sign of snakebite.

"Where exactly?"

"On the arm," she said wiggling it at me again. Still nothing.

"Are you sure it bit you?" I asked. "I'm not seeing—"

"It bit me!" she shrieked.

"Fine," I said, trying to calm her. "Just show me which suitcase you were looking at."

She pointed at a huge, gray American Tourister that was lying on the floor closed. I wasn't about to open it there, so I snapped the locks, picked it up and stashed it behind the counter.

While I waited for the paramedics to arrive, I called Jane and told her what had happened. She spoke calmly, but I could tell this was a very bad event to have happen at any time, much less the week before Christmas.

"Let's not call in the police just yet," she said. "I'll talk with the executive board and see how they want to handle it."

"Yes, ma'am," I said. "I'll hang onto the suitcase and find out what I can down here."

When the paramedics arrived to cart the woman off, the one in charge asked me what type of snake had bitten her.

"I have no idea," I said.

"Well, you better find out so we know how to treat her. Could be poisonous," he said. He handed me a card. "Call this number and tell the nurse on duty what you find out."

"How do I find out what kind of snake?" I asked, as he was leaving.

"Animal Control."

"Phone book?" I said to Rogers.

"Right over here," he gestured behind the counter.

I dialed Animal Control and was told they'd send out an agent within two hours. I grilled Rogers, finding out little about the suitcase, other than it was made in Singapore and had been stocked three weeks previous. Until the Animal Control folks arrived, it was going into my office for safekeeping. I also told Rogers to check the other suitcases.

"But, uh, what if there's another snake?" he asked, worried.

"Just shake them," I said. "If you hear something bouncing around, put them aside."

Heading back up to nine, I shook the suitcase, just to satisfy myself that there was still something in it. I thought I heard a rattle but couldn't be sure. I dumped it in the corner with the dead mannequin.

Donning the rest of my Santa suit, I contemplated the problematic days that lay before me, now with a trio of unsolved events hounding me. I prayed that nothing else would happen but had a nagging feeling there was more to come.

Having a cell phone at hand seemed like a necessity, even with my temporary gig, but Jane had told me explicitly that Santa didn't carry a phone, and any calls would be routed through my main elf.

At the North Pole on the first floor, the kiddie line again stretched out for miles. Bambi was back at her post—with makeup hiding the evidence of Tuesday's fracas—keeping the rowdy group organized. I winked at her and got a slight smile back in return.

Poor Bambi. She also had been pulled away from her main duties, negotiating with couture salesmen, and although her business slowed down during the holiday shopping season, I'm sure she felt as fish-out-of-water as I did.

My third petitioner of the day landed in my lap, the rank aroma of stale kid hair offending my olfactory nerves. He had just started into his list when I heard Bambi's cell ring. The look on her face made me say "oh no" out loud, confusing the youngster on my lap.

"Excuse me just a minute, folks. Santa has a call from the North Pole," Bambi announced, handing me the phone.

Dumping the kid and moving around the back of the throne, I said, "Beers here." There were voices talking in the background, then to me: "Jim, this is Salmon Foster. We have a situation."

Gulp. Salmon Foster was vice president of finance, probably the most powerful of all the veeps since he controlled the lifeblood of the business: money.

"Yes?"

"I need you to come up to nine right away."

"Uh, what about Santa?"

"Santa? Oh, that's right—you're filling in this week. Well, find someone to give the suit to and get up here."

"Right." I passed the phone back to Bambi and told her I needed her to find a Santa fill-in. This sounded serious.

"What?" Bambi said. "No, you can't leave me here again, not after yesterday." Bambi looked and sounded desperate.

Then Bambi's phone rang again. She just handed it to me.

"Beers."

"Hi, Jim." It was my Dad calling, which seemed really odd. He never called me—just dropped into my office occasionally on his break.

"What's up, Pops?"

"Uh, Jim, I was wondering if you could come to the shoe department…"

"I can't right now, Dad. Got to go up and see Salmon Foster."

"Oh. I see." There was a worried sound to his voice.

"What's going on?"

"Well, we have a little problem that I think you need to see. We've got a bunch of broken shoes."

"Broken shoes."

"Yeah, they're broken all right. Looks like someone broke them on purpose, too."

"How many shoes are we talking about?"

"Not sure. We're still going through boxes but we've found about a dozen so far. But there's something weird about this."

"Weirder than a bunch of broken shoes?"

"Yeah, it's only the rights."

"Just the right shoes are broken?"

"Uh-huh. I think it's just high heels, but we're still looking."

"Dad, I gotta go. I'll get there as soon as I can."

"OK, son. Bye."

Now the next dilemma: go up to Foster's office in the Santa suit, or try to find a fill-in? Better check in with him first, then find a sub and change, go down to the shoe department and…yikes.

Got to get out of this polar duty. I started to hand the phone back to Bambi but reconsidered. "Let me just have this for a second," I said, and walked off quickly despite her objections.

I glanced back briefly and saw her staring daggers at me, as a rising clamor of voices came from the Santa line behind her. I walked faster.

6

Wednesday midmorning
Temperature: 38, partly cloudy; wind chill, 37

The vice presidents were what was known as the 4-F Club—finance, fashion, facilities and fogies. The two veeps who comprised the fogies were inherited from old man Scalabrino, and did little in the way of day-to-day operations, I was told, but they were certain to show up when executive bonuses were distributed.

There were a few more vice presidents—human resources, sales, marketing—but they seemed to be the third tier in the power hierarchy. At the top was Salmon Foster, then the other members of the 4-F Club. All this comes from Tina, naturally.

I had no idea what Jane's real function was until she explained it to me one day. She had a huge assignment, one that's not so apparent on first blush. Everything to do with the physical structure of the store was her responsibility, from interior renovations to the integrity of the outer walkways, rights of way, governmental regulations such as handicapped access, parking restrictions and furnace emissions. I had a small slice of that duty – the security of the building and merchandise, plus a few other tasks she offloaded to me.

Arriving at the executive suite in costume, I was ushered in by Salmon Foster himself. He had a stern look on his face.

Foster was about my height, considerably older and looked a bit like Leslie Nielsen, without the humor. As a matter of fact, I'd never seen him smile, much less crack a joke. He was reputed to be the highest-paid employee of the La Scala empire.

The size of his office attested to that fact.

"Jim, we've got a serious situation. I need you to look into it ASAP."

"Uh, OK, Mr. Foster, but I'm a bit under the gun right now playing Santa…"

He sized me up and said, "We'll get that taken care of ASAP. Meanwhile, here's the situation." He motioned me into his spacious office and we sat down at his conference table, where several stacks of printouts lay. "Someone's been destroying records. The accounting department gets a printout every morning from the overnight report. This morning's report had selected entries zeroed out." He pushed a stack to me and I could see red circles around columns of zeroes.

"Isn't that an automated process?"

"I thought it was. The data processing folks tell me there's no way the programs can be hacked because they're password-protected. So that means it's an inside job. Someone with access screwed up the code."

"Are they sure the code's been tampered with? I mean, couldn't it be some machine crashed and caused some code not to run properly? You know PCs are always screwing up…"

"They don't think so," he said. "They're going over the code line by line right now. I need you to find out—discreetly—how many people know the passwords and who they are. If we've got a saboteur in our midst, we need to hang him ASAP."

I thought about how to conduct such an inquiry without tipping off the suspects. "Who do you trust in the computer department?"

Foster stared grimly at me. "No one," he said.

The two words I feared I would hear. Now the challenge went from merely incredibly difficult to absolutely, totally, impossibly difficult, considering my computer cluelessness. Well, if Santa can perform his yearly miracle, and I'm Santa—wait, I'm not Santa. Not even close.

"Mr. Foster, do you think we need to get the police involv—"

"No police," he cut me off. "We cannot have police traipsing through here at the peak of the holiday shopping season. That's death to sales!"

"OK, but I really need to get out of this Santa duty if you want me to conduct this investigation. Can you make that happen?"

"I can make that happen," he assured me. "I'll talk to Jane. ASAP."

"Thanks." I'm sure you will, I thought. "And you need this investigation done—ASAP?"

"Exactly," he said. "Just get back to Santaland for now, and we'll send someone down shortly."

I headed sullenly off to my post on the first floor, which I hoped would be my last visit inside the domain of the jolly olde elf. On my way down the elevator, the phone rang again.

"Jim here."

"Hi, Jim, this is Sandy. There are some people here from Animal Control…"

"Be right up," I said, punching the ninth-floor button. Santaland would have to wait.

When I arrived at my office, two guys in gray overalls and nametags that said Myron and Clark were leaning against the wall in the hallway. Clark was standing next to a large duffel bag.

"Hi, I'm Jim Biersovich," I said. "Snake's in my office."

"Didn't know Santa was a snake-handler," the one named Myron snickered.

Opening the door, I ushered them in and pointed to the suitcase. "Right in there," I said.

"Right," Clark said, unzipping the bag. "If you could just leave us alone for a minute, we'll get this taken care of." He pulled out a plastic trash bag, a canister and assorted other gear.

When I walked out, he closed the door. I could hear some soft talking, a few bumps and after only a couple minutes, the door reopened. I looked in and saw Clark tying a string around the plastic bag, with the opened suitcase lying in the corner—sans snake.

"Got it," he said.

"In the bag?"

"Yep."

"What kind of snake is it?" I asked.

"Not sure," Myron answered. "Let's just take a peek."

"Whoa! Don't open that in here," I said.

"It's OK, Santa, he's knocked out. Just put your sleeve over your mouth for a second."

I did as instructed, he peeked in the bag, then closed it again.

"Looks like we got us a *Sistrurus c. catenatus*, commonly known as the swamp rattler. Fairly poisonous."

"Good God!" I fished the card out of my pocket and rushed to the phone, relaying the information to the duty nurse at the hospital as instructed.

"It bit someone?" Clark asked after I hung up.

"Yes, a customer. At least she said it bit her. She was looking in the suitcase."

"Wow."

"Any idea where such a snake would come from?" I asked.

"Well," Myron said, "they're usually found in swampy areas. Could have come from near the river."

"Wouldn't have come from overseas?"

"Nah, it's domestic."

"OK, thanks." They packed up their gear and left with the unconscious critter. Now I had to figure out why and how someone smuggled a snake into the store and hid it inside luggage. Since it was a poisonous snake, I had to assume the perpetrator meant to seriously injure or kill someone. But why? Why a customer? Or was the customer really an innocent victim?

I was great at coming up with questions. Now I needed to find someone who could come up with some answers. I pulled out my notepad and wrote the name of the snake and some other details.

As I was shutting the suitcase to stand it up in the corner, something caught my eye. There was a mark on the inside lid near the hinge. I looked closer and saw two small letters, apparently written with a blue marker: CC. Odd.

Stacking it in the corner, I glanced down at the crumpled mannequin and wondered... Carefully removing the bra, then tugging the panties down, I found the same letters on the mannequin's rump. There was a connection! While I was contemplating this new clue, Dad walked into the office. I didn't register his presence until he cleared his throat.

"Oh. Hi, Dad."

"Jim, I can come back later—" He seemed a bit embarrassed at catching me with someone else's pants down.

"No, I was just...this mannequin was damaged and there seems to be a clue."

"Uh-huh." He was looking at me sort of funny. I flashed back to my childhood, when big brother Tom and I shared a room. Mom had discovered a Playboy under his mattress and sent him to Dad for "the talk." I didn't understand at the time what was going on, but later when I figured it out, I felt embarrassed for him for years.

"Really. Look right here." I was pointing at the mark on the derriere, but Dad barely glanced at it. I know he was thinking, "I've raised another pervert."

Time to bail and change the subject. "Never mind. What's up, Pops?"

"Well, I didn't know if you were coming."

Oh hell. Forgot about the shoes. "Sorry," I said, following him out the door.

As we exited the elevator at the second floor, I could see a mountain of shoeboxes of all colors and sizes, some open, some not, with a variety of shoes scattered about. It looked like the stockroom had erupted. A couple of employees were funneling customers away, telling them the shoe department was temporarily closed.

"What's the deal here?" I asked as we arrived at the shoe volcano.

"It's bad. We've been going through the stockroom"—he motioned toward his associate, a middle-age woman named Marly, who was carelessly tossing shoes into two big piles—"and it seems like a majority of the dress heels are broken."

"Hmm. Is it just one brand, maybe a defective batch?"

"No, several brands," he said. "This is a major problem. We're talking thousands of dollars' worth of damaged merchandise."

I picked up a couple of broken shoes and examined them, looking for a hint of how they were damaged. There didn't seem to be a smooth cut, like there was with the mannequin.

These shoes probably were just broken by hand, with the heel left dangling.

"I'm sorry, but the shoe department is temporarily closed. You'll have to come back later." A sales associate borrowed from women's fashion was assisting with crowd control.

An irate woman was bellowing, "I'm on lunch break! I need to shop now!" She left in a huff and vowed to complain to the store manager.

"Notice anyone suspicious hanging around the shoe department?" I asked Dad.

"Not really. We've been swamped with the Christmas shopping. I wouldn't notice if Santa himself walked through here. Wait, I'm noticing now," he quipped.

"Funny. Let me just look at these shoes a minute." I poked through the pile, looking for a clue. It took a while, but I found it on a green, strapped open-toe.

"Here's what I need." I showed it to my father.

"What is it?" he asked.

"See that under the broken heel? The letters 'CC'," I said.

"What's that for?" he asked.

"I don't know, but I've seen this elsewhere. We had some other incidents in the store."

"Like what?"

"Can't say right now. But maybe the same person is doing these things. Maybe he's leaving his mark."

"So this creep wants to get caught?" he asked.

"Or maybe mislead us so he can continue his crime spree." I stood up to go. "I need to take this. Let me know what the final tally is."

"OK, son. It'll be a while, though." He gave me another odd look as I left. I know he was thinking about my hand on that mannequin's butt.

7

Back on the Santa throne, business proceeded as usual. Lots of screaming brats, scads of impatient moms, and no sign of relief. Also, no sign of Bambi. When 3 o'clock rolled around, I skedaddled back to my office and collapsed in my comfy chair.

The phone was blinking at me but I ignored it. This called for music and I knew the right song for the occasion. In short order, George Harrison was singing *If you don't know where you're going, any road will take you there.*

I looked around the office. The mannequin still lay in a clump in the corner. The suitcase sat open beside it. I pulled the broken shoe from a Santa pouch and dropped it in my inbox. My computer, as is the norm, was off. Something was ringing. I reached in my other Santa pouch and pulled out Bambi's phone.

"Beers."

"Where the hell are you with my phone?" Bambi didn't sound happy.

"Sorry, I forgot. I'm in my office. Come on up." She slammed down whatever phone she was calling from.

Just then, Jane Mertin walked into the office.

"How are you holding up?" she asked.

Hmmm, that seemed like an odd question. "Fine, I guess. I'd sure like to get back to my normal duties so I can figure out what's going on—"

"About that." She folded her arms and paced to the corner of the room, looked down at the mannequin and the suitcase. Walked back and stood in front of the desk again. Glanced down at the shoe and raised an eyebrow. "We need you on Santa Claus duty through the end of the week. Then we'll have someone else take it from there."

"But Mr. Foster said—"

"Right, Mr. Foster, I know about the reports." She paced back and forth again. She stared at me a couple beats, then said, "Just through the end of the week."

As I was pondering my dismal fate, Bambi burst into the office. She didn't seem to notice Jane. "I need it back." I pushed the cell phone toward her and she snatched it up.

"Y'know," she said. "I don't appreciate it."

"Look, Bambi, I'm sorry. I got called away and forgot about the phone."

"Not that. I mean abandoning me with the damn kids and mothers! I could've been hurt!" Her lip was trembling. Another emotional scene. Sigh. It seemed like it was one after another this week. For a fleeting moment, sportswriting didn't seem like such a bad career after all. It was fleeting, however—I quickly remembered why I chucked it for this security gig.

"Is there a problem?" Jane asked Bambi.

"You're damn straight there's a problem!" she screeched.

Obviously, Bambi didn't know or didn't care that she was addressing a VP in such a shrill manner.

"Jim, you shouldn't be leaving Bambi in the lurch. You have a responsibility...we have a responsibility to the public."

"I'm really, really sorry. I shouldn't be Santa anyway," I offered lamely, casting a glance at Jane.

Bambi gave Jane a small smile of thanks for going to bat for her, then gave me a look that could strip the paint off a fuselage and stomped out. I put my head down on my desk.

"Hang in there, Jim," Jane said. I thought she was going to say she would work something out, get me some relief, but she didn't. She just left.

When I lifted my head, I was groggy and somehow the clock had moved ahead two hours. Lacking further duties at the North Pole or any compelling reason to stay, I locked up and went down the service elevator to the street.

It was snowing, and Hennepin was lit up for Christmas. The sidewalks were full of shoppers and Holidazzle parade-goers.

I felt disconnected. Normally, I would hang around to watch the parade, then pop into The Crater for a quick one, but I just wasn't in the mood. I felt drained, and disgusted, and totally whipped by circumstance. I headed home.

Suddenly, I remembered the clue. CC. I practically ran back to La Scala. Headed straight for FOS, unlocked the door to the display window and made a beeline for the Christmas dinner scene. I walked around the female mannequin, looking for signs of tampering. Nothing obvious. There were people passing on the sidewalk, glancing in. I knew I'd get strange looks but I had to do what I had to do.

Lifting the mannequin's skirt, I did a quick visual scan.

Nothing. A couple of people were staring in at me. I shrugged, then pulled down the pantaloons. Very small, in a very private location: CC. Bingo.

Ignoring the stupefied stares and snickers from outside, I put everything back in order, but when I looked up, Dad was on the other side of the glass, staring at me. He just shook his head and walked away.

I locked the display and exited the store. All the incidents were definitely the work of a single saboteur, or group of saboteurs, and the letters CC had something to do with it. I made some notes.

My cell phone rang. "Beers here."

"Hi, Jim." It was my girlfriend, Rosie.

"Oh, hi, Rosie. I was just thinking about you." Not really, but...

"When are you coming over? I have something I need to ask you about." Uh-oh. I think I've heard this before. I hadn't planned to see her until Friday, but this sounded like it could be serious. Just what I needed—another crisis to add to the growing list.

Then I remembered I was supposed to meet with Tina and Lena at 6 o'clock.

"What do you need to ask me?"

"I'd rather not say on the phone. You coming over?"

"Well, I have a meeting I need to go to at 6. Maybe after that."

"I have class at 7:30, so if you don't get here before then..." She was taking a continuing education course on female perceptive continuity, whatever that was.

"I'll try."

"OK. Later."

"Later."

It was almost 6, but I was too exhausted to meet with the girls. I called them and told them we'd have to postpone it a day. I went straight to my apartment to rest for a bit before my rendezvous with Rosie.

I needed a little pick-me-up, so I put on a pot of coffee. Sitting on the sofa, reading a magazine and waiting for the brew cycle to end, I fell into a dead sleep. The only rendezvous I had was with the sandman.

8

Thursday morning, Dec. 16
Nine shopping days till Christmas
Temperature: 23, cloudy; wind chill, 20

My term of employment at La Scala had been relatively brief, but the director of personnel, Sarah Oglesby, arrived three months after I did and immediately shook up the place.

A vehement reformed smoker, she set in place a policy of no smoking in the workplace, including the immediate exterior of the building, where smokers always seemed to congregate adjacent to entrances. No longer would patrons have to wade through a curtain of smoke to enter the store, which made customers and the majority of the employees happy but a hard-core group of puffers miserable.

Of course, it also gave them a perfect excuse to take longer breaks as they would have to wander off the block to indulge their habit. After punching off the clock, that is. Violators were suspended, and a handful found it too much to bear and quit.

Being an ex-smoker myself, I understood their dilemma. Nowadays, I could satisfy my tobacco cravings by merely making the block with an unlit Swisher Sweet clamped between my teeth.

Usually on the way to work in the morning, I make a couple rounds of the building with my Swisher. It's a twofold routine.

First, to clear my head of any cobwebs from the previous day, and second, to check for any strange situations on the perimeter of the building. Of course, this routine failed me the day the FOS display was tampered with. I guess I wasn't paying attention.

As I was rounding the last corner on my way into the building, I spotted an exceptionally shapely young blonde walking toward me, wearing a polar jacket, miniskirt and boots. It was an odd (but pleasant) sight for winter, even if temperatures were still on the balmy side (double digits above zero). I waited a beat as she passed me, then turned to stare at her departing figure. Oh my, that is some tight miniskirt, I thought.

While admiring the view as she crossed to the next block, I heard my name called, followed by a whistle. The girl turned around and gave me an icy stare, like I was the one who produced the wolf whistle. I shrugged sheepishly. She quickly turned and hurried away.

With my concentration broken (damnit!), I looked around to see the source of the whistle. A woman in dark glasses across Hennepin was gesturing wildly at me. As I crossed the street, the figure looked familiar, and when I approached, I saw it was Tina.

"What's with the sunglasses?" I asked.

"Beers, can't stay long," Tina said. She was in patched jeans and an old paint-splotched gray sweatshirt under a long coat.

She was puffing on a cigarette.

"You going to work dressed like that?"

"Not today."

"You got a day off the middle of the week at Christmas?" I asked, incredulously.

"Got a couple days off. Suspended."

"Suspended?!" I said. "What happened?"

"Accused of a third-degree KMA."

My puzzled look told her she needed to explain.

"You know how there's three ways to say 'kiss my ass'? Like just joking 'kiss my ass,' or kinda half-joking, half-serious 'kiss my ass,' or the really-mean-it, go-to-hell 'kiss my ass'?"

"If you say so."

"Well, my boss took it the third way when I really meant the second way."

"You told your boss to kiss your ass?"

"Just sort of half-joking," she said. "She wanted me to come in an hour early to inventory. I would've had to skip my workout."

"Tina, you don't tell your boss to kiss your ass," I said, shaking my head.

"Aw, kiss my ass. That's the second way, by the way."

"So the glare bothering you?"

"No," she said, without further explanation.

"Y'know, folks who wear sunglasses when it's overcast are movie stars or criminals or addicts. I don't think you fit into any of those categories—last I checked."

She sighed and took off the glasses, revealing a black left eye.

"What happened?"

"Biff the troglodyte smacked me," she said.

"Biff? He a boyfriend?"

"We just had a couple dates. Discovered he's got a little temper problem. Won't take no for an answer."

"You need to report this."

"No, I've got it under control," she said.

"Obviously, you don't," I replied.

"Don't make a big deal out of it. I can take care of myself." She put the shades back on. "Look, I gotta go take care of some things."

"When are you going to return to work?"

"Supposed to work late shift Saturday. I'm not sure..." she trailed off.

"Tina, just chill out, take it easy—and by all means avoid this Biff."

"His real name's Jorge."

"Jorge. Stay away from him, or I'll have to do something about it if you won't."

"Thanks, Beers. You're a friend. But really, I've got it under control."

"If you say so. Can you meet me at The Crater this evening?"

"Sure." She smiled and walked off with a wave.

I decided with all the occurrences of the past few days I would carry my cell phone, regardless of standing Santa policy.

BAMBI WAS A LOT CHEERIER this morning, apparently having forgiven me for abandoning her to rabid urchins so many times.

I gave her a jolly fat man thumbs-up as I took the throne and began the arduous task of providing Christmas cheer to greedy, spoiled children. Ah, joy!

Today, I felt magnanimous, and let them ramble on until they exhausted their full lists of demands, much to the consternation of the parents waiting at the back of the line. I assured the youngsters they would probably get everything on their wish lists, ho ho ho! The mothers must have forgotten that they were young once. Two of them, in fact, rather nice-looking women, gave me the middle-finger wave as they departed with their young ones. Tsk tsk, naughty girls.

The store was busy but strangely quiet. It was noisy, for sure, but nothing unusual was happening. No calls. When break time rolled around and I hit the employee lounge on seven for a snack, I felt confident the worst was over, and the store would return to the normal business of separating customers from their money.

Oh, how naive I was.

I was departing the lounge when Jane rushed in.

"Beers! Come quick!" She headed off into kitchenware and I followed, into the elevator and down to six. There was a commotion around the candy counter. We made our way through the crowd of people to find an elderly woman lying on the floor. The clerk was in a frenzy.

"Hi, folks," I said, addressing the crowd. "Could you move back please? We've got it under control. Please go back to your shopping. Thank you." Slowly, people started moving away.

"I called EMS," Jane said.

"Good idea." I addressed the clerk. "Hi, I'm Jim Biersovich, store security." Her nametag said Risa. "Can you tell me what happened, Risa?"

The nervous clerk could barely speak. "She was...I wasn't looking...she ate the candy. Then she fell." The clerk pointed to a tray of chocolate bonbons.

The candy looked innocent enough, but it may have been tampered with. I slipped behind the counter, grabbed a store bag and put the tray in it.

"Are there any other trays?" I asked.

"No, that's the only sample tray. I put it out just a little while ago. Ohhh, I feel sick about this." She was holding her abdomen and looking a bit green herself.

"You didn't eat any, did you?" Risa shook her head no. "Did anyone else eat any?" She shook her head again. "Don't worry, we'll take care of it."

The woman on the floor was coughing and breathing irregularly.

I pulled clerks from other areas and stationed them around the candy department to funnel customers away from the scene, and to let Risa take a break to regain her composure.

EMS finally arrived and carted the woman off. As I was about to hand a technician the bag of candy, I saw Jane frantically shaking her head. I gave him my card instead and asked that I be contacted as to her condition.

After they left, Jane motioned me to follow her. We went up to her office and she closed the door.

"Jane, don't you think—"

"We can't have a scandal this close to Christmas, Jim," she said.

"But what if the woman is seriously ill? Because of the candy?"

"What if she's not? What if she has a pre-existing condition, a heart problem. Maybe she had a stroke. The candy may have nothing to do with it."

She had a point but it still seemed mighty odd to me. "Jane, why can't we call in the police? We've had too many incidents at the store for this to be random or coincidence. Something is going on."

"We can't, Jim. Mr. Scalabrino doesn't want the trouble."

"Well, he's got the trouble. It's right here in his store."

"You don't understand."

"Enlighten me. I don't get it. Why is Scalabrino so scared of calling the cops? Don't tell me he's in the Mafia…"

Jane's look showed she was appalled. "Jim! That's a terrible thing to say!" I waited. Jane was quiet.

"So what do I do?"

"Just keep a lid on this for now. I'll call Mr. Scalabrino and see what he wants to do," she said. "If the hospital says it was something she ate, tell them about the candy."

I was skeptical, but she was my boss. And Scalabrino was the owner. If they said to stifle it, I'd stifle it for the time being, until I heard from the hospital. But I was nervous about it. I didn't want to end up in a cement mixer, or whatever those guys used nowadays. I brought the candy up to my office and locked it in my file cabinet.

Santaland was a zoo again when I finally got back there.

The natives were restless, and Bambi gave me a nasty look whenever I caught her eye.

Somehow, I spent a couple more hours playing Santa, but my mind was further away than the North Pole. I kept returning to the series of events that formed an ever-expanding puzzle, with pieces that didn't seem to fit into a coherent picture.

By the time my shift ended, I had formulated a game plan. At least it was a plan of action.

9

It had taken me an hour and a half to make all the calls and visit the hospital, but I was prepared when I walked into The Crater and spotted the ladies assembled at a corner booth.

Tina and Lena had that expectant puppy look, obviously eager to hear my latest news.

"Beers, the king of beers! Those your girls?" Sam asked, raising his eyebrows, as he lifted a frosty mug and pulled a Summit porter.

"Just co-workers," I explained.

Sam glanced at them and grinned back at me. "Nice. Two for one. I like it."

"Co-workers," I repeated. Sam snorted as I gathered my beer and headed for the booth.

"Ladies," I said, sitting down and taking a big swig. I paused for dramatic effect and glanced back and forth between the pair before announcing, "I have two letters for you."

"Yeah?" they said in unison.

"CC."

"Huh?" Tina said. "What's that supposed to mean?"

Recapping the events of the previous few days, I brought them up to speed on all the incidents in the store.

"Then I found the CC. It was on the mannequin when I removed the panties."

Lena's eyes widened. "You been gettin' it on wit' a mannequin? Freaky!"

"No," I said. "The broken mannequin. The letters were hidden."

"So?" Tina said.

"So I thought it looked strange. So I checked the suitcase that had the snake in it and guess what I found?"

"CC?" Lena asked.

"Bingo. And I also checked the mannequin in the front window. Ditto. And a shoe in women's shoes."

"I'm not following," Tina said.

"I think whoever is behind all these events put those letters there for someone to find."

"Oh, yeah, that's right. 'Let me commit multiple crimes and just leave my initials on my handiwork.' Good going, Sherlock," Tina said sarcastically.

"Crooks are stupid, but who would be dat stupid?" Lena asked.

"I don't know that they're the perp's initials," I said. "Could mean anything."

"Did you check the employee directory?" Tina asked.

"Of course," I said. "First thing. And no, there's no one with those initials employed here, although there are eight CCs scattered among the other locations."

"OK, so we check them out and—" Tina began.

"Already did that. I called the other branches and got confirmation either from the person himself or the supervisor that they were all on duty at the store the last three days. They couldn't have been here."

"OK, so maybe it's someone tryin' ta pin da crimes on one a deze people," Lena offered.

"Could be," Tina said, "but I'm thinking that's too easy. It's too easy to check and see if any of them were here, which they weren't, you said. I think it may be something other than an employee's initials."

I smiled. "That's what I was hoping you'd conclude, because I think that's where we've got to go. We need to come up with every possible meaning and follow it to a logical conclusion."

"Brainstawm," Lena said.

"Exactly," Tina added. "So maybe it's not a nobody employee—maybe it's like a celebrity's initials. Chevy Chase."

"Chuck Connahs," Lena said.

"Cheech & Chong," Tina countered.

"Charlie Chaplin...Christopher Columbus...Charlie Chan," Lena recited.

"Hold it, girls," I said. "Think about it. Why would some celebrity be blamed for these things?"

"Bad acting?" Tina suggested. "How about Courteney Cox?"

"Yeah," Lena added, "I hated her in 'Scream.' "

"Just a minute," I said. "Let me think." I poured down the rest of my beer and signaled the waitress for another round.

"We're overlooking something obvious," I said. "When I think of CC, something immediately comes to mind."

"Carbon copy," Tina said, slapping her forehead.

"And what is a mannequin but a cawbon copy of a human?" Lena added.

"Exactly. So maybe that's the message. Maybe the person who did this is a carbon copy of the mannequins, like in that Seinfeld episode," I said.

"Or the suitcase," Lena added with a snide smile.

I frowned. "Hmm. There is that suitcase. That couldn't be a carbon copy of a human, or anything else for that matter."

"It had a snake in it," Tina said. "What could that be a copy of?"

"Yeah," I said, "you're right. Come to think of it, the two mannequins don't look like each other." There must be a connection, though. "Hold on a sec. Let me check my notes." I flipped through my notepad and found what I was looking for.

"The snake that bit the customer was a swamp rattler. *Sistrurus c. catenatus*, the Animal Control guy said. Two more C's." We sat in silence until the next round came and drank for a couple of minutes before Tina started shaking her finger.

"Wait a minute. There's another obvious meaning for CC—cubic centimeters. Like 10cc."

"Medicinal doses."

"Don't see a connection dere," Lena said.

"Wouldn't snake venom be measured in CCs?" Tina asked.

"Still don't explain da mannequins."

"There was a band named 10cc," I said.

"Before my time, cap," Lena replied with a smile.

It was quiet again for a minute before Lena said, "Awright, dere's gotta be some more obvious CCs we not thinkin' 'bout. How 'bout chambah a commerce?"

Tina and I glanced at each other, then shook our heads.

Another thought was forming in Lena's head.

"Could be something related ta da holiday season—Christmas carol," she proposed. "Or candy cane."

"And that would somehow be related to criminal activity because....?" I asked.

Lena frowned. "Yeah, boss, it's a stretch. But why else would it be at Christmas season?"

"I saw a Christmas movie a few years ago, named 'Candy Claus,' " Tina said. "Very bad. That would make me want to commit crimes."

"Y'know, this is all happening while I'm playing Santa. You think it's about me being Santa?" I asked.

"Naw," Lena said. "Dey'd be doin' somethin' ta you if dat was da case."

"CC...CC...CC Rider?" Tina said.

"See what you have done," I said.

"What she done?" Lena asked.

"No, that's the lyrics," I said. "See what you have done. Maybe there's something there."

"Like someone is being blamed for causing someone else to do these things," Tina offered.

"Someone who's been forced to do something," I said. "But who? And why?" We were silent for a few minutes, thinking about the possibilities.

"Those other incidents at the store today—I'm not sure they're related to these. At least I have no evidence to that effect."

"Which ones?" Lena asked.

"The lady who collapsed at the candy counter. Apparently after eating some bonbons."

"Candy made her sick?" Tina asked.

"Don't know. They carted her off."

"Dat's a CC," Lena said. "Candy countah."

We pondered that in silence a minute.

"Also, those financial records that got scrambled. Mr. Foster suspects sabotage."

"Maybe it's dat WhyTooKay," Lena offered.

"Yeah, that's coming up," Tina said.

The puzzled expression on my face must have tipped them off that I had no clue what they were talking about.

"Beers, ya gotta turn on ya computah every now and den," Lena said. "Ain't ya heard 'bout da WhyTooKay?"

"No. What is it?"

"It's nineteen ninety-nine. Turn of the century supposed to cause computer programs to fail," Tina explained. "At least that's the theory. No one knows what's going to happen."

"Hmmmmm …," I suggested.

Lena went into some explanation that sailed far over my head about programming and dates and how everyone was worried that computer systems would fail one second after midnight on December 31, 1999. She said she'd been talking with the guys in the database department, Dweep and Kweep, and they were on top of it.

"Should I worry then?" I offered sheepishly.

Lena shook her head and rolled her eyes.

"Tell you what, let's all think some more, come up with other possible meanings, and get back together tomorrow morning. OK?" I said. "Coffeeshop at 8."

When I got home, there was a message from Rosie, wondering where I was earlier. She said she'd call tomorrow and perhaps we could get together finally for dinner. I was beginning to forget what she looked like, it had been so long since we actually had a date. Sheesh.

10

Friday morning, Dec. 17
Eight shopping days till Christmas
Temperature: 11, clear; wind chill, 2

The morning dawned with a jumble of thoughts shouting for attention in my hurting head. Since I only had a couple beers the previous night, I wasn't hung over but I sure felt like it. Grabbing some aspirins from the medicine cabinet, I downed them with orange juice and tried to sort out the notes I had taken the night before.

CC ... Actors? No likely connection.

Christmas related? Well, possible, since it was close to Christmas.

Medicinal dosage? Nothing apparent.

Song lyrics? Hmmmm...

We were overlooking something obvious, I knew, but that's usually the way things are. The solution always seems obvious after it's found.

Over three cups of coffee, I came up with a few more possible meanings for the cryptic initials. I hoped my associates were doing likewise and we could discover that missing key.

While pondering the mystery, I also made a mental note to check in with Rosie this morning. Our relationship seemed to be on hiatus. Not that we were burning up the road, but ever since we got together in August, the frequency and intensity of our dates had been on the uptrend. Until all this stuff started distracting me.

My cohorts were waiting for me at the coffeeshop, Tina in her sunglasses and sweatshirt casuals, Lena in her dressed-to-sell slinky dress and pearls, and me in my normal nondescript black guy-wear.

"Hey, ladies," I called, simultaneously approaching the table where they were sitting and motioning to a waitress for coffee.

"Hey, cap, how ya doin'?" Lena asked.

"Hi, Beers," Tina said. She took off the sunglasses and I saw that the shiner looked even worse today.

"Good. Let's get to work, shall we?"

"OK," Lena said. "I got a list. First one—Countin' Crows."

"Counting Crows?" I said.

"Yeah, dey a band..."

"I know who they are. I just don't see the connection. What else you got?"

"Candid Camera," she said. "Like da old TV show."

"You think someone's taping this?" Tina asked. "Seems a bit extreme for Candid Camera."

"They wouldn't damage other people's property. Maybe their own. Besides," I said, "there would be too much liability if some prank, like the snake, went wrong."

"Yeah," Lena said, "you right. Besides, I don't even think da show's on anymore."

"Anything else?" I asked.

"Just one. Crispy Creme."

"Krispy Kreme is spelled with K's," Tina said. "I should know. My mom worked at one in college. She still has the hat."

"Maybe da crook don't know dat," Lena responded.

"OK," I said, "let's assume we have an illiterate criminal. Why in the world would he be creating havoc here if he had a vendetta against Krispy Kreme?"

"If he works at Krispy Kreme—a baker or icer—maybe he got fired from La Scala. Disgruntled ex-employee."

"There aren't any Krispy Kremes within 500 miles of the Twin Cities," Tina said. "And that bums me out, by the way. According to my mom, they're fabulous doughnuts."

"What do you have, Tina?" I asked.

"Well, I did some asking around and I got a few ideas. Not sure how good they are," she added, "but here goes: country club."

I waited for Tina to continue.

"Doesn't Scalabrino own a country club down in Florida?" Lena asked me.

"I don't know. I'm the new guy, remember?"

"Yeah, he does," Tina said. "And get this—it's called Costa Claire."

Lena started laughing. "Oh my God! Dat's too funny!"

"What? What's so funny?" I asked, looking at Tina. She shrugged her shoulders.

"Don't you get it?" Lena asked. "Costa Claire? Coast is clear? Like a Mafioso telling his capo 'da coasta clear.' I don't know if dat's what he intended, but it's still pretty hilarious."

I frowned at Lena. "Let's keep this serious, OK?"

"Lighten up, Beers," Tina said. "It is pretty funny when you think about it."

"All right," I said as they giggled. "What else?"

"Well, here's an obvious one: Coca-Cola."

"Yeah, dat guy what stocks da Coke machines is pretty creepy," Lena added.

"What guy?" I asked.

"Da guy wit' da scraggy beard, wears shorts when it's 10 degrees below. Got dat Charlie Manson stare." Lena's eyes glazed over, demonstrating the creep's demeanor.

"Know his name?" I asked.

"Nevah noticed his nametag. Too creeped out by da eyes," she said. "But I can find out."

"OK. What else?"

"Comedy Central."

"Good network," Lena said. "But dat doesn't seem like a connection."

"Just throwing out ideas here," Tina said. "Chicago Cubs. Maybe a long-suffering baseball fan?"

"Lord knows Cub fans have felt the pain. But again, what's the connection? Why take it out on a department store in Minneapolis?"

The more ideas we came up with, the further it seemed we got from the solution.

Tina went down her list and fired off a few more candidates: "Chief clerk...common carrier...cold cash...community college."

Lena and I remained silent, straining our brains to come up with some logical link between any of these CCs and the events of the last few days. The silence lengthened, until finally I said, "Well, those are some ideas. Plenty of ideas. Maybe too many."

"Y'know, Jim, maybe you need ta call da cops," Lena suggested.

"No way!" Tina shouted. "Don't you know what'll happen if the cops get involved? You won't be able to tinkle without explaining in detail why."

"What do you mean?" I asked.

"There was an incident a few years ago, before you started here, Lena, and before we had a security position on staff," Tina said, pointing at me. "Someone painted an obscenity on a display wall. No one knew what to do, so they called in the cops. First, we all got a 'private interview' with investigators. Then everyone had to buy see-through purses, so they could spot the spray can I always carry around."

"You were da sprayer?" Lena asked, incredulously.

"No, dingbat," Tina responded. "But they treated me, and everyone else, like a criminal. Like I'm gonna carry a can of paint in my purse after defacing a wall. Idiots!"

"They woulda hadda make me wear a see-through dress," Lena said. "No way would I carry a see-through purse!"

"Good thing you weren't working here then," Tina said. "But they backed down after a couple weeks when everyone threatened to walk out on a Saturday. One good thing about the union—it cuts through the bullshit."

I glanced at my watch. "Look, girls, I've got to make some calls. Keep thinking and let's get together again this evening. Say about 6, at cosmetics?"

"I'm off at 6," Lena said.

"I'm off all day," Tina snickered.

"Oh, that's right. We'll have to meet you on the sidewalk," I said.

"Just don't light dat stogie," Lena said.

Lena and I headed to the store, and Tina took off on her forced holiday. Since I had 15 minutes before my Santa duty began, I hit the phone.

First, a call to Freddie. Got his answering machine and left a message asking him to find out all he could about a former pro football player named Gerald Difansa.

Next, a call to Jane. She wasn't in yet, but her secretary, Sandy, assured me she was working on relieving me of my temp duties, that a couple of Santa candidates were being interviewed today. I didn't ask whether Jane had talked to Mr. Scalabrino about the in-store incidents.

Then I called St. Alphonso Hospital to check on Mrs. Dallon, the snakebite victim. The nurse told me she had checked out. "Was she OK?" I asked. "I didn't even see a bite mark."

The nurse was coy and wouldn't provide any information about her condition. Damn patient privacy. I arranged to have a $100 La Scala Spree card sent to Mrs. Dallon, along with a bouquet of roses. I was also concerned about the woman who had fallen ill at the candy counter, but didn't have any information on her—not even her name.

A quick check of my notes got me the name of the medical technician I had given my card to. I dialed the EMS office, got him on the line and explained who I was. I told him I didn't have the name of the woman, but the store wanted to send her a gift card.

He audibly sneered, told me he couldn't give me that information and suggested that I have someone in authority submit a formal request in writing. When I told him I had that authority, he sneered again and hung up.

Finally, a call to Rosie to find out whether we could postpone our date one more night. I figured this might be a good evening to stick around after hours and see if I could discover any further clues. I felt bad about putting Rosie on the back burner. She might get the idea that I didn't have time for her, and at the moment, she would be correct.

Bambi seemed chipper this morning as I ascended the steps to my post. She actually smiled and winked at me. The usual interminable line of fidgeting children and their moms stretched out before me, like a train barreling down the tracks toward my stalled vehicle.

The first hour passed without incident, giving me a false sense of security, rather ironic since I was security. Then the excrement hit the rotating blades again. My cell phone began to ring, deep in the recesses of Santa's pouch, and I hesitated a moment before grabbing it.

"Santa here," I answered, to the delight of the young cherub in my lap.

"Is this Jim?" the voice asked.

"Yes, that's correct."

"I want a tractor!" the urchin yelled.

"Be quiet, please. Santa's talking."

"Hello? Are you there?"

"Yes, I'm just trying—"

"But I want a tractor!" the tyke hollered.

"This is Anne LaTour in the bedding department?"

"Would you be quiet?!" I said more forcefully.

"I beg your pardon?"

"No, not you, Miss LaTour. I meant—"

"Mommy! Santa yelled at me!" The kid started tearing up. The mother squinted at me and looked like she was about to sock me.

"Is this a bad time?" Anne LaTour asked.

"No—just wait—would you stop it please?" I pushed the wriggling, now crying kid off my lap and put my hand up to stop the next young beggar.

"Now, Miss LaTour, you were saying?"

"We have a situation here? I think we need some assistance?" Every statement sounded like a question.

"Well, Anne, this is Santa, on duty here at the North Pole. Can you be a bit more specific about the situation?" I smiled down at the brats waiting in line.

"I'd rather not—on the phone?"

"Can it wait until a bit later when Santa returns to his workshop?"

"No, I don't think so. I was told you were the one to call when we had a situation?"

"Yes, that's right," I said, glancing at Bambi, who by now was visibly agitated that I was still on the phone. I think she sensed what was coming.

"I'll be right up. Eighth floor, correct?"

"Yes, I'll be waiting." I hung up and shrugged at Bambi, pointing upward. She was shaking her head, trying to silently talk me out of leaving, but she just didn't understand that store security was my top priority.

"Santa needs to take a short break," I announced amid a chorus of groans. "Even Santa needs to answer the call of nature," I added with a ho ho ho. The mothers seemed to understand.

I didn't glance back at Bambi to see her reaction—I just split.

Predictably, on the ride up to the eighth floor, my cell rang again.

"Beers here."

"Jim, this is Don in maintenance. I need to talk to you about a problem we're having with locks."

"I'm in the middle of a call right now. Can it wait?"

"Sure, but we need to do something soon."

"What's going on?"

"Broken locks. Looks like someone's been trying to break in overnight the last couple of nights."

Break-ins! That might explain what's going on. "So was there a break-in?"

"They didn't get in through these doors, but they messed up the locks trying. We had to get a locksmith to replace one Wednesday and one today."

"The guard didn't hear anything?"

"Don't know. I'm just telling you what we found when we came in and tried to enter through the back doors."

"OK, I'll come down after I finish up on the eighth floor." I hung up and tried to figure out whether that was related to the open cases piling up on my plate. If no one got in, how did they cause the damage in the store? Normally, I would be the one arranging for a locksmith, but with all this Santa duty, I was out of the loop. Maybe the request was in my e-mail, which of course I hadn't checked.

Arriving at the bedding department, I discovered the First Sentinel security guard posted at an aisle. I'd never seen him before.

"I'm Jim Biersovich, store security," I told him. "Where's Ms. LaTour?" The guy pointed behind him toward a woman standing in front of a row of beds.

"Ms. LaTour?"

"Hi. It's Anne?" She stepped aside and motioned toward the sleeper sofa behind her. In a corner close to the back cushions, the mattress had a red stain the size of bowling ball.

"Is it blood?" I asked.

She shook her head and shrugged, but the worried look on her face said what else could it be?

"I'll take care of it," I assured her.

"It has to be gone soon," she said. "I have customers?"

"I know. I'm going to get it moved." I dialed Don Anderson and asked him to send up someone with a cart, assuring him that I'd be down as soon as the mattress was moved.

"Do you have another mattress to put in its place after we move it?" I asked Anne.

"My assistant, Carl? He comes in in about an hour. Maybe he can do that?"

"Good. OK. The cart's on the way."

While waiting for the cart to arrive, I walked around the sofa, looking for the telltale clue to link it to the other cases of vandalism. I didn't see it, but it had to be there, perhaps on the underside.

"Yo. Whoa, what happened here?" I turned to see Bradley and Sergei from maintenance with a cart, obviously too small to pick up a king-size mattress.

"A spill, that's all. I don't think that cart's going to handle it," I told him.

"What, this mattress? Piece of cake." They grabbed it by the side grips and manhandled it onto the top of the cart, which disappeared from view. I didn't ask how they were going to move it.

"OK, where to?" Bradley asked.

"My office?"

"On nine, right?"

"Yep. Just drop it by the door." Bradley and Sergei moved off toward the freight elevator, somehow guiding their cargo like a tugboat pushing an ocean liner. They disappeared into the elevator as I turned to look for Anne LaTour, but she was nowhere around.

My visit to maintenance was short. Anderson showed me where the door locks had been damaged in failed attempts to break in. There were lots of scratches on the door but no other telltale clues.

By the time I got back to Santaland, Bambi was at her wit's end.

"You can't keep doing this to me, Beers. I won't stand for it!"

"Bambi, let's talk about this later," I said, resuming the post and greeting my first visitor. Bambi glared at me before pasting on her elf smile and turning to reorganize the snaking line.

Fortunately, there were no more incidents before my shift ended. After ditching the fatman suit and finding the expected initials on the underside of the soiled mattress, I headed out to the sidewalk with my Swisher. I made some notes about the latest events, trying to find any kind of logical link, other than the initials. Nothing. Nada. Doughnut.

The Crater beckoned. I had a few beers while waiting for 6 p.m. to roll around.

11

Friday evening
Temperature: 14, clear; wind chill, 7

Lena met me at the corner, carrying a large shoulder bag and
wearing a big smile.

"You look happy."

"I am," she said. "Dis is gonna be fun."

"Want to tell me what the mystery is?"

"Not yet."

"OK. As soon as Tina shows up, we can brainstorm again."

"No Tina. She called me. Had a thing."

"A thing?"

"Yeah. Just you and me, *kemo sabe*. You got ya caw?"

We walked to the parking garage, rode up to the fifth floor and
piled into my antique Dodge Dart.

"Where?" I asked.

"You know where Tangletown is?"

"Never heard of it."

"Get on da intahstate, east ta St. Paul, get off at Snelling,
south."

"OK."

We headed out of downtown Minneapolis, across the
Mississippi River and toward the smaller twin of the Twin Cities.

As we were crossing the bridge, Lena suddenly leapt into the
back seat, opened her bag and started pulling out clothes.

"Don't look, now." She hunkered down in the seat and I
peeked to see her pulling her dress over her head. "I said don't
look!" She threw the dress at me and I almost veered off the road.

71

"Sorry," I said. "Usually I'm in the back seat, too, in these situations."

I heard her struggling to get changed, but tried not to glance back again for fear of causing an accident. Finally, she said "all done" and somehow crawled back over the front seat with a La Scala bag in her hands, wearing a knit top and some tight blue jeans.

"What's that?" I asked, indicating the bag.

"Secret ingredient," she answered. "You'll see."

We were heading down Snelling and she guided me into the heart of Tangletown, a hidden neighborhood enclave that I'd never explored, full of twisty streets. This must have been the area the governor, Jesse Ventura, was talking about when he said Saint Paul streets were laid out by a drunken Irishman.

"Roun' da cornah dere, see where da big totem pole is?"

I turned the corner around a house that had a 15-foot totem pole in the front yard, carved with eagle heads, rabbits, a bull and assorted other animal visages. "What the hell …?"

"Don't ask. People round heah got dem a weird sensa humah," Lena said. "Park ovah dere on da right, a little furthah."

We stopped and I turned off the ignition. "Now what?"

"Now watch," she said, opening the bag and taking out a pair of high heels. She slipped them on, opened her door and exited, crossing the street carefully on tiptoe, which wasn't easy to do since there was old, packed snow in the road. Making it to the sidewalk, she marched up to the front steps of a tidy Tudor-style house, then turned around and gave me a thumbs-up sign. Suddenly, she let out a yelp and fell on the bottom step.

Concerned that she had hurt herself, I opened the car door to go to her aid, but she frantically waved me back into the car.

As I closed the car door, the front door of the house opened and a middle-age, balding man in khakis and a red plaid shirt stepped out. I couldn't hear what was going on, but after a few seconds he helped Lena up and escorted her inside. I decided to sit tight for a while and see what happened. After two minutes, however, I began to worry that she had really hurt herself or maybe had stumbled into the clutches of a serial killer.

I started imagining all sorts of horrors—a basement torture chamber, blood-smeared walls, dismembered victims…

As I was about to rush up to the house and bang for entry, my cell phone rang.

"Beers here."

"Hey, Beers." It was Lena.

"You OK?"

"Yeah, fine. I was lookin' for ya house and I musta landed on da wrong street. Dis nice gentleman helped me when I tripped on his stoop. Told him I was lookin' for my cousin's house and got dropped at da wrong spot by da cabbie. Ya got a lotta foreignahs drivin' round heah, y'know?"

"Yeah, OK." I wasn't sure what this game was but I was going to play along.

"Anyways, dis nice man says I'm on Amherst Street. Dat near your house?"

"Riiiiiight."

"Oh, good," she said. "My cousin says he's like five minutes away." She obviously said this to the resident of the house, because I could hear a mumbled response in the background.

"OK, then, Jimbo, can ya come and pick me up? I know Aunt Gertie is worried 'bout where I am."

"Five minutes, eh? OK, whatever you say."

"Bye." I hung up and checked my watch. It was torture sitting there another five minutes but by this time I was so curious about what Lena was doing, I wasn't going to blow it.

After waiting six minutes, just so it wouldn't be so obvious, I walked up to the front door and knocked. The man answered the door, asking, "Are you Jim?"

"Yep." As he stepped aside to let me in, I spotted Lena sitting on a couch, drinking a glass of red wine. She had one foot up on an ottoman, sans shoe.

"Jimbo, good ta see ya," she said.

"What's happening, cuz?"

"This here is Rod," she said, motioning to the man. I turned to shake his hand. "Rod helped me when I twisted my ankle on his step. Darn high heel broke!"

Lena's game was beginning to sink in. "Gee, is it bad?"

"Naw, just a twinge. I'll be OK."

"Good," I said. "Well, you ready to go?"

"Your cousin was just telling me about your project," the man interjected.

"Oh?" I said.

"Yeah, how we lookin' fa somethin' ta pull da glue residue off dat china." She was nodding at me now.

"Right," I said.

"Rod here works at dat 3M."

"Oh?" I said.

"Research," he said.

"Yeah, he knows lotsa stuff dat might help us. He's even inventin' somethin' just for dat, right, Roddy?"

"Well, I can't say anything about that now," he said. "But I do have an idea for your problem." He grabbed a pad and pen and started writing. "There are many commercial applications that are useful in removing unwanted substances from surfaces, but most are messy. Here's a little something you can concoct on your own that's pretty neat. What I'm developing is a bit more advanced, but these are the basic ingredients." He finished writing, tore off the sheet and handed it to me.

It was a list including spray-mount adhesive, lemon juice and a couple of chemical compounds I'd never heard of. "Isopropylene mechta—what?"

"Now, you may have to visit a hobby shop to get the last two on that list," he explained. "There's one near the university, Babban's, that carries all sorts of minerals, compounds and assaying equipment for chemical engineering and geology majors. I'd try there. Just show them that list. They'll know."

"Hmm," I said.

"Dintja say somethin' 'bout fingahprints?" Lena said.

"Side benefit," he answered. "This mixture is so good, you can lift fingerprints with it. Add a little talc into the mix and they show up perfectly. It's basically what law enforcement agencies use."

"Cool," I said, for lack of a better response. "So I just mix these ingredients…?"

"Mix everything but the spray-mount in a glass dish," he said. "Proportions are shown. Paint it on with a small brush, spray the spray-mount, wait three minutes and it peels right off."

Now I was getting excited. "That's excellent!"

"Yeah," Lena added. "Aunt Gertie gonna be happy ta get her garage sale dishes cleaned up." She winked at me behind the man's back.

"Right, the dishes. We'd better get going, Lena." We thanked the man profusely as I helped Lena up and on her wobbly way to the car. Heading back across the river, I said, "That was fun."

"Yeah, not too shabby," Lena said. "'Course, he probably wondered why we have different accents..."

"I have an accent?" I asked, jokingly.

"And why you called me Lena. Told him my name was Betty."

I winced. "Crap. You didn't tell me."

"No biggie." She shrugged. "Probly thought it was a family nickname."

"Well, why was I Jim and you're someone else?" She didn't have an answer for that, just shrugged again.

"Did you really hurt your ankle when you fell?"

"Naw. Actin'." She beamed. "Got a pair a doze broken heels from ya dad. A little maskin' tape kept it tagethah till I made my move."

"Brilliant," I said, chuckling. "Now we need to work on this formula. You got time to do that?"

"Hmm. Guess I could get ovah dere and pick up da ingredients."

"All right. That works. Maybe we can get together and give it a shot when no one's around tomorrow morning."

"I hafta work inventory," she said.

"OK, I'll check with you tomorrow about your afternoon schedule."

"Hey, y'know, I thought a somethin' that shoulda been obvious to Tina," she said.

"What?"

"She works da cosmetic countah, right?"

"Yeah?"

"You'd think she woulda suggested Coco Chanel for da CC," Lena said.

"Yeah," I said, pondering that. Should have been the first thing she suggested. Why didn't she? Puzzling, and disturbing.

After dropping Lena off at her parking garage, I headed home to my apartment. The answering machine blinked three rapid pulses. The first call was from Freddie, asking me to meet him at The Crater for beers. He said he had some interesting information for me.

Tina left a message saying she had a couple more ideas and would talk to me tomorrow. Yeah, and I've got an idea for you too, I thought.

Finally, Rosie called to say she was out right now but would like to get together tonight, if possible. And could I please change the message on my machine: *Watch out where the huskies go and don't you eat that yellow snow*. Guess she wasn't a Zappa fan.

I called Rosie but got her answering machine, naturally, and told her to call my cell when she got back in. Then I called Freddie and told him I was on my way. After another day and night of mayhem, I could use a few more beers.

12

Freddie was camped out in a booth near the bar when I arrived at The Crater. He had two mugs, one full and one near the bottom.

"You got me one. Great," I said, sitting down across from him.

"Mine," he replied, pulling the full mug closer. "Get your own." Freddie was puffing on a particularly nasty stogie, much to the chagrin of the women at an adjacent table who kept shooting him nasty glances.

Sam was walking over to give me his trademark greeting when he was waylaid by one of the put-out patrons.

"Can't you do something about that?" she asked, jabbing a finger in Freddie's direction.

"Ma'am," Sam said, "the owner gets to do pretty much what he wants in here." He shrugged and turned to face me. "What'll ya have, Beers?"

"Surprise me," I said. "Maybe some kind of Summit."

"Damn lesbians," Freddie muttered.

"Hey, go easy," Sam said.

"And what's that 'owner' stuff?" I asked.

"Well, I'm the owner, right?" Sam asked.

"Yeah—oh, I thought you meant Freddie."

"Right. That's what I wanted them to think. Takes the heat off me, y'see?" Sam headed back to the bar, shrugging again to the hard ladies, and I turned back to see Freddie deliberately blowing a smoke ring toward their table. They got up and moved further away, glaring at him the whole time.

"Freddie, what's up?"

He set the cigar down and leaned toward me. "Beers, you got a crusade?"

Confused, I just shook my head at him.

"A crusade," he said. "What pushes your buttons, makes you go on the warpath, what weighs on your mind and makes your blood boil."

"I'm not sure what you're getting at."

He picked up the cigar, tapped off a long ash and took another pull. "Here's the deal. I know an old sportswriter who's launched a campaign aimed at reducing the length of halftime at football games. His name's Derrick Ambrose.

"Ambrose covered college and pro football games for years without giving a second thought to halftime. That's because he was busy pumping the sauce from his briefcase. But guess what? He gave up drinking, then he started noticing how long college football halftimes were getting to be.

"He did a lot of research—actually he had the sports clerk at his paper do most of it—"

"Where's this guy work?"

"He's retired. Most of the time was in Rochester, spent a few years with AP Northeast, retired in Colorado Springs."

"Never heard of him."

"That's not the point. Anyway, so he gets some research on length of halftimes and he traces it back to Super Bowl Ten at the Orange Bowl, 1976."

"Let me guess. Up With People?"

"Good guess! The Super Bowl had this huge production with fireworks and dancers and Up With People and everybody sane was appalled, but apparently the advertisers and a certain demographic loved it. Because that became the standard for halftime excellence."

"Yuck."

"Yeah, yuck. So he put about a decade's worth of televised games into a spreadsheet and charted it and he came up with an alarming pattern. Halftimes have been gradually getting longer through the years, mostly due to advertising, much to the chagrin of Ambrose and the rest of the non-drinking press."

"So what did he do to try to reverse the trend?"

"Lobbied with the NCAA, lobbied with the conferences, wrote some bitter columns, most of which got spiked, and generally let everyone he met know how disgusted he was.

"Other writers started avoiding him like the plague. Nobody wanted to sit next to him in the press box. Almost knocked him off the wagon. He was a bitter old man when he retired.

"Of course, he had a valid point."

"A voice crying in the wilderness."

"Exactly." Freddie took another deep draw on the cigar.

"Damn shame. Ironically, length of halftime for regular season pro games is a tight 12 minutes. College games are all over the map. But he's not the only lonely voice. I've got my own crusade, y'know."

"Yeah? What is that?"

Freddie waved for another round. "Beers, y'know how you pull into a mall lot or parking garage and you're driving around and around looking for a free spot, and you finally see one, and you ease up to it, start to pull in—and discover that some monster SUV idiot is taking up two slots and there's not enough room for your subcompact? Some bozo who can't steer an 8-foot-wide vehicle between parallel white lines 12 feet apart."

"You want to be a parking instructor?"

"No, goofball. I want the people who run the lots to wise up and start penalizing unskilled parkers by charging them double or having them towed."

"That won't work."

"Wanna bet? You go in these parking garages and they've got signs posted all over saying 'Vehicles taking up more than one space are subject to towing.' I just want them to enforce that."

"You think they ever will?"

"Nope. But I'm on a mission. Every time I see an illegally parked car, I leave one of these on the windshield." He reached in his shirt pocket and pulled out a folded slip of yellow paper.

On it in bold letters was a warning:

YOU ARE IN VIOLATION OF PARKING
REGULATIONS. THE RULE IS: ONE SPOT PER VEHICLE.
YOUR LICENSE NUMBER HAS BEEN NOTED AND YOU
WILL BE TOWED ON THE NEXT VIOLATION.

"Wow. You've got balls."

"Why? Doesn't cost me much to mass produce them—free, in fact, on the office copier—and if it reforms even a small fraction of the inconsiderate parkers, the world will be a better place."

"So why not just ask the management of the parking garages to enforce their rules?"

"Are you kidding? They put up a sign, but they're so afraid of losing business that they don't want to upset the bad parkers. That's a huge chunk of their clientele."

"But that's not logical," I said. "What about all the good parkers, such as yourself, who are pissed because the idiot is allowed to take up two spots without penalty?"

"Which is exactly my point. But parking garage managers are all pansies. No guts. They won't confront anybody. They buy these 'no double parking' signs in bulk, post them, and hope people conform. Doesn't work."

"I see you didn't go on the wagon when you started your campaign."

"Beer helps me think clearly."

"Right," I said, taking a guzzle myself.

"You may not know this, but there's a whole website where people can talk about their campaigns, mycause.com, and enlist support from other obsessed folks. You'd be surprised at some of the things people go on a rampage about."

"No, I wouldn't, after talking to you."

"Very funny," Freddie said. "I'm mainstream, dude. You wouldn't think my campaign was very weird next to some of them."

"Like, for instance….?"

"Like the guy who wants to make Big Bird the national symbol, instead of the eagle. Pacifist, I guess."

"No…nut case," I said.

"No kidding. And the woman who wants automakers to build cars so the engine quits when music is played beyond a certain decibel level."

"That's futile."

"And the group in Utah—and I swear this is not a hoax— who wants to change federal law to allow cannibalism of criminals on death row."

I didn't know how to respond to that, so I was quiet for a minute, sucking down my beer like Sam was about to run out, which I was pretty sure he wasn't.

"So this all has some meaning to me, I guess. Eventually, you'll get to the point, like your stories sometimes do if an editor sees them before they go to press."

"Ha ha. You're hilarious. This has lotsa meaning," Freddie said. "But first, lemme ask you a question. What's your cause?"

I blinked a few times and looked around the bar, probably seeking a clue. "I don't know."

"Yes, you do," Freddie answered. "You know."

"No. I don't."

"Beers, you know. Say it." He stared at me. "For God's sake, man, you told me a bunch of times about it."

"You mean my classic music collection?" Freddie had spent a lot of time drinking beer and watching football in my apartment, so he was quite familiar with my extensive selection of classic rock LPs, 8-track tapes, cassettes, reel-to-reel tapes and assorted stereo equipment from the ancient past, rescued from ungrateful owners at garage sales and thrift shops for a fraction of their original cost. It filled an entire wall of my den, and the second bedroom was full of unsorted finds. I envisioned myself as a rock historian. Too bad there wasn't a career path for that.

"No, no, no, not the music. But speaking of that, I've got a clue for you, Beers. There's a new gadget, been out for a while now, called a portable disc player. You put a thin circle of plastic in it, turn it on, and you can take your music with you wherever you go."

"Amazing!" I replied, matching his sarcastic tone. "But I've already got a Walkman."

"This is better than a Walkman. You decide what music you want to hear. Put your CD in there and hear the whole record."

"Sorry, CDs aren't very collectible. Tapes, yes. Vinyl, absolutely."

"You need to step up to the 19th century, Beers. You're living in the past, man!"

"The past was better."

"I give up. You're hopeless," he said in exasperation. "Anyway, that's not your cause. Not the one I'm talking about. You know."

His wide-eyed gaze demonstrated an assurance that I didn't share. What was it? I couldn't remember telling Freddie anything about a crusade. I wasn't like him. No obsessions….wait.

I knew. Yeah, now it was coming back to me. On the sports staff, working nights, manning the phones, taking high school football stats…

"You mean…"

"Yeah?"

"Joe Pyne?"

"Bingo!"

"Freddie, that's not a campaign."

"You told me you wanted his shows back on TV. That you tried to find out who owned the rights…"

"OK, but I'm not obsessed to the point…"

"Nobody's heard of the dude and you're campaigning to get him back on TV."

"People of a certain age have heard of him—my parents talked about his shows all the time—and I'm not trying to get him back on TV. He's dead. I just want to see reruns of his shows."

"A campaign."

"Well, yeah, OK. I mean, you've got a million cable channels with all sorts of old shows, and…well, I guess I've told you all this before."

"There ya go! OK, so you got a campaign, I got a campaign—everybody's got their own campaign."

"Some stranger than others," I added, raising my eyebrows.

"You got that right."

"Freddie, did you call me down here to talk about my obsessions, or to buy me several beers." I shook the empty mug at him.

"I'll get this round," he said, waving toward the bar again. "You're gonna need at least one more to wash down what I'm gonna tell you."

OK, so now I was interested in Freddie's inane patter. But he was going to make me wait until the next round came, holding up his palm toward me as I began to tell him what a lousy bum he was to keep me in suspense.

"Now," he said, setting down his new and quickly half-empty mug. "You've got the background. Nutty people, obsessions…"

"You're including yourself in that category, not me."

"Whatever. People with a cause. So I'm looking through this website, amusing myself with some of the wacky campaigns that people want to get me juked up about, and guess what I come across?"

No, I wasn't going to guess. I stared at Freddie without twitching.

"Not gonna take a guess, eh? Well, let me just give you a name: Bambi Schroeder."

"Bambi?"

"Bambi."

"OK, Bambi," I said. "What about her?"

"She's your assistant, right?" Freddie wiggled his eyebrows suggestively.

"She's playing an elf. I'm playing Santa. She's not my assistant. She works in a different department. I barely know her."

Freddie laughed. "Riiiiiight. That's what Santa wants us to believe. Well, here's a news flash, Saint Nick. Your Bambi is moonlighting, and I don't mean in the elf toy workshop."

"So what? Lotsa people have second jobs, and just because—"

"Not what I mean, big guy. I thought her name looked familiar, then remembered you mentioned her the other night. Her name's on the website because she has this secret obsession."

Freddie downed more beer and smirked, keeping me in the dark a while longer, trying to get a rise out of me. I played it cool, taking a long gulp of my own and looking around the bar again.

"And this secret obsession?" I asked calmly.

"Her employer might frown on her off-duty activities. Especially seeing as they fly in the face of La Scala's stated purpose of making money."

"She's a socialist?" I asked.

"Close, but not quite."

"Communist?"

"Strike two!"

"Well, who else is opposed to making money?"

"You're missing a bet."

"Freddie, some of us have to get up in the morning and 'ho ho ho.' You're going to have to get to the point or I'm—"

"She's a free trader."

"A what?"

"Free trader. Group that promotes barter, opposes all use of currency and, of course, paying taxes."

Now I knew there had to be a mistake. As far as I could tell, Bambi picked up her paycheck every two weeks like everyone else. Taxes were deducted from her paycheck, just like everyone else's, I was certain. She was a buyer, for God's sake, which meant she dealt in high finance with outside vendors, who certainly didn't barter their goods. Freddie was a couple irons short of a full bag, with logic that flowed like a sand trap.

I was about to tell Freddie as much when I saw a hand grab his mug and splash the contents in his cigar-chomping face.

"You're a pig!" one of the hussies from our earlier confrontation screamed. The pair stomped out as Freddie and I sat too stunned to respond. Sam saw the action and rushed over with a bar towel to help clean up the mess.

"Hey, sorry 'bout that, Fred," Sam said, dabbing at the beer dripping from his face while trying to suppress his laughter. "Those kind explode when you least expect it. Maybe you were right, Beers—had all the hallmarks of a lesbian drive-by. Let me get you another round—on the house." He rushed off to pull a fresh Leinenkugel and Freddie started giggling.

"What's so funny?"

"First free beer in The Crater," Freddie said. "And it only took a beer shower from a militant dyke."

"Man, you need to lighten up with those cigars. Non-smokers can't stand the smoke. Anyway, I think there's a movement under way in the Legislature to outlaw smoking in bars."

"You're shitting me, right?" Freddie said. "That will never get off the ground."

"I think it'll pass. Pretty soon you'll be huffing that stinky stogie out on the street."

"It's a bar, Beers. That's what bars are for."

"One of the papers I worked at before I came up here put in 'smokeless' ashtrays in the newsroom. They were supposed to suck all the smoke in so as not to offend nearby workers. That didn't fly, because you pick up the cigarette to take a puff and the smoke goes up into the airstream. Someone got rich off that stupid idea."

"This is Minnesota. Half the people in the state smoke just to keep their insides from turning to ice cubes in January."

"Non-smokers, and ex-smokers, are a tenacious lot."

"You're an ex-smoker. I don't see you throwing suds at me."

"I place a higher value on beer, obviously."

"You can't tiptoe around every hothead your whole life. You'll never have a real life if you do," he said.

"Yeah, but I may live longer—and less beer-drenched."

"Anyway, back to Bambi." Sam set down his fresh beer and Freddie resumed his spiel. "You were looking for someone with a grudge or an agenda that might be causing trouble at the store, right?"

"Who told you that?"

"Ran into Tina at lunch. She says you got your hands full, bunch of sabotage threatening the smooth flow of commerce."

"There have been a few incidents."

"And who might object to La Scala making money, other than someone who's opposed to the traditional exchange of goods for money?"

Freddie's smug look told me he was pleased with his analysis. I wasn't sure he was on the right track, but it was an interesting piece of information to try to fit into the puzzle.

"Freddie, what do you think about Y2K?" I asked, changing the subject.

Freddie's brow furrowed. "The year two thousand bug? The geeks at the paper are swarming the building like a stepped-on ant pile. They're hauling old Selectrics into the newsroom in case the computer system goes toes up. Down on three, they're setting up a bivouac room. They're hauling in cases of bottled water, granola bars and sleeping bags. They must think I'm holing up in there when the shit hits the fan, but they got another think coming."

"You think something's gonna happen?"

"I have no damn clue. I'm a writer. I write what happens. I don't make predictions, especially about computer operations." His look told me he was pretty concerned.

"I asked Lena how serious it was. Could the world come to a grinding halt at the turn of the year? She laughed and said Dweep and Kweep assured her nothing was going to happen."

"Well, there's your answer," Freddie said. "Who's Dweep and Kweep?"

"Freddie, I gotta go."

"Sure. But think about what I told you."

"I will. Say, did you find out anything about Gerald Difansa?"

"Damn. Forgot about that. What was it you wanted?"

"I need to find out anything I can about his sports career. Somewhere I heard he was a pro football player for a short time."

"Anything else you can tell me? College, address, where he works…?"

"La Scala."

"Ahhh," Freddie said. "I understand. On the QT. See what I can find out."

As I was leaving, a thought hit me. "Hey, Freddie? What do you think of when I say 'CC'?"

"CC. Carbon copy. Like you're e-mailing, right?"

"Yeah, that's right. Well, see ya."

"Si, si."

"CC what?"

"No, si si. Like Italian. Or maybe Spanish."

"Oh, right." Yet another possible meaning for the letters. Yes in Italian. Could there really be a Mafia connection? What other meanings had we missed?

"Si si ya, Freddie. And keep quiet about this, will you? I don't want to see this stuff in the paper one morning. Unless you want an unemployed ex-sportswriter moving in with you."

"Mums the word," Freddie said. "For now."

ON THE WAY HOME, I stopped to get gas. Thankfully, the small tank on my Dart ensured that I could get by with a single Jackson, whereas my gas-guzzling friends were feeling the pain of their road hog lifestyle. It was still hard to surrender to the highway robbery of almost $1.50-a-gallon gas.

While the tank was filling, I dialed Rosie again, but she still wasn't home. At the rate we were going, I might not even recognize her the next time I actually got to see her.

Arriving back at my apartment, I discovered the door ajar. This was not a good sign, unless of course Rosie was here and had just entered. Maybe she had her hands full with groceries and forgot to close the door. Yeah, she was going to cook me a nice meal.

"Rosie?" I called, nudging the door open a bit wider. No answer. All quiet. I reached in and flipped on the foyer switch and pushed the door all the way open.

"Rosie, I'm home." Still nothing. I peeked around the corner into the living room, but it was dark and quiet. Carefully opening the foyer closet, I armed myself with my ski pole and edged into the apartment. I flipped on a table lamp and looked around. It was deadly quiet. After another minute of hesitation, I tiptoed my way down the hall, turning on lights as I went. Bathroom, clear. Bedroom, clear. Hall closet, clear.

Satisfying myself that I was alone, I pondered the meaning of the open door. Could I have left it open in my preoccupied rush to meet Freddie? Or maybe Rosie had come by, then left.

I looked around for a note but didn't find one. The answering machine had no messages for me.

After casing the place one more time, I called Rosie. This time, she was home.

"Hey, Beers. I'm glad you called."

"Hi, Rosie. Were you here earlier?"

"No.

Why?" No need to alarm her if I had just stupidly forgotten to close the door. "Nothing. Thought you might come by at some point. What's up?"

"Well, it's been a while since we got together ..."

"No kidding. What color is your hair again?" I asked, making a stab at witty repartee.

"Purple. Same as always," she said, playing along with the joke. "I need to ask you about something, but I'm exhausted tonight. Can we get together tomorrow morning?"

"Just ask me now."

"No, I want to ask you in person."

Uh-oh. I had forgotten about her need to ask me something in person. A face-to-face usually meant heavy conversation, a serious topic and generally bad news. With several more hours to worry about what it was, I'd be a wreck by the time we talked.

"If it's that important, I'll come over right now."

"Now's not a good time. Meet me at the spoon tomorrow. Say 11?"

Why was now a bad time? I wondered. This must be really bad. "If it's something I did..."

"No, no, nothing you did. I just need some advice, and I'd rather not discuss it on the phone, OK? Everything's cool."

This was some small bit of relief, but that wouldn't stop me from worrying. "OK, 11 at the spoon. Good night."

"Good night, Beers. I love you."

"Love you too, babe." I hung up and walked to the sliding doors leading to my nosebleed deck, my vista on the world 22 floors below me.

Gazing out toward the museum, I spotted the giant spoon in the sculpture garden, with the enormous cherry balanced on the tip. Life is a spoonful of cherries, I suppose, when things are going smoothly. But right now it seemed to be the cherry pits.

13

Saturday morning, Dec. 18
Seven shopping days till Christmas
Temperature: 15, heavy snow; wind chill, 6

Dawn brought with it fresh snow, the kind of downpour that blankets the blackened road sludge and drapes the landscape with those idyllic scenes conjured up by advertisers that never quite jibe with the reality of plowing and white-knuckle commuting.

Seeing as it was my day off, and my first day free of the red suit, my mood should have been conquer-the-world. But there was that meeting with Rosie that I was dreading, even though she assured me all was OK. The unknown frightened me.

While guzzling my morning brew, perusing the Herald and listening to "More or Less Hudson's Bay Again" by the Masked Marauders, snatches of a dream came back to me.

Concentrating, I pulled together details from my subconscious and remembered I had been dreaming about camping out with one of my classmates from high school. It wasn't even someone I hung out with, just a guy who was in the same class.

We were at a campsite in the Smokies, and I thought it odd that he was wearing snorkeling gear. When I asked him why, the landscape suddenly changed to a snowy scene, but it was snow in place of sand at a beach. He proceeded to dive in the water and swim off.

That was it. At least, that was all I could remember. Sometimes it seemed my dreams were just strange randomness, like scenes from a Fellini film. Maybe that's where Fellini got his ideas. Maybe I should become a filmmaker, make films based on my dreams. Or maybe I should just keep them to myself so people won't think I'm nuts.

One of these days, I told myself, I'm going to start writing these dreams in a logbook. Perhaps they hold some clue to a deep mystery that's only solvable after all the scenes are considered together. Then I would have something, if not a real film concept.

My reverie was interrupted, naturally, by the phone. I decided to let the answering machine pick up. As Rosie had requested, I had changed the message.

"*Beers here. Actually, Beers not here. If you want Beers, try the liquor store. Or place your order for Beers.*" *beep* "Hello. Is this Jim Biersovich? You don't know me, so I won't bother you with a name, but I have a musical message for you, since I believe you like rock 'n' roll. It goes like this: You're gonna lose that girl. Oh, also? Butt the fuck out." Click.

Huh? What was that all about? Someone trying to move in on Rosie? Could that be what all the mystery with her was about? On top of everything else I had to worry about, I certainly didn't want to lose her.

The voice wasn't familiar, but I detected some undertones of an accent. I replayed it and gained no further clues. Just what I needed—more disturbing information to add to my rapidly growing mountain of bad news.

If I had caller ID, I might be able to figure out who that was. But I'm a little too cheap to pay for usually unneeded services. My callers normally consist of Rosie, Freddie, Dad, Jane and way too many telemarketers.

Then I recalled that there was some code I could punch into the phone to return the last call. Star-something. After pondering that for a minute, I remembered and punched in star sixty-seven. I got Rosie's answering machine and hung up before leaving a message. Obviously not the right code.

I called my go-to guru for all technical matters, Lena.

"Yeah, boss, jus' hit staw sixty-nine an' it rings da last numbah." She warned me that it didn't always work because some numbers were blocked or unlisted.

When I tried that, a recording told me the number couldn't be reached. Figured.

This was a time for consolidating my thoughts, so I sat down with a legal pad and began transcribing my notes, organizing the events of the past five days, along with the brainstorming sessions with the ladies and Freddie's weird theory. By the time I looked up, I had six full sheets of notes and the time was fast approaching 11.

I headed down and out toward the sculpture garden to learn my fate. Expecting the worst ensured that I wouldn't be disappointed, and might be pleasantly surprised. If I was going to get dumped, it was probably fate in this season of non-stop trouble. The silver lining: one less present I'd have to buy for Christmas.

Nearing the spoon, I had just about worked out my relationship resignation speech when I spotted Rosie. She was sitting on a bench across from the sculpture and its frozen reflecting pool, huddled against the falling snow. For a few seconds, I seriously considered turning around and leaving before she saw me, but figured that would just be postponing the inevitable. Might as well get it over with.

"Rosie." She turned and stood up, waiting for me. An awkward hug followed, then I noticed she was crying.

"What's wrong?" I asked.

"Beers..." She bit her lip.

"What?" Just say it—dump me and get it done with, and we'll live miserably ever after, I thought.

"I've got a problem."

Oh boy, here it comes. "What kind of problem?"

She glanced around the garden, then started walking down a path. I followed.

"I'm afraid," she said in hushed tones, constantly looking behind her.

Huh? This wasn't what I expected. "Afraid of what?"

"Not what. Who. I think..." She started sobbing quietly. "I think someone's stalking me."

"What?!"

She reached in her purse, pulled out a tissue and dabbed at her eyes. I started glancing behind us also as we walked.

"I've had some weird calls, hang-ups, strange wrong numbers. For the last couple of days, I've felt like somebody's following me. I know it's crazy. Then someone left a package on my desk yesterday. No name."

"Package? What was in it?"

"I don't know. I'm afraid to open it."

"Rosie, I'm sure it's nothing to worry about. I get wrong numbers all the time. Some even leave messages on my machine, like I'm supposed to know them." I wasn't going to alarm her with the latest message I received, but I was certain it had to be her stalker. "And the stuff that's been going on at the store lately, well...."

"No, Jim, this is different. I can't explain it, but it feels creepy. I've had wrong numbers too, but not as many as I've had in the last week or so. And I don't think it's just coincidence that it all started after the policy change."

"Policy?"

"Office of International Student Services. You know, my employer?" Rosie's job at Duvet Community College was always full of foreign intrigue, seeing as she was like a den mother to the hordes of international students that arrived on campus each fall. Helping students find housing, employment and other essentials while dealing with language and cultural barriers kept Rosie in a state of high alert—and stress—during most of our courtship.

"So, what policy?"

We were walking toward the museum entrance and Rosie motioned me to follow her inside. She led me over to a bench against the wall across from the door and we sat. A couple with three young children were exiting the exhibit hall and a few others were chatting near the front desk. Outside, the garden was draped in white against a dark gray sky, framing a steady snow shower.

Rosie leaned closer and began whispering, her eyes darting between me and the entrance. "A couple weeks ago the dean decided the college needed to keep closer tabs on international students. Something mandated by the federal government, I guess."

"Yeah, your college is a hotbed of radical unrest," I said with a grin.

"Beers," she said sternly, "I'm being serious." Her gaze told me to cut the crap and just listen. I lost the grin. "We had to get every foreign student to fill out a new form, and believe me, they were none too happy about it. I'm not sure if a lawyer has gone over it carefully, but it seems to sign away just about all their rights."

"Can I see this form?"

"I'll show you when you come up to my office."

"OK, and we can open that package..."

"I don't think that's such a good idea."

"Why not?"

Rosie was silent so I repeated my question.

"Because I think I want someone from security there when it's opened."

"And I am...?"

"You know what I mean. Campus security. I want an official witness in case..." She trailed off.

"Just what are you expecting to be in there?" Rosie didn't say anything. "And is there something else you need to tell me?"

After a few seconds, she said, "Yes."

Kaboom. Here comes the bombshell. "Well? What is it?" Might as well get it over with now so I can get on with my life, I thought.

"No. Not here. Let's go to my office." She got up and started walking to the entrance, leaving me gaping after her. Either the suspense was going to kill me or I was going to strangle her. Gritting my teeth, I followed her out to the parking lot.

We got in her car and drove in silence to the college. She pulled into the administration lot, empty except for an old van, and quickly jumped out. She unlocked the building's back door, then relocked it once we got inside.

Light seeped into the darkened hall from one lone closed door at the far end of the corridor. Rosie headed off to the right, down a completely dark hall, which she flooded with light by hitting a switch near the door to her office. International Student Services was stenciled on the frosted-glass upper half of the door. She unlocked it and headed in, casually flipping on a bank of light switches that blinked fluorescents over a maze of half-walled cubicles.

She headed through the office straight to her closed inner-office door. Pausing to turn and glance at me, she unlocked her office, flicked on the light and pointed to a small brown box sitting on her credenza.

As I walked closer to get a better look, she blurted, "Don't touch it!" She saw the why on my face, then added, "Because I've been threatened."

"What? Threatened? Who?"

"I don't know," she said. "But with the other things going on, I think it's best if we just..." She started crying softly. I pulled her to me and let her cry on my shoulder. Of all the things I expected to deal with today, this wasn't one of them.

"Why didn't you tell campus security about this and let them take it away?"

"Because it just showed up on my desk late Friday. I was in the ladies' room, and when I got back, there it was."

"What makes you believe…"

"I had a call earlier in the afternoon. I thought it was a prank or something at first, but he said my name, and he said I was going to be sorry if I contacted the authorities." She started sobbing harder.

After escorting Rosie to a chair, I leaned over the box to examine it from several angles. It didn't seem very ominous, and there wasn't any ticking, so I was pretty sure it wasn't a bomb.

It looked like it had been wrapped with a plain brown grocery bag, sealed with strapping tape. No return address, just Rosie's office address and enough stamps to start a small post office. The postmark was from downtown Minneapolis. If there were clues hiding in the exterior packaging, I wasn't seeing them.

Eventually, Rosie's crying stopped and she sniffled a few times before standing up.

"I don't hear any ticking sounds. Why do you think this is related to the phone call?"

"I don't know," she said. "I just have a feeling."

"OK, if we're not going to open it, let's get out of here."

Rosie pointed to a stack of paper in her inbox. "That's the form." I had forgotten about the form already. Picking it up, I read through the list of questions and felt my blood pressure rising at the obvious invasions of privacy the college was sanctioning.

Most forms nowadays seemed to want more than I was willing to tell—phone number, Social Security number, best times of day to reach me—but this went far beyond that, asking for names of good-character references and neighbors, titles of recent movies seen and books read, and preferences in music, among other things.

"Does anybody fill all this stuff out?" I asked. "Seems like the semester would be half over before you'd finish."

"Looks a bit excessive, doesn't it? Now you can understand the students' objections. For some of them, it recalls the oppressive governments they've escaped. Now they're getting the third degree all over again. This is supposed to be a learning environment, not a concentration camp."

"Well, it's not that bad," I said, trying to put a positive spin on the seemingly indefensible.

"Try telling that to the students," Rosie retorted. "I'm thinking one of the students is taking it out on me."

Then my cell phone rang. "This is Jim."

"Hey, son. You want to come over for supper? Just gonna throw steaks on the grill."

"Hi, Dad. Little busy right now. Let me call you back. You at home?"

"Yep."

"OK. Call you back shortly." I hung up.

"Jim, I was hoping we could go out tonight. It's been a while…"

"I know, Rosie. My Dad wants me to go over there for steaks. I'm sure he wouldn't mind if you—"

"I was hoping we could go out alone."

Dilemma. I hadn't had a date with Rosie in a week, so I knew our relationship needed a refresher. But that was just due to a coincidence of events. Wasn't it?

"Let me call him back and see if we can do it tomorrow." As I was chatting with Dad, telling him I'd pick him up for church, then we could grill, I got another call. "Call coming in, Dad. Pick you up tomorrow at 10:15, OK?"

"Sure, son. Bye."

"Beers here."

"Jimmy Jet, it's Tina."

"Hey, Tina. What's up?"

"Can you meet me in about an hour? Got some new scoop I want to share."

"Uh…I don't know…"

"You're going to want to hear this. Can't talk right now. Meet me on the west end of the High Bridge. There's an overlook." She hung up before I could further object.

"Was that Tina?" Rosie asked.

"Yeah. Wants me to meet her at the High Bridge. You know where that is?"

"Near downtown St. Paul. What does she want?"

I knew Rosie wasn't too keen on Tina, thinking her a bit rough around the edges and somewhat of a foul mouth. But I hadn't really explained to her our working relationship, or the details of the current crises at work.

"Let's go get a cup of coffee," I said, "and I'll fill you in on what's been going on at La Scala. You may not believe it."

"What? What is it?"

"Let's go. I need some coffee. It's been a long week."

We left the office and headed a short three blocks to the nearest Muggles, settling in with hot, black Colombian. As I recounted the string of incidents, her expression changed from amusement to puzzlement to horror.

"So you see why I've been busier than I'd care to be. And having to play Santa on top of all that certainly doesn't help."

"You're still Santa? I thought you were trying to get out of it?"

"Well, they said it was only for a week, so hopefully that's over with. Anyway, Tina has been helping me look into some things, and I think I need to go see what she's got. So, the High Bridge…?"

Rosie explained a simple route, then dropped me off at my apartment building. Having explored St. Paul only briefly on my initial foray into the Twin Cities, I still got lost despite having Rosie's directions, but eventually stumbled on the critical landmark she said would lead me to it: a giant green Adirondack chair. The art piece graced a small park at the lower end of the High Bridge, looking like a gaudy prop from a bad sci-fi flick.

The bridge rose ahead, shooting straight up toward the west side. Abutting the bridge on the other side was the overlook, a parking area with benches and garden that afforded a nice view of the Mississippi River and the downtown skyline. I made the block and approached from the opposite direction, then parked to take in the view and wait for Tina.

Snowfall had resumed, and as I gazed out over the river from the railing, it struck me how puny the Big Muddy looked this close to its source. Perhaps it was the fact that the frozen edges, soon to meet in the middle to form a solid mass until spring, made it look even skinnier than it was. Nevertheless, it seemed a mere shadow of the massive expanse of water I became accustomed to living in the Crescent City for a few years.

As I concentrated on the girth of the riverbed, I didn't notice Tina until she elbowed me and said, "Nice, huh?"

"Pretty cool view from up here."

Tina was breathing heavily, obviously having jogged up, from the looks of her outfit. She was sporting a dark blue Polartec vest over a gray sweatshirt and black Lycra tights, with what looked like football cleats on her feet.

"I didn't know you were a runner," I said.

"There's probably a lot about me you don't know," she answered.

"How can you smoke and run?"

"Don't do 'em at the same time."

"You shouldn't smoke at all."

"Yeah, well, everyone needs a vice or two. Otherwise, how could you live with yourself?"

Tina was employing her usual logic, which left me without an answer.

"So what have you got that I need to know about?"

She began stretching to keep limber. "Some papers I ran across. You might find them interesting, maybe even too coincidental."

"Well....spit it out."

"I'll have to show you. It's back at my apartment. Just live a few blocks up from here. Meet me there in 10 minutes."

"Where?"

"Go up two blocks, take a left, then a right on the first street. No. 639 on the left, Apartment 3B. I'm running back." And she took off.

I watched her run for a block, then turned back to the river. Its tranquility, frozen in time, was a jarring juxtaposition to my current state of agitation. On the far side I could see a group of kids walking out onto the ice, gingerly testing to see how far they could go. Their folly could be rewarded with a tragic plunge into freezing water if the ice broke. I couldn't bear to watch.

Hopping in the Dart, I headed up the road and found Tina's street. I parked across from a nondescript red brick building and looked to see if she was approaching. She either already made it there or had taken a more circuitous route, because there was no sign of her. There was, however, a disturbing note—the front door to the building was ajar, which seemed strange on such a cold day.

Heading carefully across the street through the new slush, I kept my eyes peeled for Tina. As I stepped up to enter the building, a loud crash came from somewhere above. I only hoped it wasn't from 3B. As I headed up the stairs, I suddenly heard descending steps. A large person rounded the flight above and barreled into me, knocking me against the wall of the landing, where I hit my head and fell. By the time I got back up and shook out the cobwebs, he was gone. Fearing that Tina might be in trouble, I ran the rest of the way and located 3B. Again, a door ajar.

"Tina?" I called, peeking my head around the door. No answer, and no sound. Looking around the room before entering, I saw papers and sofa cushions and other items on the floor. Either Tina was a messy housekeeper or someone had just tossed the place.

Gathering up the tiny bit of courage I had left, I pushed open the door and looked around again before entering.

"Tina? You here?" Still nothing. Carefully inching my way through the room, I checked the kitchen, then the bathroom, and finally the bedroom, which was also in disarray like the living room. Strange. Where was Tina?

I was afraid of foul play at this point, worried that whoever that was that knocked me down may have done something to her. Maybe she was tied up in one of the closets, knocked out. Or maybe he pitched her out a window. As I was walking to the side window to check, I heard a voice behind me, scaring me so badly I knocked over a table lamp, which went crashing to the floor.

"Beers! That's my favorite lamp!"

Thank God it was Tina. "Jesus, you scared the hell out of me!"

"Sorry. But you broke my lamp."

After a couple of deep breaths, I began picking up the pieces of the mangled lamp. "Where were you? I got here and the door was open and—"

"Did you see a guy in here?"

"No, but someone knocked me down in the stairwell on my way up. A big fellow."

"Oh no." Tina groaned. "I thought I saw him exiting the building as I was jogging up the street."

"Who was it?"

"Jorge."

"Jorge? Who's that?"

"Biff? The troglodyte boyfriend? Now ex-boyfriend."

"Oh."

"We had a little disagreement—actually a huge one, the final one, I hope. Last night I left him a message telling him to return my apartment key, leave it in the mailbox. Guess he was a bit pissed."

"Wow. So that was Biff." I glanced around at the mess in the room. "Looks like he was more than a bit pissed."

Tina picked up a shard from her prized lamp, looked around and sighed heavily. "I guess…"

"You need to file charges. This is criminal."

"No, Beers. I just want to be rid of him." She touched the side of her head, where her black eye was starting to fade. "I just want him gone."

"Tina," I said, spreading my arms, "this doesn't look to me like an amicable separation."

Tina sniffled a bit, turned and walked out her front door.

"Where are you going?"

"Be right back," she called. Footsteps trailed off down the stairs, and I plopped heavily on the sofa. In 30 seconds, she was back up the stairs and slammed the door behind her.

"Bastard."

"What now?"

"He didn't leave the key."

"So he'll be back."

"Yeah," she said, looking off toward the kitchen. "Look, I gotta take a shower. Let me show you why I asked you over."

She went to the kitchen and opened a lower cabinet next to the stove. Pots and pans came crashing out on the floor— might as well, I thought, since everything else seemed to be there. Then Tina stood up holding a cardboard box.

"Take a look at this," she said, dropping it on the counter. "I'll be out in a bit."

She zipped off to her bedroom, peeling her vest on the way. Sitting on one of her barstools, I opened the top flaps and discovered a thick stack of paper. It looked like a computer printout of some sort, the old kind using fanfold paper fed through a dot-matrix printer. There must have been several hundred pages of it.

Of course, most of it was foreign to me—seemingly random globs of letters, numbers and symbols that could have been some sort of spy language as easily as a manifesto produced by little green men from the planet Fripplemoo.

However, something in the first few lines looked awfully familiar. Could this be the key to solving the crime wave at La Scala? Was Biff the behemoth behind all the incidents? I pored through page after page but could find no other intelligible data.

My concentration again proved a little too intense, as I didn't notice Tina behind me until she said, "Well, what do you think?"

Turning around, I faced an incredible sight—Tina had a towel wrapped around her waist, her arms up drying her hair with another towel—and nothing else. A pair of exquisitely shaped breasts stared back at me and my brain went into instant gawker meltdown. Tina didn't seem at all self-conscious, although I couldn't pull my eyes away from the bounty of bosom before me.

"You notice anything?" she asked, still working on her hair.

"Uh...I...uh..."

"Top of the first page," she said, pointing.

I forced my eyes to follow her arm down to her hand and willed them to look at the paper. Barely cooperating, my eyes regained focus and I zoomed in on what she was pointing to.

"Uh...yeah...C&C." It was repeated several times in the first few lines of the printout. "This document is somehow the key. So Biff's our guy, eh?"

"No, silly," Tina said, folding her arms and partially obscuring my view. "This isn't Biff's. It's Bibb's."

Now I was really confused. "Bibb Tokan? The slob in programming?"

"The one and only."

Bells went off in my head. "This is a copy of the damaged finance report—and he's the one that sabotaged it! Now it's starting to fit together."

"Did you see the other one?"

"What?" Tina lifted the pile of printouts from the box to reveal another, almost identically hefty printout underneath. "Look at the first line of this one."

"CC Tool. Crap. Now I know we've got him!" Tina resumed her hair-drying, leaning to the left to let it hang down and squeegieing it with the towel. Her perky friends came back out to visit.

"Uh...we...uh..."

"He doesn't live far from here. We should go confront him," Tina said, shaking her head and in the process causing her breasts and my heart to bounce in unison. A surge of adrenalin found its way down my torso and I felt a building pressure in my jeans.

My imagination leapt to attention and concocted a vivid scenario that played out only in my head: Tina glances at my bulge and smiles. She drops both towels. Pulling me toward her, she turns her face up to kiss me and I let go of all rational thought as she slowly guides me to her bedroom.

Mick Jagger croons *Let's spend the night together, now I need you more than ever…*

After a vigorous workout on Tina's mattress, I am pleasantly spent. While I lay panting, trying to return to some semblance of a normal-breathing human, Tina hops up and I notice a tattoo on her left cheek, a small green triangle enclosing these words:

SLIPPERY WHEN WET

Then the guilt sets in as Rosie's scolding visage replaces the afterglow, and the hallucination fades to reality.

14

Saturday afternoon
Temperature: 24, snow; wind chill, 8

In reality, and regretfully, Tina went to her bedroom solo, got dressed, emerged and said, "C'mon, Beers. Let's go catch us a crook."

While I was still in the heavy-breathing stage mentally, Tina dropped on the sofa to put on her sneakers and gazed wistfully at the lamp parts. "It's gone," she said with a heavy sigh.

"I'm really sorry. I'll get you a new one."

Tina hopped up and put on her jacket. "Nope, you can't replace that. I've had that lamp since I was a kid. Oh well, forget about it."

She grabbed the box and opened the front door. "Coming?"

Piling the guilt of destroying her family heirloom on top of the guilt of mentally ravishing her, I slunk out of the apartment, down the stairs and to the car, promising myself I would somehow purge myself of such thoughts. Somehow.

Tina guided me through the back streets of her neighborhood, past rows of uniformly small houses, an ice rink on the grounds of a grammar school and a corner playground, to a main thoroughfare dotted with old-time service stations and mom-and-pop businesses. It looked like Smalltown, USA.

We stopped at a block of nondescript brick apartments. "Go around back," she said, pointing to a side parking lot that was packed with vehicles. "Over there."

She pointed to a cedar-fenced area adjoining the corner of the building, with an open gate. I parked alongside it and we hopped out.

"That's where I found the box," she said, indicating one of the two Dumpsters in the fenced area.

Good. Now I had to add consorting with a Dumpster diver to my resume of guilt.

"So you know this is Bibb's because...?"

"I saw him dump it," she said. "Sometimes I cut through parking lots on my jogging route. I was coming around the far corner over there and I saw this guy that looked familiar. The Goth Vader outfit is a dead giveaway from a long way off.

"Anyway, I watched him and he looked a little skittish while he was dumping this box, like he wanted to make sure no one was watching. But I was."

"OK. Then let's go ask him about it."

We waited until someone left the back entrance and casually caught the door before it closed and locked us out. The standard wall of mail drops was right inside the entrance. Affixed to #22 was a smudged white label with TOKAN printed on it.

Down the long hallway we went, heading up the stairs when we hit 20 and ran out of doors. No. 22 was a number short, but the outline of the missing 2 made it clear this was the right apartment.

Tina rapped out a beat just below the NO SOLICITING sign pasted under the peephole. After 10 seconds and no sounds, she knocked again, this time with both fists, until we heard heavy footsteps approaching and "All right! All right!" from the other side.

Bibb opened the door and a strong aroma—cooked beets, incense, something—hit me like a wave. He stood there scowling at us, sporting a funky-looking Gilligan hat, Deputy Dawg T-shirt, safari pants and socks with toes built in.

"Hello, Bibb," I said.

"Whaddaya want?" Right friendly chap.

"Can we come in? You know Tina, right? We need to ask you about something."

"I'm pretty busy," he said, eyes darting back and forth. "What's this about?"

"We caught you," Tina said, gloating.

"Wha...?"

"What she means is," I said, frowning at Tina, "you might want to explain a few things to us about what Tina found."

"I don't know what you're talking about."

"If we could just come in…"

Bibb wasn't having any of that, however. He looked back into the apartment, then stared directly at Tina. "No. Go away."

As he started to close the door, Tina pushed her way inside and marched into the living area before Bibb could react. I followed, toting the box.

"You can't just barge into someone's home like that!" Bibb was sputtering. "I'll call the cops. I'll…"

"You aren't gonna do any such thing, Bibbster," Tina responded. "Show him, Beers."

I set the box down on the corner of a coffee table cluttered with newspaper, glasses and dirty plates. The apartment was furnished with bachelor pad leftovers, not surprising since it was hard to imagine Bibb dating a woman, much less getting married.

A brown couch with rips in two of the three cushions sat facing a drink-ring-stained console TV. Next to the console was a computer station with a monstrous monitor bigger than the TV screen, a keyboard mostly buried under paper, and shelves stacked haphazardly with manuals, games and assorted action figurines. Luke Skywalker and Speedy Alka-Seltzer were the only two standing, and they seemed to be posed in some sort of to-the-death standoff. I was afraid of what I might discover if I looked into the kitchen.

"We'd like you to tell us about this," I said, pulling out the first printout and showing it to him. Bibb took the pages and plopped heavily on the couch, glancing nervously between us.

"Where'd you get this?" he asked after a quick glance at the second page.

Tina smiled broadly. "You're in huge trouble and it'll be a lot easier if you cooperate and tell us everything. We may not have to get the cops involved."

He looked at us oddly and said, "I don't know what you're talking about. I didn't do anything."

"Oh yeah? Well, we have the printout—" Tina began.

"Hold on, Tina," I said. "Bibb, we know what's been going on at the store. This document links you to those events. You need to tell us what you know now, and why you did this stuff. Maybe the bosses won't press charges—"

Bibb sat stonily staring at me, then at Tina. "You're both nuts. I haven't done anything… What do you mean 'what's been going on at the store'? What does that mean?" He was playing dumb, so I supposed we had to play along.

"You know. We know you know." I pointed to the pages he was holding. "We know what 'CC' means." Not really, but a little fishing might land a big one—and Bibb was enormous.

"Yeah, so?"

"You're in deep doo-doo, buddy." Tina was scowling now, getting impatient with his act.

"Look, I didn't do anything with C&C. Someone asked me if it could be done. I was just dinking around with it," he said, casually tossing the printout back in the box.

"I wouldn't call destruction of property and assault with a deadly weapon 'just dinking around,' " I said.

Bibb stood up abruptly. "What the hell? You better get out of here now before I kick your scrawny asses." Which sounded like a hollow threat coming from the Pillsbury Doughboy, but if he sat on us, we were goners.

"So you're gonna make us go to the cops, eh?" Tina said, smirking again. "OK. C'mon, Beers. Let's go see what the cops think about this." She grabbed the box and Bibb quickly snatched it out of her hands.

"Wait. Wait." He sat back down with the box on his lap. "Let's just hold on a sec. You got me mixed up with someone else."

"I know these are your printouts. I saw you dump 'em," Tina said. "Maybe we should look in your computer..." She started walking toward the workstation.

Bibb dropped the box back on the table and jumped up to head her off. "OK, OK. So I did a stack dump into my decompiler—big deal. I didn't pirate it, if that's what you think. It's just binary code. You could get the same thing if you dropped the exe in a C++ module...."

He went on spouting more gibberish, and I had no idea what he meant, although I gathered it had something to do with computers.

"Wait, wait, wait. We don't care about that. We want to know why the criminal activity."

"I told you—it's not criminal unless I replicate it and sell it. What are you talking about? I'm talking about C&C."

"Yeah. CC. At La Scala."

His face screwed up in perplexity. "La Scala doesn't sell C&C."

"Sell? Who said anything about selling?" Now I was getting even more confused.

"Let's go, Beers," Tina said. "We're not making any progress here." She grabbed the box again. "Management will be interested in seeing this, I'm sure."

Before Bibb could object, we were out the door and back down at the car. My thoughts quickly returned to events at Tina's apartment. Tina, however, was elsewhere.

"Y'know who needs to see this? Lena. She's the computer whiz." Tina riffled through a few pages. "Yeah, Lena would know."

I started the engine and headed out to the street, hesitating before broaching the subject. But it had to be said.

"Tina, back at your apartment…"

"Beers, don't worry about it. It's just a lamp, OK?"

"But what I was trying to say…"

"Look. It happened. No big deal." She smiled.

I didn't know how to explain how guilty I felt, not only about breaking her lamp, but also about lusting after her. Not to mention being so incompetent as a security agent. Powerless. Caught in a vortex of bad karma.

Tina guided me back to her apartment, then jumped out with the box. "I'll call Lena, see what she thinks. See ya."

She closed the door and headed off a few steps before turning and coming back to the car and rapping on the window. I rolled it down halfway. "Beers, forget about it. No biggie."

She turned and hiked into the building, and I watched her all the way, wondering how human chemistry could turn relationships on their ear in a matter of minutes. Now I knew I would feel awkward being around her. I would be picturing her topless, and wondering when it could happen again.

PREDICTABLY, THE PHONE RANG as I worked my way back to the larger of the Twin Cities, trying to figure out how I was going to face Rosie without letting on what had happened with Tina. It was Freddie.

"S'up, Beers?"

"Hey, Freddie, what's cooking?"

"You and me need to go out this evening. I got something to show you."

Here we go again. "Not tonight, bud. I think I need to see Rosie." Although if this was work-related, it might be the perfect answer to my current dilemma.

"It's work-related. I think you're gonna want to see this."

"Where we going?"

"Casino. I'll pick you up at 6:30."

"Uh, that's not such a good idea…"

In addition to my former addiction to tobacco, I had a small dependency on one-armed bandits that took most of my spare change back in the good old days of carousing with fellow sportswriters.

"Don't worry—we're not going to gamble. In fact, leave your wallet home. But you need to see this, and I need to tell you something I found out."

After hesitating for only a few seconds, I said, "OK. 6:30. See you then." Rosie wasn't going to like this, but it would give me more time to digest today and plan my next move.

Now, how to break the news to Rosie. She could be home, in which case her cell phone would be off and I could leave a message. Or she might be out with her cell, in which case I could interface with her answering machine. Mentally flipping a coin, I went with the cell number on the odds that she was lying low due to the perceived threats, and also waiting for my call to go out.

"Rosie, it's Beers. Got to take care of some work-related stuff this evening. I'll call you tomorrow." I hesitated a moment. "I'm really sorry." Another pause. "I'll definitely call you tomorrow, noon latest." And hung up.

That should buy me some time. Better turn off the cell, in case she tries to call back. And better not go home. Where to? Not back to Tina's, that's for sure. Maybe I'll just pop in on Dad. He'll like that.

After only doubling back a little, I pulled up in front of his place, in the Highland Park section of Saint Paul, about a three-iron shot from the Little Muddy. When we lived in New Orleans, it was the Big Muddy. Up here, it's a mere creek.

Dad was, as usual, tending to the patch of winter peppers he was growing on the back porch. He took great pride in his peppers, cultivating one of almost every variety, from bell peppers to banana peppers to hot peppers. His patch was the neighborhood supply for all things peppery. And his prize recipe, pepper-wrapped rib eye, was certainly the menu he planned for our weekend cookout.

"Hey, Dad. How you doing?"

"Hi, Jim. Didn't expect you today."

"Just in the neighborhood, thought I'd pop in. Peppers are looking good." He had about two dozen pots, with a profusion of green, red, yellow and purple peppers just begging to be harvested. My eyes began to water just looking at the habaneros.

"I might have to work tomorrow, so I thought I'd at least try to come by today."

"Work? That's too bad. I was going to grill you up a steak."

"Well...."

"Got time for one this afternoon? We could still have our cookout today."

"Sure. Can we make it before 6:30? Going out this evening."

"Oh, right. How's Rosie?"

Uh-oh. Better not get into this right now. "Uh, I'm not going out with Rosie tonight. It's...work-related." The look on Dad's face told me he knew not to inquire further.

That's what I loved about him—he gave me space, unlike Mom, who was always giving me the third degree. Poor Mom.

With the snow still falling, Dad fired up the grill in the garage. In no time, the smoke and aroma of grilled meat wafted out through the open door, certainly stimulating salivary glands up and down the block.

"Tom and Jean are coming up for Christmas. Jean said she'd cook dinner here. Hope you can join us," Dad said.

"OK, I'll bring Rosie. I'm sure she'd like to meet the nieces." Tom and his wife, Libby, had a 10-year-old, Daisy, and lived in Des Moines. Jean and her husband, TJ, had 4-year-old Samantha and 2-year-old Dorothy. They were driving up from Wichita. It had been a year since I saw her kids and maybe three since I last saw Daisy. I probably wouldn't recognize them.

A few brews and a fine steak and baked potato later, along with a post-meal nap, I was mellowed out and ready for the evening's adventure with Freddie. Making my farewell and promising to stay longer next weekend, I headed back to the apartment, timing it to arrive just minutes before Freddie, so as to avoid any possible Rosie confrontation.

15

Saturday evening
Temperature: 11, snow; wind chill, 4

Freddie was already there, waiting in his car at a meter in front of the complex. I gave him the "one minute" signal, pulled into the underground lot, raced up to the apartment, dropped my wallet, ignored the answering machine and ran back down.

"OK, Freddie, this better be good."

"Beers, trust me. You do trust me, don't you?"

He started laughing as I frowned, and we started out for the evening's "work."

The casino was a 35-minute drive north of the city. Freddie loaded a Steely Dan CD and we rode without talking, spurred forward by the jazzy guitar licks of Walter Becker and bouncy keyboard of Donald Fagan.

In the distance we saw the trio of intersecting spotlights, forming a tepee to mark the location of this Indian-owned establishment. As the strains of "Katy Lied" emerged from the speakers, we pulled off the road into the rolling acres of casino lots, which seemed to only have open spots in the adjacent county.

Boarding the shuttle with a retired couple and a trio of coeds, we gazed at the sea of cars, noting the clustering of buses and limos near the entrance.

Disembarking, Freddie took off through the casino and I followed. He seemed intent on reaching his destination before dropping any clues to the information he had for me. Oddly, he headed straight into the bingo parlor after grabbing a matchbook from a change station on the way.

The room was auditorium-like, with banked seats 30 across and 20 deep, each with its own small table, facing a stage where the numbers were posted. A large grid showed the numbers already called for the game in progress, and casino personnel manned the ball cage, microphone and cashier's station.

Predictably, Freddie marched up toward the front and took a seat directly across from the spinning cage. As I sat next to him, Freddie pulled out a long cigar from inside his jacket and offered it to me across his arm like a sword.

"I don't think we can—"

"Sure, we can, Beers, it's a casino." He pushed it into my hand and pulled out one for himself.

After we lit up, sending a mushroom cloud of smoke across the stage, almost obscuring the view of the action, Freddie flipped his book of matches onto my bingo desk. "Take a look." My head was already light from the first few puffs. Smoking one cigar every six months did that to me.

It was an ordinary-looking book of matches sporting the logo of the Fortunate Son Casino. I opened it and noticed the absence of a secret phone number inviting me to a randy rendezvous.

"Cool matches. You collect?"

"Look on the back." I flipped the matchbook over and saw what Freddie was getting at—the letters CC in a florid script. Hmmm. This was interesting.

"Chippewa Corporation," Freddie said. "That's the name of their company. They own this casino and two others, one up toward Duluth and another near Fargo."

"Indians? That's weird." This was a link I hadn't considered, although now that I thought about it, there were a lot of Sioux, Ojibwe, Chippewa and other tribes in this neck of the woods.

"They call them Native Americans nowadays. I know you want to be politically correct," Freddie said, chuckling at the irony.

"I don't know if there are any Native Americans working for La Scala," I said.

"You probably wouldn't know unless you asked them. It's not like they go around in feathers and war paint." He blew another large plume toward the board, which was filling up rapidly with numbers. "Let me tell you a few things about Minnesota that maybe you don't understand."

"Way back when, this state was chockfull of Norwegians and Irishmen. The Norwegians, of course, were hardy souls used to the frigid winters. They felt right at home. The Irish were usually too drunk to notice the cold, but they made good use of the Mississippi, when it wasn't frozen, to establish bootlegging operations and make a good living.

"For years, Minnesota was seen as a lily-white state—lots of Caucasians and very few of other races. That's been turned on its head. Now there are huge immigrant populations, mainly in the Twin Cities. You've got Hispanics, Vietnamese, Laotians, Somalis, Russians, blacks, Italians, you name it, in large quantities. They've all got their own little society, their own culture and their own crime. Of course, the Indians—I mean Native Americans—were here before them all."

"Wait. Russians and Italians? They're white, right?" Freddie puffed and continued while I scribbled notes.

"You've said you suspect some Mafia connection because of who Scalabrino is. But don't rule out other ethnic groups— they've all got some sort of Mafia. Even the Indians."

"Bingo!" someone yelled from the back of the room. We turned around to see an elderly woman in a hideous green polka dot dress with a breathing apparatus attached to a portable oxygen tank waving toward the stage. A drink girl paused in front of Freddie's table, and he ordered scotch, neat, and a Cold Spring Moonlight Ale for me.

"Mafia. Huh."

"Yeah, Mafia," Freddie said. Smoke curled up toward the high ceiling of the bingo cavern. The smoke was getting thick in here, much like the growing cloud of confusing information cluttering my cranium. The winner continued crying "Bingo! Bingo!" between racking coughs, long after the bingo pit boss delivered her winnings.

AT LEAST FREDDIE HAD THE DECENCY to stay away from the real gambling tables. Knowing my weakness, he showed a great deal of restraint. That didn't stop him from pushing another cigar and more drinks my way as he enlightened me on his version of Twin Cities history.

Coming from what the locals quaintly refer to as "outstate," Freddie had spent most of his life in and around the metro area, picking up more than his share of urban lore and especially sports knowledge from his constantly changing beat. He was the kind of guy who could get the most recalcitrant public or sports team official to spill his guts by sharing a dirty joke, offering a fine cigar or springing for a couple of martinis.

Being an outsider, I had not bothered to learn much of the political, criminal and cultural history of the Twin Cities, so Freddie's crash course at the casino was quite enlightening.

He told me about the Hmong gang, Ntshav Tsev ("House of Blood"), that roughed up partying college students the night the university won the hockey championship. A Somali group calling itself Ciwo cizo ("Biting Pain") that torched a meat market because the butcher shorted someone's mother on pork loin. An Indian gang, Brotherhood of the Flesh, that slashed tires at a competing tribe's casino. The Russian Sacred Union, causing a rumble with an Irish group called Iron Shamrock, resulting in lots of broken storefront windows in the Lake Street market corridor.

Then the payoff for all this education, smoke inhalation and brush with temptation: Freddie finally got to what journalists call the "nut graf," the piece of information that defines the story.

"Here's what you really need to know," he said. "You asked me to find out what I could about Gerald Difansa and his 'illustrious' football career. Well, there ain't a whole lot to tell. But it is interesting.

"Gerald was the prototypical late bloomer. In high school, he mostly rode the bench as a third-string defensive back. His coach thought he was too scrawny and slow to make an impact. But something happened between high school graduation and college."

"He finally reached puberty?" I guessed.

"Funny. No, he shot up 6 inches to 6-foot-1 and gained 30 pounds of muscle by working construction. He walked on at Mankato State and quickly became the starting tight end as a freshman. His fierce blocking and dependable hands caught the notice of lots of Big Ten coaches, and he transferred the next year to Northwestern.

"Then he grew 4 more inches, bulked up to 260 pounds and got switched to defensive end. His junior year, he was second team All Big Ten. A broken foot halfway through his senior year prevented him from getting more honors, but he did get drafted by the Denver Broncos."

"Oh...my...Elway!"

"Yeah, well this was before Elway hit it big. In training camp, he was so tenacious, he knocked two tight ends out of commission. So they switched him to offense to fill the gap, since they already had more than enough defensive linemen.

He was turning heads in exhibition season—four touchdown catches, lots of de-cleaters, even played a bit on defense—and was projected to be All-Pro when the season began. And that's when it hit the fan."

Freddie signaled a cocktail waitress for another round and pulled out his third cigar of the night. I declined to join him this time.

"The Friday before the opener, he was suddenly cut. Very hush-hush. He kicked around for a couple years in Canadian football but didn't really live up to the promise he showed in that first preseason. Then he abruptly retired from football and went to Europe for a few years. When he came back, he was a couture display designer—window dresser, to you. The rest, as they say, is not worth mentioning."

"So what's the mystery?"

"Rumor was he got back involved with his high school gang. And I mean a wop gang, kind of Mafia prep school. Knocking heads, threatening a few shop owners, some petty larceny. Word was the Denver mob found out he was inside— the NFL, that is— and made him pull a few jobs. Team kept the cops out of it, but gave him his walking papers when it all came out."

" 'It' being...?"

"Burglary. Two players' cars and head coach's home. Probably would have gotten away with it, but the coach's wife was hiding in the closet with her boyfriend and ratted him out."

"So you think Gerald has some gang ties."

"Yeah. Might want to follow that up. He might be trying to get caught so he can get out."

What Freddie said made about as much sense as any theory we'd come up with yet, but not being trained in forensic investigation, I could only absorb any information I could get and hope inspiration or divine intervention would show me the solution. Logic wasn't cutting it so far.

"Listen, Freddie, what do you think about Scalabrino?"

"Scalabrino? Mafioso," he said. "Big time."

"How do you know?"

"Oh, I've heard things."

"Such as?"

"Well, this Dayton's chick I dated once or twice told me he was involved in some mob thing."

"Rumor and innuendo."

"No," Freddie said defensively. "No. It's true."

"Proof?"

"Well, not per se…"

"As I thought," I said. "Anyway, you have to promise me something."

"Sure, Beers."

"None of this is on the record. You can't write anything about this or tell anyone at the paper about this."

"Or you'll get whacked?"

"Worse. I could get fired."

On the ride back, Freddie regaled me with his latest batch of dirty jokes. Why he didn't go into standup comedy I'll never figure out. I was laughing so hard, I almost forgot the highs and lows of this busy Saturday.

Almost.

When I finally got back to my apartment, thoroughly whipped, I opened the door, flipped on the light, dropped my keys on the table and noticed I was standing on a folded sheet of paper, obviously slipped under the door. Picking it up and unfolding it, I found a simple message formed from torn pieces of newspaper: DROP IT. And underneath that, in the now familiar blue marker, CC. At least this time he had the courtesy not to break into my apartment, if CC was the intruder last time.

The message machine was blinking. One from Rosie that I skipped for now. One from a telemarketer—delete. And one from Lena.

"Hey, Beers, gotcha printouts ovah heah dat Tina found. Dey's sumphin' ya need ta know 'bout dis heah. It's not whatcha think. Call me."

10:45. Too late to call tonight. Catch her tomorrow. Today was a day of information overload. Perhaps tomorrow would bring a little enlightenment.

16

Sunday morning, Dec. 19
Six shopping days till Christmas
Temperature: 6, light snow; wind chill, -2

After a fitful night, I awoke to the sound of my cell phone ringing. Looking out my bedroom window, I was greeted by another frigid, overcast, snowy day. Resisting that inner voice telling me to ignore it and escape under the covers, I flipped open the phone and uttered a barely audible "Hello?"

"Jim? This is Jane. What can you tell me about the situation at the store?"

Barely coherent at this point, I surmised she was talking about the ongoing question of who was behind the various incidents.

"Well, I've got some leads, but nothing solid."

"They're telling me we may have to close until—"

"Close? What for?" Now I was awake.

"The structural engineers are saying the fire may have—"

"Whoa! Whoa! Whoa! Hold on. What fire?"

"This morning's fire in the deli."

"I didn't know there was a fire." Now I was panicked. I was supposed to know, but how was I supposed to know? "First I've heard."

"I guess the guard forgot to call you. Anyway, the fire may have caused some smoke damage on the first floor, but we think it was contained pretty quickly. I need you to get down there and see what we can do to stabilize the situation. It's too close to Christmas to be closing. We'd be murdered!"

That's the only thing that hasn't happened yet, I thought.

"OK. I'll get over there."

"And call me at home." She rattled off her number.

"Right." I hung up, threw on some clothes and raced the short distance to La Scala. The parking garage was practically vacant on a Sunday morning, so I got a nice prime spot on the first level. Normally, I have to circle down to the fourth level of hell to find a spot. The first level is reserved for store muckamucks, a category that excluded me due to my subordinate status.

Arriving at the store entrance, I found a fire truck, emergency lights still sweeping the building, and a hose snaking through the open door. I followed it down to the deli. My "La Scala Security" badge got me through the barricades.

The smell of smoke thickened the closer I got, and I could tell from the aroma there was going to be a fire sale soon. Smokers might not notice the lingering smell on their clothes. Look for the silver lining, I say.

Turning the corner, I came across the fire scene. The deli was in shambles. Several ax-wielding firemen were slogging across the wet floor, and one began rolling up the hose. Most of the counter was charred and it looked like one of the yogurt machines had exploded. The sea of flotsam included plates, utensils and boxes, and there was a large hole chopped in the back wall leading to the kitchen.

I approached the nearest fireman. "Do you know how it started?"

"I'm sorry, sir. You shouldn't be in here. No civilians—"

"Jim Biersovich, store security." I flashed my badge. "The vice president for facilities asked me to assess the situation."

"Well, you might want to talk to that guy over there." He pointed at a First Sentinel guard. "He's the one who reported it."

The guard was sitting at a table, smoking, staring at the demolished deli, when I approached. He was in his 50s, overweight, with bushy gray eyebrows and jowls that bookended a dour expression.

"Jim Biersovich, store security. You on duty when this happened?"

The guard glanced at me, then back at the deli counter. "Yeah. Helluva thing." His nametag said James Beam.

"Jim Beam. Like the bourbon. Guess you get people commenting on your name all the time."

He glared at me a couple beats, then went back to puffing and staring at the smoldering mess. "Yeah. Bourbon."

"Uh, Jim. Can you tell me what happened? I kinda need to know so I can report to the VP. And just FYI, store policy prohibits smoking."

The icy glare again, then he flicked the cigarette onto the wet tile. "Who's gonna know?" he said. Water was advancing through the carpet into the adjacent sporting goods department.

"So, can you tell me what time...?"

"About 6:30. Just coming down from my half-hour check on 9. I get off the elevator and smell something. Smoky. Not like a cigarette. Bigger. I come around here and, whoa Nelly! It's lit up like a blowtorch! The sprinklers were shooting water all over creation. I hit the fire alarm, then got that extinguisher"—he pointed at a red canister lying in a pool near the counter—"and tried to put it out."

"Could you see where it started?"

"Not sure, but there was big flame coming out of that grease vat." He pointed out the french fry vat next to the yogurt machine.

"Did you see anyone or hear anything?"

His face suddenly soured. "Listen, mister, I do my job. If I'd a seen someone, I'd a reported it, like we're supposed to."

"OK, thanks. Just call me if you remember anything else." I gave him my card, then ran out to catch up with the firemen.

"Excuse me, just one more question."

They all turned around. "Yeah?" the one carrying the hose said.

"Did you see anything to suggest...uh...I mean...could the fire..."

"Arson? You'll have to speak to the FI. He's on the way." They turned and headed to the truck.

"FI?"

"Fire investigator," he called over his shoulder.

While waiting for the investigator, I thought I'd take a closer look at the scene. Beam had departed when I returned.

The stench was overpowering; I pulled my jacket up over my nose and headed behind the counter. Good thing I wore snow boots, because shoes would have been ruined as I waded through the floating litter and stepped up into the kitchen.

In contrast, the kitchen looked spotless. Nothing seemed out of place. Pots and countertops sparkled in the soft glow of fluorescent lights. Unfortunately, I didn't notice a spot of grease on the floor—oblivious until I skidded into a dish caddy on wheels, knocking it over and sending a sizable stack of dinner plates crashing to the floor. Now it was a mess. Damn.

As I picked myself up and tiptoed across the shards, I spotted a smudge on the back of the kitchen door. I looked closer and saw that it wasn't a smudge, after all. Just under the doorknob, a blue CC. Our fiend had struck again. I exited the kitchen and dialed Jane.

"Hi, Jane. Beers here. Just talked with the guard."

"And?"

"He didn't see anyone, but the fire investigator is on the way. May be arson."

"Arson!"

"There's another thing. I think this is related to the other stuff that happened last week."

"You mean the mannequins?"

"Not just the mannequins." It was time to bring Jane up to speed and push for police involvement. I detailed the rest of the incidents I hadn't told her about, including the damaged shoes, the bloody mattress and the mysterious initials left as a signature to the dastardly deeds. Plus there were the attempted break-ins, which may or may not have been related, and now a possible arson, which was certainly perpetrated by the same villain.

When I finished outlining the series of incidents, there was a deadly silence on the other end of the line. "Jane? You still there?"

"Yes. Jim, I'm going to have to get back to you. It may be time to call in the authorities. If we've got a nut case targeting La Scala—well, we need to make sure our customers and employees are safe. I need to talk to Mr. S first. If you need me, I'll be at home for a while." She gave me the number again. "Oh, by the way, we found someone else to play Santa this week, so you're off the hook." I did a silent leap for joy.

I hung up feeling reassured that Jane would bring the pros in, since I was a bit overwhelmed with questions that didn't yet have an answer. If Bibb was behind the incidents, that would explain his access to financial records. It would be harder for him to cause the other mayhem undetected, since he moved through the store like a plodding buffalo. Gerald could certainly sabotage his own mannequins, but didn't have access to the computer room. Bambi, with her alleged disdain for capitalism, might have motive to sabotage financial records, but again, no access. Plus she was nearby in Santaland when most of the problems were discovered.

Anyone in maintenance would have access to every department, but why would they want to break in when they have all the keys? Could be a security guard. They're here all the time. Note: Check the First Sentinel schedule for the past week. Mafia connection? Random nut?

While pondering the possible conclusions to be drawn from all this confusion, I didn't notice the fire investigator until I heard a crash behind the counter as a bowl hit the tile and shattered. The guy was huge, at least 6-6, with an Afro straight out of the '70s.

"Sorry," he said.

"You the FI?" I asked.

"Yeah. Dominick Freson. And you are...?"

"Jim Biersovich, store security." We shook hands. "I was just talking with the guard on duty. He said he didn't see anyone. He punched the alarm."

"Hmmm." Freson looked at the seared wall behind the counter, bent down and scraped a spot with his pen, then wrote some notes in a small pad. "This vat, yogurt, I guess, exploded from the heat."

"Know what started it, Mr. Freson?"

"Detective. Looks like you have an accelerant in a Type C container, delayed combustion, flash burst..."

"Huh?"

Freson frowned at me. "Bomb. A crude one. Pretty small, but effective. I need to collect some samples here. You planning to clean this up soon?"

"Uh, yeah, I guess. We need to open at noon." I glanced at my watch. A little over three hours to get things cleaned up.

"I'll need 15 minutes. Then you can have it." He turned back to continue collecting samples, and I dialed Jane's home number and filled her in.

"We've got a team on the way over, Jim. Just hang around until they get there. Then you can take off."

"I can stay if I'm needed..."

"Not really necessary. The cleaners will take care of everything, and we've got a construction team that's going to block off that wing for now."

"So we're planning to open on schedule?"

"That's the plan."

"OK. I'll hang around here till l they arrive."

"Thanks, Jim." I watched Freson a while and then walked up to the front entrance to see if the fire engines were gone. They were. Just one fire car, probably Freson's, with a light flashing on the dash. On cue, my cell rang.

"Beers."

"Hey, Jimbo, what's happenin'."

"Hi, Lena. You wouldn't believe."

"Yeah, I might," she snickered. "Where y'at?"

"I'm at the store. There was a fire…"

"A fire! No!"

"Yep. Deli. Fire investigator's looking at it right now. Thinks it was set off by a bomb."

"A bomb! No way!"

"That's what he said. I gotta hang around for a bit until the cleanup crew gets here. Whatcha doing?"

"Well, I talked wit' Tina last night 'bout dat printout…"

"Yeah?"

"Wanna show ya what it means. If ya hang dere fa 15, I'll come by."

"OK. I'm waiting near the deli."

"See ya shortly."

When I walked back in, Freson was on his way out. He told me he'd be in contact with the store manager. He asked who that might be. I gave him Jane's name and number.

The cleaning crew was just setting up their gear. It was Don Anderson and his maintenance underlings—Bradley, Sergei and Pyotr— plus a couple from the overnight cleaning crew. Anderson was talking on his cell phone. Pyotr had a shop vac, trying to stop the incursion of water into sporting goods. Sergei and Bradley were tossing scrap into a pile. When Anderson got off the phone, I asked how long he thought it would take to clean up.

"We got a grade A mess here," he said. "I just talked to the trade office. Need to get a carpenter, plumber and electrician in here. Maybe by Tuesday we can get this back into shape."

I felt a panic coming on. "No, Jane Mertin says we're opening on schedule today."

"What? That's nuts! No way they can open this store." As he was ranting, I saw from the corner of my eye a couple of people approaching. All activity stopped as soon as we realized who it was—Johnny Scalabrino himself, along with a couple of young suits.

It was the first time I saw Scalabrino in close proximity. He had a face like a bucket of mud, eyebrows like buck moth caterpillars and a serious suit that said Big Money. It was a talking suit. Probably had a little string up one sleeve that he pulled.

Everyone stood staring at him, waiting to see what he was going to do.

He was carrying a putter, which he waved at the deli counter. I turned to face him in case he swung it in my direction. I wanted to make sure my head wasn't on the tee.

"What's the situation here?" he asked the room in general.

Anderson and I looked at each other, then he addressed Scalabrino. "Well, sir, we're going to clean this up best we can, but it's gonna take a while. I've got calls in to an electrician, a carpenter—" (*If I were a carpenter, and you were a lady...* Damnit!)

"We open at noon," Scalabrino said matter-of-factly.

Anderson glanced at me, back at his crew, who were still standing and staring, and yelled, "Get to work, people!" Then to Scalabrino: "Sir, that may not be possible with all the damage—"

"Noon," he said. "Jason, see they get whatever they need."

"Yes, sir," one of his toady assistants said. Scalabrino and the other yes-man turned to leave.

"Mr. Scalabrino?" He turned back and gave me a look like he had just stepped in gum.

"Yessir?"

"I'm Jim Biersovich, Mr. Scalabrino, and—"

"Johnny."

"Sir?"

"It's Johnny."

"Johnny... I don't know how up to speed you are on all the events that have been happening..."

"I've heard things."

"Well, I just think maybe it's time to bring in the police."

He gave me another look, like he was trying to figure out what I wanted for Christmas. I could hear gears whirring under his scalp. "All I Want for Christmas Is My Two Front Teeth" spun up on my mental music box. After three choruses, he finally spoke.

"Mr. Biersovich—"

"Jim. Or Jab."

"Mr. Biersovich, I think you can understand why I don't want to involve the authorities in this, being that it's Christmas season and all." He winked at me. "Any other time of year and I'd say yes. We just can't risk the potential effect on our customer base. You understand?"

"Yes, sir."

"I know you probably could use some help on this, so I'm gonna send you an assistant…"

Uh-oh.

"My cousin Joseph. You give him a call. OK, Mr. Biersovich?" He snapped his fingers and the assistant called Jason handed me a card. It said simply Joe T, with a phone number underneath.

There was a twinkle in Scalabrino's eye that made me think he would make a better Santa than anyone around.

"Yes, sir," I answered after three short lifetimes.

"Good. You have any problems, you call Joseph. Don't call the cops, your boss, your girlfriend or Ghostbusters. Call Joseph."

The conversation was over. I knew because he promptly turned and left, with the unnamed toady floating in his wake.

This was something. Now I had to bring on a new assistant, probably mob connected. Things were getting dicey.

The remaining lackey, Jason, surveyed the scene, trying to figure out what to do next.

"Jason," I said, "I'm Jim Biersovich, store security." He looked puzzled. "Jane Mertin is my boss."

The light went on. "Oh. Good. So, what do you need here to stabilize the situation? Mr. Scalabrino wants—"

"Understood. Let's let Don and his crew get to work and they can tell us what they need."

"Right. OK. Well, here's my number, if anyone needs anything construction related. Especially if you need to pour cement." He took a card out of his wallet and handed it to me.

"Thanks," I said. Then he left.

Anderson was sneering at him all the way out the building. I handed him the card and asked what he planned to do. He said he'd have the carpenter basically build a temporary wall around the deli; then they could clean up without interruption.

He flicked the card into the growing pile of debris and walked over to join his crew.

Sergei and Pyotr started tossing scrap into a rolling bin while singing the "Volga Boat Song" or some other popular ditty at the tops of their voices. Bradley was nodding to some unheard sounds in his earphones connected to a Walkman.

All I heard in my head was Jimi Hendrix wailing *Let me stand next to your fire.*

17

Sunday late morning
Temperature: 11, sunny; wind chill, 8

The maintenance guys had just rolled off two carts full of splintered wood, broken glassware, plates (thanks to me) and other assorted mess, and finished sucking up the water with a shop vac when Lena breezed in. She was wearing a strapless black formal, slit up the right side, festooned with sequins across her bust line. I fought hard to stop the strains of "Pretty Woman."

"Hey, Beers, come see what I gotcha heah." She plopped the stack of printouts on one of the deli tables and hiked up her dress as she sat down. "Jeez, what a mess!"

Looking up to avoid staring at her legs, I said, "Yeah. Looks like our perp struck again."

"Perp! Man, you talkin' like dem duhtectives now." She gave me that raspy, staccato laugh that was her trademark. "You find some lettahs?"

"Yeah. Kitchen door. FI says—"

"FI?"

"Fire inspector. He found signs of accelerant...something about Type C..."

"Dat's a bomb all right!" Lena blurted. "Damn!"

I gave Lena one of those surprised-but-not-really looks. Of course she knew about bombs. Lena knew lots of stuff that she had gleaned from the web.

"I'm thinking it's time to bring in the cops. Scalabrino thinks it's time to bring in his cousin. He's apparently my new assistant." I showed her the card. My frown showed her my disgust.

Lena thought about that for a second, giving me a chance to ask about her getup. "You look really nice. Just coming in from the symphony?"

"Naw." She offered no further explanation, leaving me to imagine all sorts of intriguing possibilities set to the tune of... On cue, my phone rang. "Jim here."

"Yo yo yo, Beers, my man, what's up?" It was Freddie. "Found out some more good stuff for you. Why don't we hit The Crater at noon, watch the Vikes and I'll bring you up to speed."

"Can't, Freddie. Got a little store problem here that needs attention."

There was dead air for a few seconds. "What now?"

"Well, we had a little fire..."

"Beers, Beers, Beers. Man. You need to get out of that place."

"I'm getting ready to go in a bit, but..."

"I mean you need out. Y'know, we've got an opening for an agate clerk."

"Agate."

"Yeah, like box scores, Vegas line, transactions..."

"I know what agate is. I'm just wondering why you think I'd be interested in that."

"You obviously need something. You're not tearing up the world as a private eye."

"Security specialist."

"Whatever. Shit keeps happening on your watch, and you're not hacking it. You're Michael Jordan in the bigs. You're Bill Murray in the PGA. You're Billy Scandowski in Hollywood."

"Who the hell is Billy Scandowski?"

"My cousin. Thinks he's a movie star. His biggest role has been delivering yellow pages to three ZIP codes every August."

"So what are you trying to say?"

"You're a fish out of water with this detective stuff. It's not your strong point. You're doomed to failure."

"I take issue with that. I think I'm holding my own."

"You couldn't hold your own if you had three more hands."

"Look, I'm not going back to sportswriting. Too many bad memories."

"Just because Davis called you a no-talent jock-sniffing hack?"

"No. Not just because of that," I said defensively. The assistant sports editor's words still stung almost a year later.

"Beers, listen to me. You're a sportswriter. It's what you do best. You need to lead with your strong hand. This department store crap is not your cuppa joe."

I wanted to continue arguing with him but he had a point, a good one, in fact. "I gotta go, Freddie. I'll call you later." I hung up and just shook my head at Lena.

"So whatcha gonna do wit' dis mess?" she asked. "No way dis store can open."

"Oh, it's opening. The big boss says so. Mustn't hurt Christmas sales, profits, y'know." I gave Lena my most sarcastic eye roll.

"Well, da cops can take ovah now…"

I shook my head. "No cops. Also per the big kahuna."

Lena was dumbfounded. "You know how crazy dat is?"

Patsy Cline crooned "Crazy" in my head as I contemplated the insanity of the past week. I had no comeback. It *was* crazy.

But it wasn't my store. Lena, Tina, Dad, Jane, Bambi, Gerald and all the rest—we were all just pawns on the big chessboard that was La Scala. And Johnny Scalabrino was in danger of losing his queen.

We didn't say anything for a few minutes, just watched the maintenance guys continue to collect and haul off debris. I glanced at Lena, thinking how beautiful she looked in her spangly, low-cut dress, dolled up like she was heading to the theater or a state dinner. Wow. Nice.

Then I noticed the stack of printouts under her elbow. "Uh, you were going to tell me about the printouts."

Lena glanced down and was suddenly animated again. "Oh yeah. Man! You not gonna believe dis." She unfolded the first couple of sheets and scooched her chair next to mine. "Now, ya see here, dis is what you saw, dat CC? Now, over here, see dis 'DecRec 2.9'?"

"Yeah. What's that?"

"Decompile-Recompile. It's a program hackahs use."

"Right."

"Bibb was usin' dis on da main servah at da store." She tsk-tsked and shook her head.

"And that means…?"

She gave me a stern look. "Beers, you don't know much 'bout computahs, do ya?"

"No," I said sheepishly. That was the same argument my last boss used against me in my unceremonious exit from newspapering. He just laughed at me when I told him the computer was stealing my soul. I always preferred a typewriter. It didn't have any secrets lurking within; you always got what you wanted from it.

"Lemme explain dis so you can undahstand." She thought for a second. "Ya know 'bout computah games, right?"

"Yeah, I know about computer games," I said indignantly. "I'm not totally ignorant."

"OK, ya know 'bout C&C?"

Now she had me. "You mean the mixed drink?"

It was Lena's turn to roll her eyes. "No. Stay wit' me heah. We talkin' 'bout games. Dere's a game called C&C—Command & Conquer. OK?"

"Yeah."

"Bibb is big into it. He's in a clan—dat's like a fraternity fa game playahs. Right?"

I kept my mouth shut and Lena continued.

"Deze clans, dey all try to, well, each one, uh…dey cheat. Yep, dey all cheatahs. Dey do anything ta win.

"Bibb, he's in dis clan dat's not too good, compared ta da othah cheatahs. Dey got tired a losin'. Da rest of da clan ordered Bibb ta cheat or dey were gonna boot him."

"I'm following so far."

"OK. So ta cheat ta win, Bibb gets dis program, DecRec. He loads it on da servah, loads da game on da servah and spends hours lookin' through da game code for ways ta cheat."

"So our store terrorist is a game cheater!" I said dramatically. "That's why he wrote CC all over his handiwork." I nodded in sudden realization. Erroneously.

"Beers!" Lena shouted. "Shut up fa a second. You all wrong. Dis got nothin' ta do wit' ya sabatoor, except fa doze blanked-out financial printouts. Y'see, while our game boy was trying ta cheat on company time, he accidentally wiped out some critical softwayah on da servah. Dat's why he didn't wanna tell you 'bout da printouts. He's afraid he's gonna get fired.

"But I got a coupla friends down in the database depawtment, Dweep and Kweep. Showed 'em dis and dey knew what ta do. Dey restored da softwayah from backup."

"Now who are Dweep and Kweep?"

"Duipnummar Bashra and Quepanzo Gozam. I think dey from somewayah else."

"How'd you find out all this?"

Lena smiled. "Latah. I got ta get goin' now." She stood to leave.

"Wait, before you go. I was talking with Freddie last night and I think the CCs may be a gang sign."

"Gang sign? Naw, don't think so."

"Why not?"

"I seen gang signs, Beers. Dey's elaborate stuff, swirls and angles and such. Artistic, like. Dis too simple ta be a gang sign."

"Maybe it's a new gang."

She just smiled at my apparent naivete.

"You have an audience with the queen this morning?" I asked, fishing for a clue to her getup.

She flashed that Cheshire grin, turned and walked off without a word. Now I was left to contemplate my next move. I guess Bibb could be eliminated as a suspect. Maybe. But that left almost everybody else in the world to investigate. Sigh.

Maybe agate clerk wasn't such a bad gig after all.

I hung around for a while longer, watching the cleanup team transform a holy mess into an empty shell of store space that could be closed off. I wouldn't have believed it could be cleaned up in time, but it looked more and more like that noon opening might just happen. When the carpenters began hammering up temporary walls, I left for home.

Dad called, wondering where I was. I forgot I had told him I would pick him up for church. I apologized and briefly explained what happened. I asked him to pray for me.

18

A rriving back at my apartment a few minutes before noon, I was already whipped, and most of the day lay ahead of me. Fortunately, it was my day off. Unfortunately, my front door was ajar, and I know it wasn't like that when I left.

I crept closer and put my ear to the crack. A man's voice emerged from somewhere near the living area, obviously talking on the phone.

"Yeah…never seen anything like it. It's wall to wall, man… Don't worry. I'm gonna take care of everything… He doesn't need to know. Trust me."

This sounded bad. Either someone was planning to rip me off or—I didn't want to think what else. As I was contemplating whether to run or confront the intruder, the door suddenly flew open and I was face to face with a short, dapper man in a pinstriped suit. He was wearing black gloves, which he started to take off.

"You just gonna stand out there, or you want to come in?" he asked.

There was a cell phone in his hand, not a gun, and he was at least a half-foot shorter than me, so I thought I might have a fighting chance. Then again…

"We have security cameras in this building. You're on tape, if you took anything or you plan to—"

He started laughing, waving me in with his gloves. "No, no, no, you got it all wrong. C'mon in, Mr. Biersovich." He knew my name, but he could have gotten that from the mail slot or the pile

129

of unopened junk mail on my counter. When he walked into the den and flopped down on my couch, I felt a bit less nervous and followed him in.

"You know me but I don't know you. Want to tell me why you broke in? A police officer lives right down the hall..."

He spread his hands. "Sorry about that. My cousin told me time was essential. I didn't wanna just wait out in the hall for you. Name's Joseph Terrazzo."

The name didn't ring a bell. He saw my confusion.

"Johnny sent me."

"Oh. Cousin Joseph." He didn't look like a big Mafia enforcer, more like an accountant.

"Yeah. Just call me Joe T, Mr. Biersovich."

"OK. And you can call me Jim. Or Beers. That's what most people call me." No sense in pushing Jab.

"Good. Now, Johnny told me we need to figure out who's causing problems at the store and terminate—"

"Whoa! No killing!"

He continued after a few seconds. "And terminate... the...perpetrator's...employment. Got it?"

"Oh. Yeah. Right." That was a relief. "But how do you know it's an employee?"

Joe T stared at me for a few seconds, then shook his head. I didn't know whether he was trying to figure out how to bump me off or teach me all the secrets of the family. In either case, it was bad news for me.

As I was pondering how to convince him I wasn't a total doofus, he stood and walked around the room. "Tell me about this," he said, gesturing to my wall of music.

"Well, I'm a collector. I've been collecting for a long time."

He picked a tape from a rack. "Strawberry Alarm Clock. You listen to this stuff?"

"Sometimes," I said. "Mostly I just collect. Some of this stuff is pretty rare nowadays."

"I'll say. What you call this...?"

"Eight-track."

"Right. Eight-track. They haven't made these in, what, 20 years?"

"More like 30."

"And you think these are valuable?"

"Well, I don't know how valuable they are. Rare, for sure."

"Huh." He was quiet for a minute or so, looking over the racks and racks of now-ancient music. Then he put the tape back. "Let's go somewhere."

"Uh, OK. Where?"

"C'mon. My car's on the street."

I didn't know if taking a ride in a made man's car was such a good idea. But he made it sound like an offer I couldn't refuse, if I wanted to stay healthy.

Before we left, I listened to Rosie's message from last night. She sounded perturbed, wondering why I was never around. I returned the call, but she wasn't there. I left a message promising to call later.

Joe T had a limo and a driver, naturally, and it was one of those enormous silver Mercedes that looked like it wouldn't fit in one lane. It was plush—black leather seats, a side console with TV screens, a fully stocked bar and a glass roof for skygazing. He sat in a seat facing mine, about a half-block away. We could have used the floor for a putting green. I thought he might offer me a drink, but no such luck. I could have used one right about then.

Our route took us through Loring Park, past Uptown and down Lyndale to Minnehaha Parkway, a popular biking, hiking and picnicking green belt on the south side of the city. At some point we turned off the parkway into a cobblestone street that I'd never seen before, winding up a hill through the trees several hundred yards and coming to a stop in the circular driveway of the most immense house—no, it was a mansion—I'd ever seen. The residence was girded by towering palm trees on both sides, with an unobstructed view of the parkway below. This must be the home of the proverbial king of the hill, I thought.

Joe T led the way up to the front door, which opened seconds before he reached it, leading into a cavernous wood-paneled hallway and eventually into a study bigger than my entire apartment. Seated at a massive mahogany desk in front of a spectacular picture window was Johnny Scalabrino, looking through a View-Master and chuckling to himself. Sitting in various chairs around the room were several other men in suits. Executives? No. Staff? Maybe. Mafioso? I didn't want to think about it.

"Hey, Joe T, you ever seen one of these?" Scalabrino asked.

"View-Master?" Joe T said. "Yeah, I had one of those when I was a kid."

"This is something. Mmm-mmm," Scalabrino said. "Whoo!" he put down the View-Master and noticed me. "Hey, kid, c'mere and take a look." He held out the device to me.

"It's Jim Biersovich, sir."

"Sure. Mr. Biersovich. Come look."

I took the View-Master and peered at the 3-D images: the Parthenon, the Colosseum, the Leaning Tower of Pisa, the Pyramids. "Great stuff," I said, handing it back.

"Damn straight," Scalabrino answered. "Beautiful! Didn't none of this look this good last time I saw 'em."

Not knowing exactly why I was here, I glanced around the room, taking in the wall of books, high carved ceiling, a blue-felt billiard table, a long bar in the back and he-man-sized leather chairs. While I was admiring the view through the picture window, one of Scalabrino's servants, or maybe an underling, hard to tell, rolled up a cart full of bottles, glasses and an ice bucket.

"Have a seat right there," Scalabrino said, motioning to an ottoman at the side of his desk. "Drink?"

Gulp. Here was a dilemma. Drink with the big boss, or not? It would probably not be a good career move to get sloshed in front of the boss. Then again, who was I to refuse an offer from someone who could possibly be dangerous, maybe more dangerous than the maniac trying to lay waste to La Scala? On the other hand...

"Hello? Mr. Biersovich, you with me? I said you want a drink?"

"Yes, sir, I would. Thank you." I was having some trouble swallowing at the moment.

He looked at me a few seconds, raised eyebrows, waiting.

"Well...am I supposed to guess...?"

"Uh, no sir. Sorry. Um, I'll just have what Mr. T is having."

He stared at me for a second, then burst into laughter. The other men in the room joined him in what soon escalated into howls and guffaws. The only one not laughing was Joe T. He was staring daggers at me. Thank God they were only stare daggers and not real ones.

"It's Joe T," he said quietly, then turned and left the room.

Scalabrino was beating his palm on his desk and some of the other men had fallen on the expansive Persian rug, laughing uncontrollably. My keen powers of analysis told me it was something I said. Eventually, the mirth died down and everyone caught their breath.

"Oh, Mr. Biersovich, my boy, that was a good one. I haven't laughed like that...," he said, leaving the thought unfinished.

"Um. Mr. Scalabrino, sir, did I...uh, something I said..."

"Mr. T," he answered, chuckling a bit more. "It's a long story, but just make sure you say 'Joe T' from now on. He's got a thing about 'Mr. T.' A bit sensitive, you might say."

"Right." This was not good. Just pissed off the guy supposed to be helping me protect the boss's empire. Not good, not good.

Since Joe T didn't return, I had to make a choice about what to drink. I didn't see any beer in evidence, so I finally settled on a dry martini. I still wasn't sure whether drinking was such a good idea, but my mouth was suddenly the Sahara.

While everyone was enjoying cocktails, Scalabrino laid out his game plan. It wasn't that he had no faith in my ability, he just wanted to protect a huge investment, a family tradition, a Twin Cities institution, blah blah blah.

I phased out somewhere in the middle of his spiel, concentrating on the bottom of my martini glass, until I came to as he was saying "... armed and posted on every floor." That didn't sound quite right.

"Uh, sir? The security guards aren't armed—"

He smiled, closed his eyes and shook his head. "Not security guards. My guards. My boys will be making sure there's no problem."

I wasn't sure who his "boys" were, but I had an idea. This was worrisome—armed Mafiosos scaring away customers, perhaps waving guns and threatening people. Maybe even a shootout. "Mr. Scalabrino, sir."

"Call me Johnny."

"Mr. Johnny, sir." I wasn't real confident about what I was going to say but I had to say it. "Armed guards might be a problem. If a customer got hurt, God forbid, you'd have a lot bigger problem than just a little vandalism. There could be multimillion-dollar lawsuits, criminal charges...who knows what."

Scalabrino chuckled again and shook his head. He looked up and I followed his eyes. Joe T was back in the room, still looking a bit pissed.

"Don't worry about it," Scalabrino said. "My boys will be incognito. Very discreet. They won't be wearing holsters and cowboy boots. You won't even know they're there."

"I don't understand," I said.

"What don't you understand?"

"Why tell me if I won't even know they're there?"

"I just wanted to let you know so if something happens, y'know, my boys will take care of it."

"That's right," Joe T said. "We'll take care of it." Joe T was looking at me with a glare that could've sliced through salami.

"How will I know who to contact if there's trouble?"

"They'll find you," Scalabrino said. "Joseph, take Mr. Biersovich back home so he can rest. Tomorrow may be a busy day."

Signaling that the social call was over, Johnny picked up the View-Master and resumed his world tour. I followed Joe T back to the car. Glancing at the trees, I made myself a mental note to get Lena to do some research, and find out what kind of palm trees grow in Minnesota. Maybe they're petrified trees, I thought.

After a quiet and nervous return trip—my nerves only, I'm sure—I was deposited back at my building. There was no further sign of trespass in my apartment, thank goodness, and after a long, hot shower, I curled up under the covers for what turned out to be a 13-hour nap.

19

The wee hours of Monday, Dec. 20
Five shopping days till Christmas
Temperature: 12, partly cloudy; wind chill, 12

I woke up in a cold sweat to the sounds of breaking glass.
Or at least I thought it was breaking glass. It was obviously
a nightmare, because it sounded too close to be anywhere but
inside my apartment, and after a quick tour, I couldn't find a
broken window, lamp or even a shot glass.

The clock showed 3:35. It was an odd time for me to be awake,
but seeing as I was too nervous to attempt a resumption of sleep, I
set about making productive use of my insomnia.

A long-overdue vacuuming led to several loads of clothes, a
blitz through the kitchen and a series of less necessary tasks,
culminating in a resorting of my extensive LP collection by date of
release.

Somewhere in the middle of the late British Invasion years, a
weird feeling set in. I felt light-headed and some color splotches
obscured my vision. Then I came to on the floor, clutching *Rubber
Soul* to my chest. This time it wasn't a sound that brought me to,
but the recollection of a dream that I had just had, or had three
years ago—who knew?

In the dream, I was floating in outer space, in a different solar
system because I didn't recognize the planets. No bright red one,
no ringed orb, no gassy giant. Just a bunch of moon-sized planets
of different colors. I was approaching an orange one, freefalling
toward a sparkling lake in the shape of a question mark. Then it
shifted, reforming itself into a crescent, then twisting again to form
a snaky S. I looked up (well, as up as "up" can be in space) and saw

my spaceship looming overhead, lights blinking and small puffs of smoke emanating from various spots. That was it.

There was something else about this dream, but I couldn't quite figure it out. It was almost as if my subconscious mind was trying to tell me something, like the mysteries of the universe, or maybe just a key to unwrapping the mysteries at La Scala. Perhaps the girls would be able to help me interpret it.

Of course, it was still a bit early to seek the assistance of the glitter twins. I'm sure Lena wouldn't appreciate a call at 6 a.m. Tina would tear me a new one. Killing time consisted of finishing up the LP reorganization, cleaning the bathroom (ugh) and recycling several weeks' worth of papers.

Finally, 7 a.m. rolled around and I figured if the girls weren't up yet, they should be. Tina was surprisingly chirpy for such an early hour, but Lena cussed a blue streak before finally agreeing to meet us at the Waffles R Us kitty-corner from the store. After getting dressed, I still had energy to burn, so I decided to bundle up and walk to downtown. Tina was already working on a huge Spanish omelet when I arrived.

"That looks yummy," I said, signaling the waitress for a coffee cup. My head was pounding.

"Delicious!" Tina replied. She seemed to be humming to herself between bites.

"What's up?" I asked.

"Huh? You called me—you tell me what's up."

"I'll get to that. I need to know why you're so chipper this morning." Tina feigned indignation. "What are you implying—I'm a grump?"

"No, just that it's early, and usually...well, I mean...sometimes you appear not quite so upbeat at an early hour." She kept on munching.

"Tina, you've worked at La Scala a long time."

"Almost six years."

"What can you tell me about Scalabrino?"

"Like is he Mafia?"

"Yeah."

"No."

"No?"

"I've been hearing those types of rumors for years," she said. "People in the store, my friends always think that. But I dated a cop. Scalabrino's just a businessman. A connected one, but a businessman."

"So no mob connection."

"Nope. Clean as a whistle," she said. "At least that's what my cop friend said, and cops should know."

"What's the story on the building? It seems a bit out of place with the rest of downtown."

"I kinda like it," Tina said. "Not what you'd expect to find in the Midwest. Old man Scalabrino worked in his dad's dry goods store in the Bronx. This is the unofficial version, of course. I heard all this when I first got hired by Dame Fritti."

"Who's that?"

"Probably the original cosmetician for La Scala. She retired the year after I started. Another white-hair, like Hantack, except probably a bit older. She had to be in her 90s.

"Anyway, Frank Scalabrino—that's the dad—used to take the subway down to Saks Fifth Avenue when he was a teenager and just walk through the place. He knew it was a lot classier than his dad's paltry store, and he decided one day he would out-Saks Saks.

"But the competition in New York was formidable—Saks, Macy's, Bloomingdale's, Bergdorf Goodman—so he looked west and saw a big city without much going on. Minneapolis.

"When he turned 18, he set out on his own with a bit of savings. His father was crushed when he left, but later, when he saw the store his son had created, he was in awe. I think Frank's folks sold their store and moved here to retire and watch the son grow his empire."

"So he built the other stores after this one?"

"Frank opened the one in Chicago, but Johnny built the two out west. Frank had a love of classical beauty and appreciation of the culture of his parents' homeland. Johnny, well…he was more into Hollywood glitz. He didn't change this store or the one in Chicago out of respect for his father, but the ones in Vegas and San Francisco have a completely different decor. You wouldn't even think it's the same chain if they weren't named La Scala."

"Well, this building is pretty nice. I'm glad his old man had good taste," I chuckled.

"Did anyone tell you about the subbasement?"

"No. What subbasement?"

"When I was a rookie, one of the girls in women's wear took me around the building but warned me to stay out of the subbasement. Said there was something dangerous there."

"Something dangerous? Like what?"

"No clue. She didn't say. I don't know if she was just putting me on or if there's some truth to it. I've tried looking for a trapdoor in the basement but have never found anything. Maybe you should find out if it's there. After all, you're in charge of safety, right?"

She smiled and attacked the omelet again. I could have sworn she was humming "It's a Beautiful Morning." Either she had hit the Powerball numbers last night or scored in some other way.

My cell phone rang. "Beers here."

"Where the hell were you yesterday?!" Uh-oh. It was Rosie. I forgot all about calling her after my visit to Casa Scalabrino.

"Hey, Rosie. Sorry about that. We had a fire at the store…"

"I don't give a damn! You said we were going to get together. I'm not sure about this anymore."

Lena walked in just then. "Yo, dawgs, wassup?"

"Listen, Rosie, I'm real sorry. I got called in to the store because of a fire, then I had to meet with Mr. Scalabrino—"

"Scalabrino? The owner?"

"Yeah, and there's lots of stuff going on that I can't really get into now. And I guess I was so worn out from all that, that I just sort of crashed yesterday. I slept all day. Didn't hear you call."

"That's because I didn't call, you asshole!" She slammed down the phone in my ear. It was like a sonic boom to my headache.

I closed the phone, placed it quietly on the table and looked from Tina to Lena.

"What was that?" Tina asked.

"Oh…"

"Sounds like trouble in paradise," Lena chimed in.

I just shook my head. "I'd rather not talk about that right now. I do have something to discuss that could be relevant to all the problems we've been having."

" 'There are no problems, only opportunities,' " Tina recited. "Company handbook, page 14. I had to read it once. Scintillating."

"Anyway," I continued, "we're a bit under the gun now, pardon the pun."

"Whatcha mean, guv?" Lena asked.

"Well, Mr. Scalabrino doesn't want to call in the cops, even though we've had like an incident a day for the past week. He's calling in his own troops."

Lena looked at Tina, then back at me. "Da Mafia?9!" Lena asked.

"He's not in the Mafia, Lena," Tina said.

"His 'associates,' " I said. "One's his cousin."

"Oh, so it's all in the family," Tina replied with a smirk.

"They're setting up shop in the store to try to nab the instigator." I told them about my visit to the big house.

"How many is he puttin' in da store? Can we recahnize dem? Are dey packin' heat?" Lena asked.

"Packing heat? Oh my God, Lena," Tina said. "I'm sure they're harmless. Unless, of course, you make a practice of putting snakes in suitcases or burning down the yogurt maker."

"He said on each floor. So I guess that's 10, if you include the lower level." I pondered a minute. No one spoke.

"I don't know if we'll know where they are, who they are, whether they'll be armed—we won't know anything, really, unless they tell us," I said. "So I guess we'd better just keep our eyes peeled and let them do what they're gonna do. It's sort of out of our hands now."

"Well, dat sucks," Lena said.

"Yeah," Tina added. "It's not like they own the place or something—oh, wait."

"There's something I want to keep following up on, though. My friend Freddie gave me a little history lesson the other night. He was talking about all the ethnic groups that have made this the new melting pot."

"No freaking kidding!" Tina said.

"Yeah, it's like dey don't unnastand English when ya tawkin' to 'em," Lena added.

I smiled at Tina. She winked back at me.

"So I want you two, in your spare time, to do all the research you can about the ethnic groups in the Twin Cities. Lena, can you dig up what you can about their history, when they came here, where they settled and so on. Tina, I'd like anything you can find out about ethnic gangs."

"Sure, cap."

"You got a lead on this?" Tina asked. "Like it's a foreigner of some stripe?"

"Maybe," I said. "I'm trying to piece things together right now. The more info, the better."

"You reporting this to Scalabrino?"

"Nope. Let's just keep this among us chickens for now."

"Hey, I thought of something that might give a clue," Tina said. "The CC is written in blue. Maybe it's 'Blue Christmas' in French. Cyan is French for blue. Could be someone who's having a sad Christmas season, or who likes Elvis."

"Or hates Elvis," I added.

"*Mais, non,*" Lena interjected. "*Le bleu est bleu pour le français.*"

"Huh?" I said.

"*Bleu* is French fa blue," Lena said. "*J'ai grandi en parlant le français.*"

"Once again—huh?"

"I grew up tawkin' French," Lena explained. "I may sound like a yat, but I was born in Abbeville—dat's in Cajun country. Mosta my kin are coonasses."

"Oh." Tina just stared with a stunned expression.

We finished up our breakfast and headed over to the store. Tina was off suspension, so she reported to cosmetics. Her shiner had faded to the point where her makeup completely covered it.

"By da way," Lena said, grabbing my arm. "Dat dummy, she's clean."

"What?"

"Da dummy in yer awfiss. Spent yestidday aftahnoon dustin' it. Nuttin'. Da perp wore gloves." She gave me a smug look. "Y'know, when I was a kid, my bruthah Jawn useta put tagedda model caws."

"Jawn??"

"Yeah, Jawn. J-o-h-n. Anyway, he put tagedda T-birds, Cawvettes, Mustangs—and he'd get all dat glue on his fingahs. He'd peel it off and you'd have perfect fingahprints."

"Hope he wasn't inhaling too deeply."

"I useta save dem from da trash and play duhtective." She waggled her eyebrows, then took off for the jewelry counter.

I headed up to Jane's office. On the way, I considered whether to call Rosie back and try to apologize. No, probably too soon. Let it cool down a bit more.

I walked past Santaland and was pleasantly surprised to see another jolly fat man preparing to assume the throne. When he turned to sit down, I saw it was Bibb Tokan. Apparently, someone had spotted his talent in the girth department and decided he would be the man for the week.

I arrived at the ninth floor and Sandy waved me right into Jane's office, where she was huddled over some papers with Salmon Foster. Well, time to clear up at least one of the many mysteries.

"Oh, hi, Jim. Salmon and I were just going over some numbers. We're on a thin margin for the season, so we really need to keep a lid on…you know."

"Mr. Foster, Jane. I think I have some information you need to know." Both turned to look at me head on. "I've found out what happened with the overnight reports."

"Great, Jim," Foster said. "Who was it? We need to set an example on this one."

I hesitated. Jane looked on expectantly. "Well, you might want to have a chat with Santa," I said.

"Santa? Is this some kind of joke? It's not a laughing matter," Foster responded.

"No, I mean, the store's current Santa, Bibb Tokan." I explained about the printouts Tina had found and Lena's discovery about what he was trying to do. "So, it wasn't really sabotage, just a hobby that kind of, y'know, got out of control."

Foster was muttering under his breath and I could hear a couple of expletives. He looked like he was about to go ballistic.

"I think we should handle this in-house, Salmon. No police," Jane said. "Mr. Scalabrino left me a message this morning and he made it clear he wants it done his way. In fact, he's beefing up store security through the holidays."

He stared at Jane, then at me before stomping out. Jane sighed. I could tell she was under the gun. The holidays had to be especially stressful for the veeps, what with pressure from the owner to meet sales goals in spite of any outside factor, including consumer stinginess.

"I think Mr. Tokan is in for a bit of a suspension. After this week," Jane added. "Let's chat, Jim."

She sat in her high-backed leather chair. I took the leatherette chair next to the credenza. Glancing out her window overlooking

Hennepin, I saw that snow had resumed, and the city was covered in a descending gloom that only lightened when it reached the ground.

She folded her hands, looked down at them for a moment before she began. "Jim, I just want to tell you I appreciate the stress you've been under with…" She waved her hands. "All this."

"Thanks, Jane."

"The board is very nervous right now. The employees have heard rumors about the incidents and they're even hearing wild stories from customers."

"Yes."

"Mr. Scalabrino, as you know, is a very private person," she said. "We must do as he wishes concerning all this."

"I know, Jane, he told me. I just wish I knew what I was doing…"

"Jim, this will all calm down and get back to normal soon. You'll see. Just hang in there. You're doing a fine job."

"What is the possibility that I can see some personnel records?"

She considered for a moment. "Why do you ask?"

"I think our incidents are almost definitely an inside job, and I'd like to see if I can narrow it down to a few suspects."

"No, I don't think so, Jim. There are strict rules about personnel files. What about a company directory?"

"I've already seen that. It doesn't help much. Names can only tell so much."

She was quiet, fiddling with a few papers on her desk. "I don't think that's possible, Jim. Federal rules prohibit—"

"OK, I understand. Thought I'd try. I'll have to figure this out some other way."

"Anything else I can help with?"

"Not sure."

"Well, keep me informed of your progress. You know, we've got 'visitors' to consider now."

"Yeah. You know if the 'visitors' will be carrying weapons?"

Jane looked appalled. Then slowly shook her head. "I hope to God they aren't."

As I was leaving, Jane said, "Oh, one more thing. The company party on Friday. I'm getting the marketing department to take that over so you don't have to worry about planning it."

Planning? What the hell? "It's my job to plan that?"

"Oh, you weren't here last year. I forgot. We had it off-site last year, but decided to bring it back to La Scala this year. It's going to be fun!"

Jane looked excited about it, whereas I could hardly muster enough enthusiasm to get up in the morning.

Heading back to my office, I discovered the door was ajar, and it looked like a box of talc had exploded in there. Powder covered most of the floor, desk, computer and chair. At first I suspected yet another case of sabotage.

My computer was on, which was unusual for my office. I can't remember the last time I actually booted it up. It's not that I'm a technophobe, I just prefer doing things the old-fashioned way.

A Post-it on the side of the monitor said: "Sorry about the mess. Be back shortly to clean it up. – L"

Lena had obviously done a bit of research on mannequins while she was there trying to find fingerprints because the screen showed several models offered by an outfit called American Form Factory.

I debated whether to try to clean up a bit, but was saved by the phone. It was Joe T.

"Mr. Biersovich, I just want you to know we've got our personnel stationed in the store, so you can carry on like normal."

"OK, thank you. Call me Jim. Where are they? I'd like to check in with them and see how things are going."

"Umm…no. That's not possible."

"But I'm—"

"You just leave the security stuff to us. Bobo, Tiny and Needlenose will make sure things are shipshape. Nobody's gonna slip one past us while we're on duty."

"Oh. OK. Well, thanks."

"Bye, Jim. And remember—Johnny's counting on you."

After I hung up, I was more worried than ever. What was that last comment about? What's he counting on me for? To cover up whatever problems his minions cause? At least now I knew there were only three of them. I wasn't sure how only three could cover 10 floors, but that wasn't my problem. I decided I would make a walk-through of the entire store and see if I could spot them.

Forty-five minutes later, after descending from nine all the way to the lower level, I couldn't tell whether I had seen any of the three. The store was fairly packed, it being just five shopping days till Christmas, and there were just too many solitary men walking around, trying to figure out what the heck they should buy the wife/boss/kids/girlfriend/boyfriend.

I passed through cosmetics and jewelry to bring the girls up to speed, and told them to inform me if they think they spotted Tiny, Bobo or Needlenose. Sheesh. Just the names were enough to wig me out.

My cell phone rang. It was Jane.

"Jim, we have another problem. Come see me." In two minutes I was back in her office with the door closed.

"We heard from Mrs. Carlson this morning."

"Who?"

"Mrs. Carlson, the lady at the candy counter."

"Oh."

"She was poisoned. They had to pump her stomach and found some pesticide in her blood. She said she was going to talk to the police. We're worried she may sue."

"Yikes."

"Fortunately, she's OK. But we have to make sure we're not liable here, Jim. What did you do with that candy?"

"It's still in my office. Locked in my filing cabinet, as a matter of fact." I was lying but Jane didn't want to hear the truth. Or at least I didn't want to tell her.

Jane was nervously tapping a pen on her desk.

"We should call Joe T," I said. "Mr. Scalabrino's cousin. He said to call Joe T if we had any problems." Jane nodded anxiously as I dialed.

"Joe T."

"Hi, Joe, this is Jim Biersovich. We have a situation here…a customer got sick after eating La Scala candy. Apparently, it was laced with pesticide."

"You sure about that?"

"Not absolutely sure, but it seems pretty likely." I explained about what the hospital found and that the store was worried about liability.

"Stay there. I'm on my way." He hung up.

"He's on his way over," I told Jane. "Should we tell anyone else? The company lawyers?" She shook her head. I headed to my office and waited there.

Now I was glad I made the right decision. It seemed apparent Scalabrino and his associates wanted to suppress the evidence, if it was indeed a crime. The Doors seemed like appropriate music for the afternoon, so I loaded the cassette player. "Riders on the Storm" was playing when Joe T walked in and shut the door.

"You got the candy?"

Urk. How to tell him I had turned it over to the hospital, who in turn had probably given it to police investigators? Only one thing to do—come clean.

"I gave it to the hospital. The woman was—" I started to explain but his look cut me off.

He closed his eyes for a second, then shook his head. Opening his eyes, he stared at me and said, "You did the right thing."

I was stunned. I thought I was a goner. "But I thought..."

He held up a hand. "We'll take care of it."

"The police are probably—"

"Taken care of," he answered. "You'll get a visit from Detective Cuccia. Show him the candy counter and—" He was interrupted by a police detective in full uniform who popped his head in the door.

"Joe T, how are ya? You Mr. Beers?"

"Yes, sir, officer."

Joe T gave him a hug, whispered in his ear and left.

"Let's take a look at that candy counter," Cuccia said.

I led him down the elevator to the sixth floor and pointed out the location.

"Were you the person on duty?" he asked the clerk.

"You mean when the lady..."

"Yeah. Your name is...?"

"Risa. Risa Emerson."

"So, Risa, there was candy out on the counter, she ate some, then collapsed. Is that what happened?"

"Yes, officer. I mean, I think that's what happened. I had other customers. I wasn't watching her the whole time..."

"And then EMS came and took her away, correct?"

"Yes, sir."

"OK," Cuccia said. "Thank you, ma'am. That's all I need."

We walked back toward the elevator.

"Thanks for your help, Mr. Beers." He punched the down button.

"Is that it? Do I need to do anything else?"

"Nope, all taken care of. We'll be in touch with Mrs. Carlson. Have a good day." He entered the elevator and gave me a thumbs up as the doors closed.

That was too easy. If I was a gambling man, I'd bet Cuccia was on the Scalabrino payroll. I wondered whether that was a good thing.

20

The afternoon was uneventful, except for another cold front moving through and causing the mercury to plummet.

Whether because of the presence of Scalabrino's enforcers or just blind luck, the store escaped without further incident. I was hopeful that the problems were behind us, and all that was left was to find the culprit, turn him over to the authorities and carry on with the business of business.

One of Don Anderson's crew came up and vacuumed my office and hauled away the mattress in the hallway. Later, I managed to get hold of Rosie and invite her over for supper, and amazingly she agreed. Somehow, after much groveling, I convinced her that the pressure had gotten to me and that was the reason I was so thoughtless, and it would never happen again. She bought it.

Now I just had to zip by the grocery on the way home, pick up some pizza toppings and salad ingredients, and tidy up a bit before she arrived. Oh, and chill some white wine.

I almost made a clean getaway at 5, but my cell phone rang as I was walking out. Groan.

"Mr. Biersinski? This is Quan with First Sentinel. I'm on the seventh floor. You'd better come see."

"It's Biersovich. I'm on my way."

The First Sentinel guards rarely called me, so this must be something serious. They were actually just for show since they didn't carry guns. A uniform is usually all the deterrent a shoplifter needs.

Unfortunately, since La Scala only contracted for one guard to cover the entire store, they weren't very effective. I could recall only once in my tenure when a guard had actually apprehended a thief, and that was solely because the idiot ran into the guard while trying to make his getaway and dropped the Cuisinart hidden under his jacket.

Arriving on seven, I was met at the elevator by Mok Quan, who ushered me through kitchenware to the break room, where a man was slumped in a chair in the corner.

"Found him like that when I came to get some coffee," he said.

I approached the man and nudged him lightly. "Sir?" No response.

There was no telltale clue as to who this was—a customer or maybe one of Scalabrino's boys. He was dressed in a brown cardigan and corduroy slacks over snow boots. I debated whether to look for a wallet but decided that wouldn't look good if he came to while I was picking his pocket. I felt his pulse. Thank God—still alive, at least.

"Thanks, Quan, I'll take it from here." He gave me an inquiring look, shrugged and wandered off on his appointed rounds. Nothing for me to do here but wait. I got a cup of coffee and sat down at the next table.

This could be one of Scalabrino's men. He wasn't that tiny and he certainly didn't have a needle nose. If anyone, this must be Bobo. Of course, it could just be a tired customer who needed a place to rest. I had great sympathy for any husband forced to accompany his wife on a Christmas shopping blitz.

Guys know how to shop: Make a list, get in, get the stuff, get out. Women like to make a career out of it. But this guy may not have been a beleaguered husband since he wasn't wearing a ring...

Several employees wandered in in the next 15 minutes while I was playing mental ping pong. They would generally glance at the sleeping man with puzzled looks, nod at me and move on. Bradley from maintenance walked in, popped a Coke from the vending machine, turned to me and said, "Who's the stiff?" while lifting his chin toward the man in the corner.

"Dunno," I said. "I think he's a visiting veep. Taking a break."

Bradley smirked and exited. A few minutes later, the man started coming to, lifting both hands to the top of his head and moaning.

"Sir?"

Moans.

"Sir? I'm Jim Biersovich. I work for the store. Can I help you? Are you OK?"

He finally opened his eyes, looked at me and said curtly, "Fine." Then he got up, a little wobbly, and left in a hurry.

I tried following him but he made a beeline for the stairs while talking on a cell phone. Since I was concentrating on where he was going, I didn't see the young customer approaching from my left. We collided, and several packages she was carrying went flying.

I apologized profusely, helped her up and collected her packages. She laughed about it, said no big deal, she wasn't paying attention either. By the time I got to the stairwell, he was two floors down and heading out into jewelry. When I got to five, he was nowhere in sight. Lena was ringing up a sale and I sidled in next to the register.

"Did you see a man come by here?" I whispered. "About 6-2, nicely dressed, tan slacks, brown and tan cardigan. Talking on a cell phone. Maybe holding his head?"

Lena looked at me like I was an alien. "Whatchu think, chief? I got two custamahs ta ring up and a third waitin' fa giff wrap. Dis place is a zoo!" She shook her head and returned to punching numbers on the register.

I walked the perimeter of the floor but didn't see him. Gone. I couldn't help thinking that if that was Bobo, he left with a booboo.

I DECIDED IT WAS TIME to wrap this case up or die trying. Wait. Wrong choice of words.

There were some obvious suspects I needed to eliminate. Not in the sense of killing, of course. Bibb Tokan was sort of cleared because of his boneheadedness. But I needed to see whether Gerald Difansa or Bambi Schroeder was somehow involved. And there were the maintenance guys to consider, along with the First Sentinel crew itself. Lots of folks to grill.

While I was heading back to my office and mentally lining up suspects, my phone rang. It was Joe T.

"Mr. Biersovich, howya doin'?"

"Fine, Joe T." I wondered whether I should ask about the mystery man in the cardigan. "What's new?"

"Well…" He paused for dramatic effect. "We sorta have a situation. Johnny is changing his approach. He wants you should do what you need to do to find out who's responsible for…y'know."

Gulp. The albatross was back on my scrawny shoulders.

"Uh, OK. Can I ask why? Did something happen?" Fishing.

"There was an incident. Johnny said he wants to pull back and let you run with the ball."

Damn the torpedoes… "Does this have anything to do with a man in a cardigan sweater, uh, I just found, er, I mean…"

"Johnny wants to pull back and let you run with the ball," Joe T repeated.

I remembered something I forgot to check. When I gave the hospital the tainted candy, I had neglected to examine the box. I asked Joe T if there had been a report on it.

"Detective Cuccia tells me there were two sets of prints on the box. I imagine they would be yours and the clerk's. The perp probably wore gloves. You can expect another visit from him so he can collect your prints."

"Did they find anything else?"

"Not really. Oh, wait. CC. The letters CC were written on the bottom of the box."

I told him about all the other CCs I found. He asked whether I checked the company directory and I told him I had, offering some of our theories about what it meant.

"Good work, Jim. Let me ponder that awhile."

"Joe T, can you answer something for me? Why doesn't Mr. Scalabrino want cameras in the store? It would make things so much simpler."

The line went silent for a moment, then he said, "I'll tell you this just so you understand, but never mention it again.

"Johnny, when he was teenager, worked at a fast-food joint before he joined the family business."

Visions of guys in zoot suits toting gats flashed through my head, but I asked, "Golden arches?"

"You got it. They had security cameras to prevent late-night holdups—in the lot, in the dining room but also in the kitchen.

"Johnny didn't think anyone looked at the tapes, but they did. They caught him and the milkshake guy playing basketball with ketchup packets and the fry vat late one night when no one was around. They'd explode and make a mess, ketchup everywhere. Looked like a bloody massacre."

"What happened?"

"Customer comes in, sees red splatters behind the counter, thinks someone got murdered. Turns out to be an off-duty cop. Pretty soon the place is surrounded by cop cars, Johnny has to talk his way out of it, which he does. Or so he thinks.

"He cleans up the mess and locks up the store for the night. Little does he realize that he didn't get all the packets out of the fry vat. Next day, vat is fired up, residual ketchup packets melt and start sending up mushroom clouds of toxic smoke. Have to clear the joint.

"Fire department comes, gets it under control, tells manager there's foreign material in the fry vat. Manager runs back tapes from previous night and Johnny is busted."

"Did he get arrested?"

"No, they just threatened to sue. Johnny's old man made it quietly go away, but warned him not to fuck up again. Let's just say it was one of the more humiliating events in his life. Johnny swore he'd never spy on his employees."

"Well, I still think this is a job for the police."

"No. Johnny doesn't want that. Handle this internally. You call me if you need anything. If it's a serious situation, I'll get the detective to visit you again." He hung up.

That clinched it in my mind. The unconscious man was one of Scalabrino's goons, and Johnny was obviously irate that the culprit had gotten the drop on him. It was an embarrassment.

Scalabrino couldn't trust his own men to take care of things. So now he thought I could do it? I wanted to call in the real cops, but that wasn't going to happen.

The phone rang again. By this time, I was back at my desk.

"Hi, this is Dominick Freson." Freson...name didn't ring a bell. "From the fire investigator's office."

"Hi, Mr. Freson. What can I do for you?"

"Well, we have results of the tests on that incendiary device at the store, and it's definitely a bomb. We're not sure of the source, but we have some leads, and it was definitely arson.

"We've called in a police detective, Sgt. O'Hare, and he'll be contacting you shortly."

Uh-oh. Could that be another of Scalabrino's men, or was this a legit policeman? "Well, Mr. Freson, it's really not necessary."

"What do you mean?"

"Well…Mr. Scalabrino is handling it."

"Mr. Biersovich, let me explain. We have a crime scene. Arson is a crime, especially one involving a bomb. It will be investigated."

"OK, but Mr. Scalabrino…"

"Mr. Scalabrino can contact me if he has any questions." He gave me his phone number.

As soon as I hung up, the phone rang again. I had to get an unlisted number.

"Beers."

"Hello, Jim. This is Gerald."

Oh, great, the temperamental Mr. Difansa. Just what I needed on top of everything else.

"Hi, Gerald. Is something wrong?" Dead air. "Gerald?"

"I want to talk to you. In private."

"About what? Where are you? I'll come down now."

"I can't talk here. I'd rather not get into it right now. Can you meet me after work?"

"Sure. Where?"

He gave me his address, in the heart of Frogtown, along with detailed directions so I wouldn't get lost. "Say 7 o'clock? I have some important information for you."

"OK, Gerald, 7." He hung up.

Curiouser and curiouser. Was Gerald going to confess to the mannequin incidents? Sabotaging his own domain? He was definitely high-strung enough to do something like that, although with his size, he probably would have been noticed by somebody.

I wondered whether he had keys to the main doors, or just his display windows. Somewhere there was a master list of who had keys to what. Probably filed in personnel.

And I wasn't getting access to the personnel records. Catch-22. Or 23.

I should have looked for a CC written on the mystery man. That would have been another clue to—what? I didn't know.

The phone rang again. I was about to shut it off completely, but decided I'd better answer it.

"Beers."

"Jimbo, Freddie. You busy?"

"I'm working, Freddie. What's up?"

"Meet me at The Crater. Now." Click.

Freddie sounded alarmed. It was well past 5, so I could leave anytime. I just didn't know whether I should. Well, a quick meet with Freddie couldn't hurt. No one would miss me. Unless the phantom struck again.

I rode down and was striding briskly out the store. I glanced over at cosmetics and saw Tina watching me. She winked, then turned back to her customer. What was that?

Suddenly, all the guilt came flooding back, and I remembered my dinner plans with Rosie. Crap. She was going to go ballistic if I canceled again. Maybe just push it back a bit. OK, here's the plan: meet with Freddie, zip to the grocery, zip home and assemble a salad and pizza, run over to Gerald's for a quick chat, then back in time to cook the pizza and welcome Rosie at 8.

Simple. I left a message on Rosie's machine to change the time, then hit The Crater.

21

I followed the cloud of cigar smoke to locate Freddie in his corner booth. As I sat, I saw an alarmed look on his face that I wasn't accustomed to. His ubiquitous playful smirk was noticeably absent.

"S'up, Freddie."

"Beers." He signaled to Sam for another round. "I got something I need to show you." He reached in his jacket pocket and pulled out a folded sheet of paper. "It's right here."

The drama was killing me. "What? What is it?" His alarmed demeanor was contagious.

When his next beer arrived, he gulped half of it down, wiped his mouth on his sleeve, then said, "Take a look at this." He unfolded the paper in front of me. There were just a few words typed on the paper:

MENTION MY NAME AGAIN AND YOU'RE DEAD

Freddie chugged the rest of his beer while waving at the bar for another.

"What do you think this is?" I asked him.

"Obviously, someone doesn't like me talking about him. And I think you know who that somebody is."

"You think this is from Gerald."

"Who else?"

"Well, you cover a lot of games. Couldn't it be an athlete?"

154

"Gerald was an athlete. He must have found out I was looking into his background. He's got a record. And now you've got a buttload of problems at his—and your—workplace. It adds up to an asshole threatening me."

Freddie might be right. Although he looked like he was harmless, Gerald was big and strong enough to put the hurt on most people if he got worked up.

"I find it hard to believe Gerald has it in for you," I said. "In fact, he called me a while ago, and I'm heading over to his place to meet with him. He said he had something important to tell me."

"Don't go, Beers. It's probably a trap and he's going to beat your ass, or worse."

I snickered and gave him a dismissive wave. But now he had me worried.

"I'll be OK. Gerald's a big pussycat. In fact, he's probably gay."

"That's not what I heard when I was looking into his pro career. He pulls more ass than 20 Mule Team Borax."

"That makes no sense, Freddie. Wouldn't the mules be the ones doing the pulling?"

"Whatever. Maybe you better call me when you're talking with him. Just so I know you're OK."

"Sure. Whatever you say. Let me have this piece of paper. I'll see what he knows about it."

Freddie nodded. I was finishing off my beer and getting ready to leave, but, predictably, my phone rang. It was Tina.

"Saw you sneaking out the store. What are you doing?"

"Just having a beer with Freddie. That's all. Nothing suspicious. Although I probably will need to chat with you later."

"About what?"

"Later. I've got to go meet Gerald—"

"What for?"

"Look, I need to get going. I'll call you later."

"Be careful, Beers."

I promised her I would, reassured Freddie, then headed to the grocery. I raced home with my bags, chopped lettuce and veggies, rolled out the dough, spread the sauce and cheese and shrimp, then chunked it all in the fridge.

I was ringing the bell of No. 24 at a Frogtown apartment building at three minutes after 7. He lived on the second floor of a nondescript brick building with an outside fenced walkway. Looked like it was a converted cheap motel.

At 7:04, I was knocking on the door of No. 24.

At 7:05, I was peeking in the window next to the door of No. 24. Through the crack between the curtains, I could see a sparse room with a worn gray couch, end table, lamp, couple of chairs, some generic wall art and a doorway leading into a hallway. No sign of activity.

The sound of my cell phone ringing scared the hell out of me. "Yeah?"

"Gerald here. Come down to the back parking lot." Click.

I wandered back downstairs and down a narrow alley to the back lot. There were just a few cars there, but no sign of Gerald.

I walked into the middle of the dimly lit parking area and spun around once looking for him.

"Gerald! Where are you?" I barked.

A light blinked twice in the far corner of the lot. I walked toward the light.

"Gerald, cut the crap. I don't have a lot of time."

A loud whisper answered, "Quiet!" When I got to where the light had blinked, no one was there. I heard footsteps running away. On the ground at my feet was an envelope. This was getting stranger and stranger, and that was saying something for the odd Mr. Difansa. I picked up the envelope and headed back to my car.

My initials were on the envelope. Inside was a single sheet of paper with the words: "For a good time, call 403-766-6551. Ask for Bambi."

Weird. My Bambi? Of course, how many Bambis were there in the world, especially in the Twin Cities area. I dialed.

"Hello."

"Hi. Bambi? This is Beers."

"Oh, hey, Beers. How are you? Something wrong at the store?"

"No, not really. I just needed to call you…" I wasn't really sure why.

"Is this about…Did Gerald show you the thing?"

"What thing? I don't know what Gerald was going to show me. I was supposed to meet him and he didn't show up. Or at least he wasn't—"

"Oh no."

"What? What's wrong?"

"I'm scared."

"Look, I need to talk to somebody about what's going on. If you have information…"

"You know where I live?"

"No."

She gave me an address in Minnetonka. It would take me 20 minutes to get there, 20 to get back, so I'd have about five minutes to chat, max.

"Can't you just tell me over the phone?"

Click.

What the hell? This was getting annoying. People wanted to talk to me, then kept hanging up. I was starting to get paranoid myself.

If I was going to find out anything, I would have to nail down someone who would be willing to talk to me. Nothing to do but race out to Minnetonka.

The snow was now blowing horizontally across the highway but I managed to get there without spinning out. For some reason, the hairs on the back of my neck were standing up, like I was being watched. Occasionally, I saw lights behind me, but I was probably just being paranoid again.

The house was on a winding uphill road back in the woods off Lake Minnetonka. It was in a conclave of huge houses, contemporary designs nestled among the trees. I pulled up the driveway of Bambi's home and wondered how the heck she afforded it on whatever salary she mustered from La Scala.

The strains of "She Is Loaded" wafted through my brain. I got out and surveyed the woods beyond the sloping front yard. Silence clung like plastic wrap to the snow-covered trees.

The front door opened behind me and Bambi was illuminated in the porch light. She was huddled against the cold and glancing furtively around her front yard. She motioned me urgently into the house.

Through a foyer wide enough to drive an 18-wheeler through, she led me into the dimly lit den, where a blazing fire cast flickering shadows across the blue leather furniture.

"Have a seat," she said. "Drink?"

"None for me, thanks."

She headed straight to a bar in the corner and poured a half-glass of gin, neat, then sat on the Indian rug directly in front of the fireplace.

I hadn't said a word to this point, but figured this was my cue. "What's going on, Bambi?"

She took a big swig of her gin. "We have a problem." She hesitated before speaking again. I gave her time. "The incidents we had last week? I think someone's trying to get me in trouble."

"Why do you think that?"

Bambi suddenly stood up, walked back to the bar, grabbed a sheet of paper and brought it to me. "Look at this."

In the middle of the sheet was typewritten:

ALL BECAUSE OF YOU

"It was in my top desk drawer this morning. I didn't know what to do with it. I'm scared."

Bizarre. Yet another cryptic note delivered by the likely perpetrator to a store employee. Wait. Freddie isn't a La Scala employee. What's the common denominator? Me. So this must be somehow directed at me. Unless Freddie is the culprit, and he's just trying to throw me off the trail by pretending he got a note from the perp. But why Freddie? That didn't make sense. I took Freddie's note out of my pocket to compare them. Looked like it was from the same typewriter.

"Do you have any idea why someone would give you this?"

Again, Bambi hesitated before speaking. "I...I used to be involved in something. Something that could be construed the wrong way."

"Like a barter cabal?"

Her eyes widened and her mouth fell open. "How do you know about that?"

"I've got sources. But I don't think that necessarily makes you a suspect for anything. Or is there something you're not telling me?"

"That has nothing to do with my job," Bambi said defensively.

"I didn't say it did." She was on the verge of tears. "Look, I'm not going to say anything about it. But you have to tell me whatever you know that may help me figure out who's sabotaging the store."

Bambi started pacing in front of the fireplace. "There are some...people...who work at La Scala..."

"Yes?"

"They have records, Jim. They've been arrested."

"Like who?" She downed her drink and headed back to the bar. I was afraid she was going to get plastered before she told me anything.

"I'd rather not name names," she said, her back turned to me. "I don't want to get involved." Bambi was worried about something more than her "hobby," and I needed to find out what.

AS I WAS CONSIDERING Bambi's deep, dark secret, the doorbell rang. Bambi froze like a deer in head—uh, she stood still.

"Aren't you going to see who that is?" I asked when the bell rang a second time.

"You get it."

I walked down the gargantuan foyer to the front door and peeked out the spyhole. Gerald was on the doorstep, looking around furtively. I opened the door but blocked him from entering.

"Gerald? What are you doing here?"

"I was in the neighborhood..."

"Bullshit," I said. "I just came from your place. You weren't around. Or maybe you were, and you followed me out here."

"Can I come in?"

I stepped aside to let him in. Bambi, arms folded, led the way back into the den.

I figured it was time to try to put the screws to them. "Interesting that I have both of you here. You seem to be the prime suspects in this case."

"What?!" Bambi shouted. "That can't be!"

Gerald's brow wrinkled. "It's not me, Jim. I can prove it."

"OK, prove it."

He hesitated. "I think I know who did it."

I waited. He wasn't forthcoming. I decided to goad him a little to get him talking.

"Let's see, Gerald. It all started when a mannequin was put in a compromising position. That's your area. Then another mannequin was damaged. That's also your area. Then you decided to get creative and spread suspicion in other areas. You seem to have a history of skating on the wrong side of the law."

Gerald was quiet, but obviously worried. His lip started trembling.

"Bambi, you had every opportunity to do the same thing. As I understand it, the buying season is dormant during the holidays, so you've got lots of free time to cause havoc. And something tells me you're not a fan of the free enterprise system."

Bambi's expression turned dark and she was wringing her hands. "But I got this threat," she said, grabbing the paper and thrusting it toward me.

"You could have typed it," I responded. "And here's another thing. The perpetrator signed his handiwork in blue marker. Don't you use a lot of those blue markers on couture catalogs? Gerald, I've taken a look at your design table. You've got some of those markers in a cup. In fact, it could have been the both of you acting as a team."

They looked at each other, then back at me. "No," they said in unison.

"OK, then who?" I plopped down on the couch, spread my arms across the back and crossed my legs. "Let's hear it. Give me your grand theory."

Gerald walked to the fireplace and turned. "I think your answer is on the ninth floor."

"A VP?" I asked. "Why? And which one?"

"I don't know," Gerald answered. "But it's got to be. They have access to the whole store. They can get people to do whatever they want. I've heard there's dissension."

"Dissension? About what?"

"I don't know, but it probably has to do with end-of-year bonuses. You know, the VPs get performance bonuses based on their department's operations for the year."

"Yeah. So what?"

"I just think that's how somebody is threatening Mr. Scalabrino. Like, pay up or else."

The theory was ludicrous. Vice presidents knew so much about the store's operations and financial structure they could cause much more damage behind the scenes. These types of public spectacles couldn't be the work of a top manager.

"That's ridiculous," Bambi said, confirming my thoughts.

"Why so?" I asked, playing devil's advocate.

"It's not a manager. It may not even be an employee."

I couldn't decide whether to give Bambi my coy look or my smug look. I settled on the penetrating gaze. "Why do you say that?"

But she just shook her head.

"She doesn't know," Gerald said. "Neither do I. But it could be anybody."

"Wouldn't an employee have more opportunity to do all this stuff?" I asked. Lacking any better intelligence, I threw out a few more names. "What about the new guy in sporting goods? What's his name?"

"Brad Conley," Bambi offered. "He's incapable of remembering how to ring up a sale, much less masterminding a criminal enterprise."

"And you know this because...?"

"We went to dinner. Once."

Gerald snickered.

"What about the guys in maintenance?"

"Those little cretins are probably behind it," Gerald said.

"They're mostly college kids, part-timers hired for the holidays," Bambi added. "Doesn't seem likely."

"I don't trust those security guards, either," Gerald said.

He might have a point there. We seldom had the same contract guard two days in a row, but they had access keys to all but the executive suite.

Suddenly there was the loud crash of breaking glass from an adjoining room. Bambi rushed out and we followed. In the library across the hallway, we looked for the source of the sound. There was no obvious vase shattered on the floor.

"The window," Gerald said, pointing. There was a large hole in the lower part of the picture window, with long cracks radiating from it and plenty of shards on the floor. But I didn't see the rock that caused it.

"What the hell? Maybe a bird flew into it?"

"No bird," Gerald said. "Gunshot." He walked across the room to the wall opposite and started looking. In the corner, behind a giant stuffed panda, he found a hole, about a quarter inch in diameter.

"Call the cops," I told Bambi, "and stay away from the windows."

She rushed back into the den and dialed 911.

A DEPUTY CORMIER ARRIVED 20 minutes later, extracted a slug from the wall, walked around the outside of the house and reported that everything seemed in order. He spent some time on the squawk box in his cruiser before returning and telling Bambi, "We haven't heard any other reports of shooting in the area. It may have been some careless hunter loading his rifle to go hunting, probably a kid. We're going to check around the neighborhood. If you hear anything else, call me." He gave her a card.

The worried look on Bambi's face delayed the deputy's departure.

"Is there something else, ma'am?"

Bambi glanced at me, then Gerald. I saw the wheels turning in her head and wasn't going to tell her which way she should go. She chose discretion.

"No. I'm fine. I'll be OK. Thank you for coming out."

As he backed out the driveway, I could tell by the look on her face she wouldn't be fine.

"Would you like me to hang around tonight, Bambi?" I asked.

"No, I'll stay," Gerald interjected. He put an arm around Bambi and guided her to the couch. I glanced at my watch.

Damn. It was already 45 minutes past the time Rosie was supposed to arrive, and it would take me another half-hour to get back, considering the weather. I decided I'd better call.

There was no answer at my apartment. Also no answer at Rosie's. Not a good sign.

The road back was treacherous both safety-wise and mentally. When I finally got up to my apartment, there was a note pushed under the door. It was from Rosie. "Don't call me. EVER."

22

Tuesday morning, Dec. 21
Four shopping days till Christmas
Temperature: 11, heavy snow; wind chill, 4

Snow began dropping furiously, descending across the city like a movie house curtain, obscuring the view of holiday hustle and bustle.

Tina was chomping on Belgian waffles and I was slugging down cup after cup of coffee to try to get over my growing winter hangover. Lena didn't make it to breakfast with us.

I filled Tina in on the poisoned candy incident and the strange man in the lounge, plus the confusing events of last night. She already knew about the former, wasn't surprised by the latter.

Unknown to me, Tina had paid a visit to Rosie on Monday to go to bat for me. That was before I stood her up last night.

She explained about the mystery box on Rosie's desk. "I opened it for her."

"You just opened it? She thought it was a bomb or something."

"No bomb. What was in the box was a Babushka doll."

"Huh?"

"A matryoshka, a nesting doll made out of wood. You've seen them. They're hollow wooden dolls, a little smaller than a bowling pin. Open one up and there's another inside, then another inside that, and so on."

"Oh, right."

"Anyway, this was an antique, made before the fall of the Soviet empire. Had CCCP stamped on the bottom. Apparently, these are rare and pretty valuable nowadays."

"Why is that?"

"Well, I read up on that last night. The Soviets wanted to create big factories to mass-produce goods. The creation of goods outside factories was forbidden," she explained. "So craftsmen were criminals. They went underground and secretly continued to make their artwork by hand, smuggling them out to the West."

"But isn't this a factory-made doll? It's got a Soviet stamp."

"Nope. This is where the craftsmen got crafty. They knew if they didn't look like officially sanctioned goods, they would be destroyed if discovered. So they created fake stamps for the bottom. If you take this one apart, and look at the innermost doll, the craftsman's name is on the bottom."

"Ah. So, why did Rosie get this?"

"Well, it seems she's got a secret admirer. One of the foreign students apparently sent it to her, asking for a date. There was a note in the innermost doll signed Misha. I think she's considering it."

This hit me like a punch to the gut. I knew we were having some problems getting together, but I thought our relationship was further along than this. Of course, she had essentially told me to drop dead.

"She told you this yesterday? Not today?"

"She didn't say it in so many words. But I could tell."

Then that was it. She was probably just coming to my place for dinner to dump me anyway. Not that that was any consolation, but at least I could justify trying to get on with my life. Such as it was.

"Here's another thing," Tina said. "I've been thinking about the sabotage and what they've all got in common. Shoes, snake, sleeper sofa, suitcase."

"The letter S," I said.

"Yep."

"Except for mannequin and deli. And the candy."

"Didn't you say the mannequin was a stork?"

"OK, sure. One of them. What about the deli?"

"Haven't figured that one out yet, but I'm sure there's something that starts with S. Who manufactured the candy? Maybe it's a company that starts with S."

I pondered that in silence. "So what does that mean? Why the S?"

"Give me your notebook and pen." I did and she started writing. She made a big S on a blank page. "What's that made of?" I stared at it, glanced up at Tina, shrugged.

"Right, 2 C's. A C up here for the top curve, and a backward one down here for the bottom curve. The S is really 2 C's."

Tina was onto something. Maybe. Or it could just be coincidence.

I would have to think about the deli and see where that fit in with her theory. But still, what did it mean? As usual, confusion equaled no clue.

THE STORE WAS BUSY. This was drop-dead time for procrastinators. Either get it now or be in the doghouse Christmas morning when the presents are opened. Needless to say, there were even more frantic men shopping than before.

Earrings were getting scooped up by the fistfuls and teddies were flying off the racks and into the clutches of ever-hopeful males. The Christmas shopping season was closing with a bull market.

My morning walk through the store's levels was one of amazement. There were lines at every register and more people than I had ever seen in the store at one time. Employees seemingly had shifted into high gear, pumping out receipts and gift boxes at an accelerating pace.

The break room on seven was being transformed into a party room. Garlands had been hung across the ceiling and posters encouraged employees to "kick off your holiday partying at La Scala." There was also a note that you had to be in attendance to get your gift, whatever that was.

I checked in with Jane late in the morning to tell her all was frenzied, but nothing seemed out of the ordinary. No incidents, at least. We were on a roll.

My phone didn't ring once. Everyone was too busy to bother me, I guess. The only message on my machine was a recorded reminder from human resources about the company party on Christmas Eve. I even booted up my computer, just to see if there were any critical emails for me to answer. Nothing. After playing solitaire for a while, I left and made another circuit of the store. Still very busy, still nothing unusual. My phone rang.

"Beers."

"Yo, Merry Almost Christmas, dude."

"Hey, Freddie. How's it going?"

"I'm starving. You up for lunch?"

"Well, it's probably our busiest day of the season so far…"

"And you're putting out fires?"

"Actually, no. It's busy but quiet, if that's possible."

"Then let's get some lunch. You can spare an hour."

Couldn't argue with that. Besides, I was suddenly starving.

We arranged to meet at The Crater. Sam had supplemented the twinkly lights behind the bar with a string of cigars. He pulled two off the string and handed them to Freddie and me as we approached the bar. "On the house, gentlemen. What'll it be?"

"Beers for Beers," Freddie chuckled.

"Original," I said. "You write your own material?"

Sam drew a pair of Summit IPAs and we retreated to a booth. Freddie had the stogie lit before his rear end hit the seat. I scanned the room for smoke-hating lesbians.

"I think I've solved your little case," Freddie said.

"What do you mean?"

"I know who's been messing up your orderly workplace and threatening me." He puffed with a contented look on his face.

"Who?"

"Not so fast, my friend. I need to lay the case out for you and build this up logically, like in the Columbo stories."

"You're not Columbo, although you do dress badly and smoke awful cigars."

"Jealousy—not a pretty emotion," he responded. "Man, I used to love watching those Columbo shows when I was a kid. He always had just one more thing—"

"Freddie. I have to get back to work before the year ends. Spill it."

His gleeful expression abruptly turned sour. "All right! It's your boss, Jane."

Flabbergasted, I responded, "You're nuts."

"Irregardless, it's her."

"That's insane and not possible."

Freddie puffed. I waited. Drummed my fingers on the table. Examined my unlit cigar. Sipped. Scanned the room a few times.

"She's screwing the CFO," he said.

"What?! No way!"

"True."

"You are insane, Freddie. Jane is happily married—" Actually, I had no way of knowing this, just assumed it to be true. I didn't even know her husband's name.

"Was happily married," he replied. "Seems there's a nasty divorce in the works."

"So what's that got to do with—"

"Like I say, she's doing the horizontal tango with Mr. Moneybags. But Senõr Deep Pockets has his eye on another of your illustrious and ever-so-busy co-workers."

"And that is...?"

"Bambi. She apparently caught him in her headlights, so to speak, stroked his ego and other things, and milked his vast portfolio for information."

"Freddie, enough with the cheap innuendos. Just say it in the King's English."

"Bambi went to bed with Salmon Foster, found out who's got his or her hands in the till, and is blackmailing them. Jane apparently is one of the folks with their hands in the cookie jar."

This all hit me like a head slap. Jane couldn't possibly be crooked. She was too sweet and naive to...wait, maybe that was all an act. And Bambi—could this be the deep, dark secret she couldn't fess up to? She's blackmailing important people in the company, including someone who's threatening to kill her? And Gerald, and Freddie and anyone else who gets in his way. Or her way.

"So let me get this straight," I said. "According to you—"

"Not me. I have sources."

"Who?"

"Not gonna say."

"According to you," I continued, "Jane Mertin is causing sabotage around the store in retaliation for Bambi's blackmailing her."

"Or as a cover-up," Freddie offered.

"A smokescreen," I said.

He nodded. "Jane isn't doing this herself. She's got a boy-toy she's directing to do the dirty work. And she's trying to pin it all on Bambi. Or actually, she's trying to pin it on someone else—she doesn't know it's Bambi who's trying to blackmail her. That's why several people got threatening notes."

"Like me."

"Yep."

"And you. And Bambi. And Gerald."

"Yep."

I considered for a minute. "Gerald told you this."

Freddie paused mid-puff. "Uh, no."

"Uh, yeah." I had caught him off-guard. He didn't anticipate my keen powers of deduction. Actually, just a guess, but probably a good one nevertheless. "Gerald isn't the most unimpeachable source, y'know."

"He's telling the truth," Freddie asserted.

"And you know this because...?"

"I have corroboration. One of my front-office sources. You can take this to the bank." He nodded and pointed his dwindling cigar at me.

"Freddie, I hate to tell you you're full of shit, but I'm sure it wouldn't be the first time."

"Listen, Beers..."

"No, you listen. Jane isn't doing this. I know her. She's a nice lady. You would never go to press with an unsubstantiated rumor like this, would you?" He hung his head and didn't answer.

"Don't believe any wild rumor you hear. Be a reporter. Get real corroboration. And believe me, you won't find any on Jane."

"Beers, you need to be a hard-boiled detective, like Mike Hammer, if you want to survive in that biz," Freddie said.

"I can be hard-boiled."

"No you can't. You're soft-boiled. You're a three-minute egg, up against rotten yeggs."

"Quite the wordsmith you are. You should get a job writing somewhere."

"That's so funny I forgot to laugh."

"Ah, you know clichés! That qualifies you to be...a sportswriter!"

Freddie didn't like being shot down. He drank mostly in silence, puffing up a huge cloud of cigar smoke. Just another smokescreen in this case, I thought.

My phone rang.

"Jim, this is Don Anderson. I need you down here pronto."

"Gotta go, Freddie." I ran out the door, leaving him with the tab.

ENTERING THE MAINTENANCE DEPARTMENT, I saw Don standing near the freight elevator in the back. As I approached, I looked down to see a large pile of dresses, pants, shirts and coats in tatters. Someone had used a sharp object to shred them. Attached to the back wall of the elevator was a note with something written in blue: съешьте меня сс

"It must be Pete," Anderson said.

"Pete?"

"Our temp. He just up and quit a while ago. Threw down his stuff and walked out. Didn't say a word."

"Where is he now?"

"Don't know." Anderson said he wasn't answering his home phone number and he didn't have a cell phone as far as he knew.

"Where's the rest of your crew. Maybe they know."

"Out to lunch."

"Let's check his locker," I said. We did, and found a slew of blue markers and a couple of box cutters, along with a loaded key ring, two screwdrivers and a small hacksaw. It looked like we found our vandal.

"You tell anyone about this?" I asked Anderson.

"Called you first."

"Good." I dialed Joe T and filled him in.

"On my way," he said.

I told Anderson to clean out the elevator and put the remnants in boxes, including the note. Meanwhile, I collected all the items in Pete's locker, wearing gloves in case there were fingerprints to be obtained.

Joe T arrived with a couple of "assistants," who collected the boxes of tattered clothing and locker items, along with Pete's address and phone number.

"So you think he's the one," Joe T said.

"I don't know. I'm pretty sure this is the type of marker that left all the CCs. And then there's the note."

"What does it say?"

"I don't know. I've copied it down in my notepad. I'm going to find out."

"Good work, Jim," he said. "Keep this under your hat, OK? I'll get Detective Cuccia to pay our friend a visit and ask him a few questions." Joe T left and I relayed to Anderson the need to keep this on the QT.

THE REST OF THE DAY was uneventful. Except for one late afternoon excursion through the store, I stayed in my office and listened to music. Mick Jagger was singing again; this time it was "Shattered," which is how my nerves felt. Shattered but relieved at the same time. Was it over? Hard to say. I was hopeful, but accustomed to not getting my hopes up.

Several times, the phone rang. I let voice mail get it. Nothing was an emergency, and I just didn't feel like talking.

Tina called to say she had gotten her cop friend to talk to the troglodyte, and he agreed to pay for the damage and wasn't going to bother her anymore. Lena called to say she landed the whale, finally, and would have a nice little commission on her next paycheck. Bambi called to complain about Bibb, and how terrible a Santa he made, despite looking right for the part.

Jane called to get an update on events, but I didn't return her call to tell her about Pete. Not that I believed Freddie's insane theory—but Joe T had told me to keep my trap shut, and that seemed like a good approach at the moment.

I still had my doubts about Bambi. It seemed odd that she would have such a nice home on a store job salary.

TWO MORE RUN-OF-THE-MILL DAYS PASSED. The hustle of Christmas shopping got furious, but shoplifters were oddly absent. Perhaps they found better merchandise at La Scala's competitors.

Preparations for the office Christmas party were in high gear, and clerks were buzzing about what to wear, whether alcohol would be served, who was planning entertainment and what kind of gift they would get.

I had asked Lena to try to find out more about Bambi, and she came through. Her research showed that Bambi was the daughter of a guy who invented a popular ice auger. Figures—family money. I couldn't picture her out on a frozen lake trying to catch walleyes, however.

Lacking any other viable suspect, I had become convinced that Pete was behind the incidents in the store. Since there were no further problems, and blue markers had been found in his locker, it seemed logical to assume that he was the culprit.

I heard no more from Joe T, so I was reasonably sure they were taking care of the situation and that was that. It was going to be a happy and peaceful Christmas after all. Except that my girlfriend hated me. And there was still the pesky problem of the meaning of those two letters.

23

Friday morning, Dec. 24
One shopping day till Christmas
Temperature: -14, clear; wind chill, -21

The eve of Christmas Eve was a lonely night. Rosie didn't call, and I didn't see any point in calling her. I screwed up, big time.

It would take a Christmas miracle for her to forgive me. But like long ago when I gave up believing in Santa, I didn't see any miracles on the horizon.

I decided to walk in to work for a change. In retrospect, not such a good idea. I didn't realize how much the temperature had dropped overnight. Although I was well bundled up, my cheeks started to burn by the time I had walked four blocks.

My fingers were in shock, as if they had been immersed in a bucket of ice water for several minutes. Apparently, my gloves were wimpy and I needed a ski mask. The sidewalks were ice floes. I was doing OK until I slipped and landed hard on my ass while trying to beat a yellow light. It was the kind of day that made me wonder whether a new Ice Age was approaching.

Needless to say, I walked as briskly as the icy sidewalks and my sore rump would allow.

Traffic in the store thinned on Christmas Eve. There were a few truly desperate individuals, grabbing things at random just to have something to give, but for the most part, it got really quiet toward lunchtime. Perhaps it was because the store planned to close early for the employee party and people had finished their frenzied shopping the day before. I made several circuits of the store but saw nothing unusual. It was the calm after the storm.

By early afternoon, the store had gone almost three days without an incident. This was a major victory in my mind. I was a hero and had solved the baffling case of the store destroyer.

Well, OK, the strange case had resolved itself as the havoc creator had checked out, if it indeed was Pete. Perhaps he had been apprehended by Joe T and his henchmen. Who knew? Who cared, as long as it was over.

The red light on the phone in my office was flashing, which meant there were several un-listened-to messages, but I wasn't in the mood. Rosie had said in no uncertain terms that we were kaput. That bummed me out. "Blue Christmas" was on repeat cycle in my brain. I found a tape in the cabinet and put it in the tape player. Better Elvis's voice than the one in my head.

The store planned to close at 3 p.m., with the employee Christmas party to follow in the break room. This being my first Christmas at La Scala, I didn't know quite what to expect, but I thought I'd better put in an appearance. It was probably mandatory attendance for management types. Any regular employee who attended was promised some sort of gift. It was probably a turkey.

Before heading down, I thought I would type up a full report for Jane, based on whatever information I had amassed in the last week or so. My reporter's notepad was full of scribblings, but it would take the skill of a veteran reporter to make it coherent. It was like covering a football game. I would take notes, but the sense of the game would come later, after I started typing. Segues and embellishments—and, of course, clichés—would round out the notes into a full story. Time to summon up my rusty reporting skills. I fired up the computer.

As I was typing, the strains of "Silent Night" started playing over the store's PA system. So far, it was a silent night, and I hoped it would stay that way, except, of course, for the merriment at the Christmas party.

I was rounding third and heading home on my report when there was a knock at the door. It opened and Lena walked in. She was smartly outfitted in a long blue dress with lots of cleavage showing.

"Where y'at, Beers."

"Hey, Lena. Lookin' good."

"Comin' down fa da pawty?"

"Yeah, just finishing up my report. I figure Jane needs something documented for the executive team to look at."

Lena walked around the desk beside me, leaned over and started reading the screen. Mass quantities of Lena bosom were inches away from my face. I peeked. I peeked again. I stared. Guilt. I looked back at the screen. Glancing up at her face, I saw she was staring at me. "What?" I said.

Once again, my brain played tricks on me, sending me into a fantasy land where passion trumped logic: Lena leans over and kisses me softly. Then she does it again, and this time with some tongue. My single functioning brain cell asks what's going on. The rest are just going with the flow.

There's a symphony playing, but it sounds like The Beatles singing "Michelle." Lena sweeps the papers and computer and everything else off my desk and starts ripping my clothes off. We make passionate love on the desk, while a half-nude mannequin watches from the corner of the room.

Then my brain came back to life. We were still dressed. Everything was still on the desktop. Once again, lust had taken me elsewhere, and left me with a load of guilt. Just like the imaginary incident with Tina at her apartment, this was a case of my flight of fancy transporting me to a place where desire eclipsed reality.

Snapping back to reality, I heard Lena say, "Nice ruhpawt." Lena gave me a chaste peck on the cheek and said, "Merry Christmas, Beers," as she left. I was alone again in my corporate cell.

The clock on the wall said ten till three. Just enough time to wrap up my report, send it to Jane's printer and hotfoot it down to seven for the party.

The party had already spilled out into the kitchenware department by the time I arrived. Threading my way through co-workers I had never met, I entered the break room. The veeps were huddled together in a corner, segregated from the rabble. Tina was holding court near the punch bowl, surrounded by a group of cackling women and a couple of leering men. But Lena was absent.

I winked at Tina and sidled up next to Jane. After a minute, she noticed me and said, "Merry Christmas, Jim."

"Merry Christmas, Jane. I sent you a report on everything that happened in the last week. Should be on your printer."

"Great, Jim. Thanks. You doing anything special for Christmas?"

I already had. In my mind. "No, no. Just dinner with my Dad and my siblings, then hanging out at home. Having some friends over. You should come. Tomorrow evening. Nothing fancy, just drinks and snacks."

"That sounds wonderful, Jim. I'll try. My kids are in from college but…" She didn't finish her thought.

"Well, enjoy the party," I said. I headed toward the punch bowl. Tina was woofing down a handful of cashews. The crowd had dispersed.

"Seen Lena?" I asked.

Tina read something in my expression. "What's going on with you and Lena?" she asked.

"Nothing. She told me she would be here, that's all." I didn't even sound convincing to myself. I felt myself blushing.

Tina grinned. "You dog!" she said, laughing.

"What?" I said, hunching my shoulders. "What?"

"Good for you," she answered, raising her glass of punch in cheers. I had to get out of there. Tina was obviously assuming something had transpired between us. She can read people like that. In this case, she read wrong.

"Gotta get something in my office," I said. "See you in a bit." She just kept grinning at me.

I headed through pots, pans, mixers, utensils and a slew of party animals to the stairwell. I walked down to the sixth floor and popped out into menswear.

All quiet. Not a creature was stirring, although there were rumored to be mice among the shoeboxes in back.

The fifth floor was fairly quiet also, except for some shuffling sounds. Lena was behind the jewelry counter, putting away some display items. She glanced at me walking up, smiled and kept working.

"Lena, I…"

"Shhhh. Nuttin' ta say, Beers. I didn't get ya a present, so…what's a little kiss between friends?"

It wasn't a little kiss to me. That was a present? Huh. More than what I got Lena, which was nothing, but now I'd better do so. Also better get something for Tina. I pulled out my notepad and wrote myself a reminder.

"Whatcha writin' dere?"

"Nothing. Just a note for my report. You heading up to the party?"

"Yeah. Catch up wit' ya in a bit." She moved down the counter and stowed more boxes.

I headed down to four. Suddenly, I realized my bladder was at the bursting point, so I headed across the floor to the men's room in the returns department.

Electronics was aglow with laser lights and every TV was lit up with scenes of "Rudolph the Red-Nosed Reindeer." Seen it a billion and a half times. Good old Burl Ives.

I followed the glowing red nose down the row of tubes to the corner, where one lone set was tuned to a different program. It looked like it was a rock video station, playing a '60s retrospective. I watched for a while as it ran through videos of the Stones, Led Zeppelin, the Who, the Kinks. It was always entertaining seeing these old clips, especially the outfits and hairdos. Hard to believe that was during my lifetime, but I was but a wee lad when the British Invasion occurred.

Then it was the Beatles. Ahh, the classics. Playing "Back in the USSR." I let the sound wash over me and smiled, leaning against the singing snowman on a 27-inch tube.

Suddenly, though, there was a moment of clarity. An image on the screen triggered something in my subconscious, a memory forgotten, a puzzle piece falling into place, a key unlocking the door to a dark passageway suddenly illuminated with possibility. Yes, this could be the answer.

Most times, logic held the key to the mysteries of life. This time, it was chance and intuition, but I felt a certainty that told me it had to be true.

After a quick trip to the men's room, I ran to the elevator and rode it up to my office. My copy of the latest company directory was buried under old memos in my middle desk drawer.

I zipped down the list and bingo! There it was. The answer I had hoped to find. Now it was just a matter of confronting the perp, wrapping this case up with a pretty bow and putting it under Johnny Scalabrino's tree.

24

After locking my office, I rode down to the basement. Peeking in the deli area, I saw work had been progressing nicely but it still had a ways to go and probably wouldn't be completed until well after New Year's. I continued through the lower level to maintenance.

As expected, there was little activity. Don Anderson was probably off for the holidays, and only Bradley was in sight.

He was sitting with his feet propped up on the crew chief's desk, boom box blaring "Grandma Got Run Over by a Reindeer." He didn't notice me until I was standing right beside him.

"Hey, Bradley. How's it going?"

"Cool, dude. Wassup? What can I do for you?"

"Can you turn that down?" I yelled, pointing at the boom box. He made a minuscule downward adjustment in the decibel level.

"I'm looking for someone. One of your cohorts."

"Hey, you the Santa dude? Almost didn't recognize you."

"Yeah, I was Santa for a few days. Jim's the name. Looking for Sergei."

"Oh, right. The guy with the mannequin. Schwing!"

I nodded. "Sergei?"

Bradley squinted and scratched the back of his head. "Uh…not sure. I think he's off."

"Is he off?"

"Not sure."

"Can you check? I kinda need to talk to him."

177

"Right. Got the schedule posted over by the door." He dropped his legs, got up and sauntered over to the wall, scratched his head again. "Hmmmm…says here he's off."

"You know when he works again?"

"Let's see, today's Saturday, so…"

"Today's Friday."

"Huh?" He looked at me like I had just shown him the invention of fire. "Friday? For true? Damn!"

"What's the problem?"

"I was supposed to be off today. Crap!"

Apparently, Bradley was a bit short in the attention span department, and maybe awareness of reality in general. I looked at the calendar but didn't see any names, just initials.

"So this SS here—that's Sergei? He's working today?"

Bradley looked where I was pointing. "Oh, right, I guess he is. Strange, haven't seen him around lately. Usually he's goofing off down here."

I didn't make the obvious retort. "Do you think he's at the party?"

"Party?"

"The company party. In the break room?"

"Oh, hell. Forgot about that. Don said I could go if I finished my work."

Again, I was discreet. "Well, you should get up there," I said. "Maybe you can help me find Sergei."

"I don't know…"

"There's food and drinks."

He was out the door before I could add any further encouragement.

I followed him back up to the festivities. The casual mingling had morphed into a crowd watching a performance.

Several people wearing signs were recreating a fictitious management seminar. The girl wearing a "Jane Mertin" sign was leading the other fake veeps in a rousing cheer for "Johnny S." Except it sounded like Johnny "Asssssssssss." Then they broke into song:

Johnny, we love you,
Not cause we have to,
You let us work our tails off.

Give us that bonus,
But you don't own us...

The rest was indecipherable because of the riotous laughter from the crowd. I signaled to Lena and Tina to meet me outside the break room. We huddled in a corner far from the crowd.

"I need you to help me look for somebody. You know the guys in maintenance?"

"Bradley?" Lena asked.

"No, not him. The Russian dude, Sergei."

"Hey, I know him," Tina said. "He was here a minute ago. Wearing a Santa hat and python boots."

"Dat's all?" Lena asked. "Freaky."

"No, he had on pants, nothing special. Jeans maybe. But the boots and hat for sure."

"OK," I said, "let's try to find him. I'm convinced he's the guy we're looking for. I don't want you going off by yourselves because he may try something. Why don't you two stick together and we'll split up the floors."

Their expressions told me they didn't like that idea. "We can cover the store quicker if we each take three floors," Tina said.

"Yeah," Lena agreed.

"Maybe I should call in Joe T," I suggested.

"No way," Lena said. "Dis is our bust."

"What if he's armed?" I said. "He could have a weapon."

"Or a snake," Tina added. She shivered.

"Snakes don't bother me," Lena replied. "Useta have a pet boa back in Metry. But I'm 'lergic ta bullet holes."

"Let's call Joe T," Tina said.

Joe T's answering machine picked up. I left a message for him to call me ASAP. Perhaps we could locate Sergei quicker with Bradley's help. I spotted him across the way in china, where he was pouring Jägermeister from a pint bottle into a champagne glass. "C'mon," I told the girls.

"Bradley, need your help," I said.

"Whassup, Santa dude. Hellooooo, ladies!" He grinned broadly and winked at Lena, threw an air smooch at Tina.

They were not amused.

"I need your help to find Sergei. Know where he is?"

"Naw, man. He ain't here. He's a party pooper," Bradley said disgustedly, swigging his contraband hooch.

"Is he in the store?" I insisted.

"Sure, bro. He's working today. You checked the sked." He was starting to pour another glassful when Lena grabbed his arm.

"Bradley, sweetie." She fluttered her eyelashes at him and put on a syrupy southern accent. "Ah'd sher lahk it if yewd hep me." He put down the bottle and glass, and started to embrace Lena. When he went in for a kiss, she twisted his arm behind his back and got him in a headlock. "Cut the crap, doofus. Find Sergei for us."

"OK, OK!" he yelped. "Lemme go!"

She released him and he checked for broken bones, flexing his arm several times. "He might be wearing a pager. I can try that." He extracted a phone from his pocket and punched in a number. "He should call me back soon," Bradley said.

"Can you help us look around the store?" I asked.

"Uh. What about the party?"

"It'll go on for a couple hours," Tina said. "Help us find him real quick and you can get back to your...whatever."

"Tina, you go with Bradley," I said. "Lena, come with me."

"What do we do if we find him?" Bradley asked.

"Just call my cell if you find him." I gave Bradley the number. "Don't do anything else. You guys start at the lower level and work up. We'll start on nine."

As Tina and Bradley headed down the elevator, Lena and I went up. We walked through the darkened ninth floor. Most of the offices were locked and no one was around. When we came to my office, I could feel myself blushing. I peeked at Lena and she was smirking. I looked inside and quickly closed and locked the door.

We walked down the long hallways of storage rooms and offices, checking each door. All but a few seemed to be locked. Again, all was quiet. As we headed to the stairs, my cell phone rang. It was Tina.

"Something weird down here, Beers."

"Whatcha got?"

"Well, everything looked normal in the deli and the basement, but someone's been playing in sporting goods."

"How so?"

"All the balls are on the floor. Baseballs, basketballs, footballs. They're all over the floor."

"Hmmmm."

"No one is down here, though. I'm grabbing one of these bats for protection."

"OK. Keep looking." I hung up and relayed the information to Lena.

"Guess da guy's got balls," she quipped.

I decided we probably should carry a big stick also but didn't want to go all the way down to the basement. We went down the stairs to eight. Immediately, something felt wrong.

We strolled through the luggage department, which seemed normal. But bedding was another matter. As we walked down toward the beds, a disturbing scenario was apparent.

Three beds were occupied. At first, I thought it was people sleeping. But as we got closer, I saw it was just mannequins. Two in each bed.

"Dem dummies having a pawty up heah," Lena said.

"Funny, they're usually well-behaved."

I noticed there was one straight, one gay and one lesbian scene depicted in the pairings by the prankster. Predictably, my phone rang.

"Got something else, Beers," Tina said.

"Yeah, us too." I described the baffling sleep-in.

"You won't believe what we got down here on one. Sweatsuits everywhere. Covering the whole cosmetics counter. Bastard."

"Anybody?"

"Not a soul here. Where's the security guard we're supposed to have?"

"Not sure. Maybe he's at the party."

"This is creeping me out a bit. We're heading up to two now."

I twisted a leg off the nearest mannequin and slung it over my shoulder. It wasn't a bat, but it was something. I decided we'd skip seven for now since everyone was at the party and we'd just come from there.

The sixth floor was Christmas central. In addition to seasonal gifts, there was a walk-through Christmas village that led directly to the candy counter. Kids loved it, parents tolerated it and candy sales soared every holiday season, I learned.

The village itself looked normal. A couple of elves were out of place, but otherwise it looked as I remembered from a previous visit. The candy counter, however, was another matter.

Dozens of candy canes had been unwrapped and hung across the front of the counter. Behind it, a huge pile of chocolate candies had been dumped from boxes, littering the floor behind the counter. Lena picked one up and bit into it before I could stop her. "Good stuff," she said. I prayed it wasn't tampered with.

Bambi's office was on six, in a suite that encompassed the return department. Nothing unusual there and all the offices were locked.

The phone rang.

"Joe T here. What's up?"

I could hear clamor in the background, voices and dishes clanking.

"Hey, Joe T. We've got a situation at the store. Thought you might like to know about it." He was silent so I continued. "Looks like our vandal is active again. We're going through the store now, floor by floor, and finding a bit of a mess on each floor. And I think I know who it is. It isn't Pete."

There was dead air for ten seconds. Finally, Joe T spoke. "Anybody hurt?"

"No, not that I know of. Like I say, we're just going through the store now and..."

"We'll send someone over." Click.

"Whaddid he say?" Lena asked.

"They're going to send someone over."

"When?"

"Not sure. Sounded like he was at a party."

"Oh, yeah. Mistah Scalabrino's havin' his big bash tonight, too."

"Ah. Well, Joe T is sending someone over, but we probably should keep——" And the phone rang again.

"Tina?"

"Yeah, Beers. On two. Ladies shoe department is messed up. Got two towers of boxes stacked to the ceiling in the middle of the floor, then sort of semi-circles around them. Weird."

"Semi-circles?"

"Yeah, not quite circles."

"What semi-circles?" Lena asked.

"Tina says there are shoeboxes stacked up, with some arranged in semi-circles around the stacks."

"Like C's?" she asked.

"Of course! Tina, they look like big C's?"

"Yeah, I guess. If you look at them from 50,000 feet, I guess they'd look like C's."

"Anything else?"

"Not yet. Keep you posted." She hung up.

Lena and I took the stairs down to five. Lena seemed especially apprehensive about what state she'd find the jewelry counter in, but was visibly relieved to find it unscathed. The purse section, however, was in shambles. Prada and Coach bags were lined up on the floor like dominoes and were covered in what looked like confectioner's sugar. It turned out to be talc.

"Damn," Lena whispered.

Yeah. Damn. I dialed Tina's cell. No answer. "Come on," I said. "Pick up."

"What's the haps, Beers?" Lena asked.

"Not getting an answer." After 11 rings, I hung up. "Something's wrong. We'd better head down." We took the stairs, skipping four and heading down to three. Exiting onto the floor in casual wear, we could hear voices, arguing, coming from the lingerie department. My phone rang.

"Down here in ladies' undies," Tina whispered. "We found him. Bradley's talking to him now. Yelling, really."

"We hear," I said. "We're on three. Heading over now."

Lena and I walked briskly toward the voices. Bras and panties were flying up in the air. I heard Bradley curse and threaten Sergei, but the commotion continued. Arriving at the scene, I saw Bradley waving his bottle of hooch at Sergei, who was sitting atop a rack, pulling off undergarments and tossing them in all directions.

"Dude, I'm telling you, you're in major doo-doo," Bradley was yelling.

"Nyet!" Sergei yelled back. "You have the doo-doo." Then a bunch of stuff I assumed was Russian expletives, delivered with vehemence. Then he talked into what looked like a walkie-talkie. All I could make out was the name Misha.

Bradley rushed him and tried to pull him off the rack, but Sergei kicked him away. I heard the elevator door open and turned to see a burly guy running toward us with a bullwhip.

Before I could react, he flicked it out expertly, caught Bradley around the ankles and yanked him off his feet. He went down with a thud, dragging a display cart down with him in a crash of glass and panties.

I pushed Lena behind me and inched backward toward the lingerie counter, giving the whip wielder room. Sergei was guffawing at the top of his lungs, continuing to strew items across the floor. Tina was trying to stare down the guy with the whip while he coiled it. Bradley's fall had apparently knocked him out.

"Sergei," I called from the safety of the counter. "The game's over. Time to give it up."

He just laughed and pointed at his cohort, who joined in his mirth. "Misha, you hear? You have what army," Sergei said to me. "Is not happen for you." Sergei jumped down, and he and Misha ran off toward the stairs.

"Stay here with Bradley and get someone to help him," I ordered Lena. Tina was already running after them.

"No way in hell I'm stayin' heah," Lena said. She took off after Tina. Bradley was out cold but breathing OK. I also headed for the stairs.

In the stairwell, I spotted Lena heading down two steps at a time. Apparently, the Russkies were making a run for it. Tina yelled for them to stop, but the trampling steps continued. I redialed Joe T and asked him to have someone cover the rear exit when they arrived.

The procession exited the stairwell on the first floor. They were heading straight for the front entrance, but that was a dead end. The doors had been locked when the store closed for the party. Sergei rattled the doors a few times, then turned to face us. He would have to go through us to get to the emergency exit. Misha pointed his whip at Tina and Lena. "Nyet!" he shouted. They held their stance 15 feet away.

In the dark outside the doors, I saw a face ease into the light. It was Joe T. He motioned me to open the door. I pointed two fingers at Misha and Sergei and mouthed, "These two."

"You can't escape," I yelled. "We've got the emergency exit covered." They took off running toward sportswear.

"Tina," I yelled, following them, "get the keys from Bradley and let Joe T in. Lena, tell Joe T I'll call him and let him know where they go." I ran off to catch up with the pair.

Of course, they headed straight for the stairs and started back up. And up. And up. By the time I got to the ninth floor, I was puffing like I'd just run a marathon. I thought my chest would explode. Definitely out of shape. Damn Freddie and his cigars! I tried to control my breathing and listen for movement.

Except for my gasping, it was quiet. I gazed around the floor. The lighting was dim in the executive suite, and the hallways leading off to the sides were dark. After another minute, my respiration returned to normal. I started easing my way down the corridor.

Beyond the glass doors leading into the vice presidents' suite, I could see the open door leading into Jane's office. The light was off and it was dark. There was light under the door of Salmon Foster's office, but the door was closed. Most other doors were closed also.

I peeked down the hall toward my meager quarters. Couldn't see anything, so I waited a minute until my eyes adjusted.

Creeping down the hallway, I listened for any sound of the vandals, but it was quiet. Eerily quiet. I could hear my heartbeat, ba-bum ba-bum ba-bum. It was going too fast. What if I had an anxiety attack, or worse, a heart attack? Calm down.

They're not armed, except for a bullwhip. Just stay out of range. Spot them, then call in the reinforcements. Don't be a hero.

My inner dialogue was shattered by a jackhammer going off inside my head. Wait. That's an alarm. A fire alarm. Oh jeez, what next? Another fire? Could be cover. Maybe they're creating a diversion. When the doors open and partygoers flee the fire, the perps will sneak out with them. Gotta stop them.

I punched up Joe T's number.

"Joe T here."

"Joe T, Beers," I said. "There's an alarm going off!"

"What? Can't hear you over the alarm."

I cupped my hand around my mouth. "There's an alarm going off!"

"No shit, Einstein," he replied. "What tipped you off? Maybe that loud, buzzing sound...?"

"They might be trying to get out. The doors are locked, but when people start leaving..."

"I follow you. Where are you?"

"Ninth floor. I followed them up here."

"Is there any way they got past you?"

"I don't think so. I haven't seen anyone get past me to get to the elevators or the stairs."

"Yeah, and the freight elevator?"

Freight elevator? Oh man! Forgot about that. "Uh…they might be heading down that way."

I heard muffled voices. Joe T was talking to someone else.

"How about the roof?"

"Dunno."

"OK. Freight elevator is probably locked off to the basement after hours. They may be heading down there. Don't let 'em get on the roof." He hung up.

The roof. Where's the exit to the roof? Oh yeah, near the freight elevator. I inched down the cross hallway, looking for any sign of activity.

Each door I checked as I went down the hall was locked, fortunately. There were a lot of doors. How could the store possibly need so many offices? Some of those offices probably contained files, records, inventory or other stuff. Still deathly quiet. Except for that eardrum-shattering alarm, of course.

Down two more hallways and I finally came to what must have been the opposite side of the building. There was a door with a thin pane of glass, and behind it a small room containing the freight elevator. It was open and vacant.

I dialed. The door to the roof, 15 feet away, was closed. I was fairly sure they didn't go that way, otherwise there would be a higher-pitched ringing sound in addition to the buzz of the alarm. I knew that because I set it off accidentally one time, and had to race to the control panel with my key to turn it off, then punch in the four-digit false-alarm code that would be transmitted to First Sentinel. I had only been working there a week and had been looking for the men's room. The large red-bordered sign that said ROOF ACCESS – ALARM WILL SOUND apparently hadn't registered.

"Joe, I'm at the freight elevator. It's still up here on 9. And the door to the roof is secure."

"Yeah, they're not in the basement, which means they probably snuck out down the main stairs when you weren't looking."

"Should I come down? Is there a fire?"

"I don't see any smoke. Stay up there. If the place starts burning down, I'll call you. We're gonna watch the front doors and the loading dock." He hung up.

Great. I sniffed. No smoke so far as I could tell. I went to a wall vent and sniffed again. OK, still nothing. Must be a false alarm.

Heading back toward the main elevators, I saw something. A glare of light spilling out into the hallway. I stopped. Listened. Deep beneath the clanging alarm, a giggle. I took my shoes off and tiptoed down the hall to the door and listened.

I heard another sound. Cards. Someone shuffling cards. They were in that room, playing cards. That seemed illogical, but not much about their actions made much sense at the moment.

The sign on the door said Old Inventory. Must be a white elephant graveyard of some sort.

I didn't want to confront them by myself, but I also didn't want them to get away again. Then I had an idea about how to slow them down until reinforcements arrived.

Doing a fast tiptoe down the hall, I crossed the lobby to the corridor leading to my office. Gathering up the broken mannequin and suitcase, I zipped back to the lobby and carefully placed the mannequin at the corner, leaning against the wall. Then I headed back down toward the door where I saw the light.

Sweating the whole time, moving a millimeter at a time, I placed the suitcase directly in front of the door. Then I slipped back to my office and dialed Joe T.

"Joe T," I whispered, "I think they're up here."

"What? Can't hear ya. Speak up!"

"Can't. Just come up to nine."

"What? Say again. Not hearing much over this alarm," he yelled.

"They're up here on nine," I practically shouted.

"Got it!" As I hung up, it was suddenly quiet again. Actually very quiet. I realized the alarm had gone off, and I was hearing my heartbeat again. Ba-bum ba-bum ba-bum. Like the lead-in to the old Genesis song "Back in New York City."

I was tiptoeing back toward the elevator lobby when I heard a door open, then a thump and several loud shouts. Someone had tripped over the suitcase.

I turned off the lights in the lobby and zipped back down the hall. From my dark hiding spot in a doorway, I could see vague figures approaching from far down the cross hallway. They were whispering something in what sounded like Russian.

Then they stopped. They had spotted the mannequin.

"Is up for you!" Sergei shouted, laughing.

"Time for whipping," Misha added. "You bad boy." Misha flicked the whip, catching the mannequin around the legs and dropping it to the floor. I wasted no time, sprinting down the hall and tackling Sergei. My old high school coach would have been proud of the way I took him down.

What I assumed were Russian expletives filled the air. But I also heard the beautiful sound of an elevator door opening.

Sergei was beating at my head, but I held on. Behind me, I heard another thud, like a body hitting the floor, then the voice of Joe T: "You lose." Two pairs of arms grabbed Sergei from under me and lifted him up. He kicked and screamed, but wasn't going anywhere. I turned around to see Joe T wrapping the whip around Misha's wrists behind his back.

"Hit the lights, wouldya?" Joe T said. I got up and hit the switch and saw him sitting on top of Misha. Two large guys in dark suits were holding Sergei, who was now in cuffs.

"Joe T, man, am I glad to see you."

"Beers. Good job. So these two guys…"

"That's Sergei," I said. "He works here. That's his friend or whatever, Misha. Not sure what his role is here, other than helping Sergei. I'm certain Sergei is behind all the incidents."

The Russians were dragged into the lobby. An elevator opened and a fireman came out in full gear, sporting an axe.

"Smoke?" he asked.

"No. False alarm," Joe T answered. "These two." The firemen looked at the now disheveled pair and said, "Assholes. I was just getting ready to play Santa for my girls." He walked down a hall, checked a couple of smoke monitors, then headed back down the elevator.

The next elevator up contained more men in dark suits, who nodded to Joe T, then took Sergei and Misha away. They were big and burly and looked like undercover cops, but I wasn't sure.

"Thanks," Joe T said.

"For what?" I said. "Just doing my job."

He stared at me a few beats. "I think you know why. My cousin needs someone who looks after his interests without taking advantage of him. Know what I mean?"

I didn't know what he meant. But I nodded anyway.

"Johnny is having a party tonight. He wants you should come up to the house. Have a drink. Know what I'm saying?"

Now that I could understand. Party. Drink. Sure. Whatever.

"Let's go."

"Just a sec," I said, scooting back down the hallway. I located my shoes and slipped them on. I peeked in the door of Old Inventory. The cards were still laid out on top of a crate. Our master criminals were obviously playing go fish. Go figure.

Joe T escorted me into the elevator, arm in arm, like we were going to a prom. Then out the front door, where most of the employees were still assembled, huddled and shivering in their party outfits in the cold, watching the fire crew return their gear to the truck.

"Beers! Ovah heah!" It was Lena, waving frantically from curbside.

Tina zipped up beside me. "You OK?" she asked.

"Fine."

"Man, those dudes were some bad asses. The veeps flipped when they saw what they did on the first floor."

"It's over now," I said.

"Yeah, we saw the cops haul them away. I think it was cops. Must've been plainclothes. They weren't in uniform."

I glanced over at Joe T, who was grinning. "Those were cops, right?" I asked. He just kept grinning.

"Beers! Dawlin', how are ya?" Lena asked.

"Good, good."

"Man, doze perps was a pair, yeah," she said.

Joe T guided me straight toward the silver limo waiting at the curb.

"Where ya goin'?" Lena asked.

I shrugged. "Gotta report to the boss. I'll call you later." We sped away from the scene and headed to the parkway.

THE SCALABRINO RESIDENCE was lit up like a Vegas casino with Christmas lights. It put to shame the meager strings adorning most of the houses along the parkway. Minnesota Nice didn't jibe with Minnesota Gaudy. The 30-foot palms lining the front drive could probably serve as landing lights for craft from Jupiter.

Mercedes sedans snaked down the drive and guests had spilled out onto the expansive side terrace, where fire pits kept it cozy despite the cold. I heard the rhythms of a jazz band playing "Girl From Ipanema" as I walked up the steps to the open front door, pulled along by Joe T. The foyer also was filled with guests, all in formal attire. I definitely felt out of uniform. But at least I was wearing shoes.

Joe T led me into a small room off the study I had visited before. "Wait here," he said, then left, closing the door.

I looked around. There was no furniture, just a lot of paintings on the walls. The floor was covered with what looked like a very old and very expensive Karastan rug. The high ceiling was stamped metal with a large crystal-laden chandelier in the middle.

Johnny Scalabrino opened the door and walked in with open arms, giving me a bear hug. He was in a Santa suit and carrying his putter.

"Mr. Biersovich, welcome to my home. And congratulations."

"Thank you, sir."

"Call me Johnny."

"Yes, sir, Johnny."

"Actually, tonight you can call me Santa. There's some nice party favors if you stick around."

"Yes, sir, Santa."

"You did a good job catching those Russkies," he said. "Joseph told me all about it. I need a man like you on my team." He pulled off his Santa cap and hung it on a wall sconce.

Team? What team? I already worked for him. Was he talking about a softball team? Or maybe a hit squad?

He walked to the wall opposite the door, where he pushed some sort of button with the end of the putter. A hinged painting flew out from the wall, revealing a safe. He twirled the dial and pulled down the handle. I wasn't very close, but I could see several large stacks of money. He took one out and fanned it toward me.

"You earned this," he said, holding it out toward me.

I couldn't move. It looked like a wad of bills big enough to endow a professorship. I was afraid to touch it.

"Sir…"

"Santa!"

"Santa. Sir, I can't take that. I was just doing my job."

He frowned. "Mr. Biersovich, consider this your Christmas bonus." He held my arm and plopped the bills into my palm. "You earned it. Actually, you can also consider it a down payment on your next project." He broke out in a wide grin.

I didn't know what that meant either.

25

Saturday, Dec. 25, Christmas Day
Temperature: 0, light snow; wind chill, -2

And you said what?"
"I was just doing my job."
Freddie shook his head and took another swig of beer.
"Man, you are a case!"

The Christmas gathering at my apartment was in full swing. My siblings had just left with the nieces—past their bedtime—so the serious partying could begin.

There was a knock at the door. It wasn't Rosie, it was Bambi.

"Hey, Beers," she said, holding up a bottle of champagne.

"Ice chest in the kitchen."

Tina was on the couch, laughing with Gerald. Freddie had moseyed over to the hors d'oeuvres to chat up Lena. My young neighbors were poring through my albums, looking for something they recognized. Currently, the Jethro Tull Christmas album was playing, the appropriate music for the occasion.

No Rosie tonight, I thought. She hadn't bothered to return my call. Guess we were finally and completely done. Sigh. Time for another beer.

As I was rooting in the ice chest for a Turbodog, Bambi said, "So tell me, Beers. How did you know it was the Russian guy?"

"Well, I didn't know until yesterday. In fact, it was during the office party," I said. Freddie and Lena wandered closer. "I was trying to piece together all the information I had gathered over the course of the past week or so. Sort of like what I did when reporting.

"All my notes were in my notepad. I was in my office typing up my report—" Lena smiled and blushed a bit when I mentioned that. I wasn't looking in a mirror, but felt like my face was on fire. I took a big swallow of beer. Gerald and Tina came in the kitchen to get another drink.

"I was typing up my report, getting ready to head down to the party. All this stuff was floating around in my head," I said.

"Mannequins." Gerald grimaced. "Shoes."

I peeked over to the den, where my dad obviously was telling Jane a joke, because she was laughing uproariously.

"Snakes." Tina shivered.

"Fire," I added. "The sofa bed. Suitcase. Candy. The initials CC. All that stuff.

"I thought the case was solved when the maintenance guy, Pete, suddenly disappeared. He looked like the main suspect. But I still didn't know what that CC meant. It bothered me.

"Then I went down to the party. I knew there was some unifying thread lying just under my conscious mind. I thought I had to apply common sense to the data, and my logic would find an answer. But I also had to pee."

"Mind over bladder," Freddie quipped. Everyone laughed.

"I was heading down to the men's room near the electronics department, and that's where I figured it out. All the TVs were on and most were playing a Christmas program. One had old rock 'n' roll on. There was a bunch of music videos. Good old '60s and '70s rock songs. One was 'Back in the USSR.' That was the one that gave me the answer."

"Beatles?" Tina asked.

"Yeah, Beatles."

"I don't get it," Freddie said.

"Well, consider this. The perpetrator left his mark on his crimes. We found 'CC' in blue marker all over the place. Lena, Tina and I spent a lot of time trying to figure out what it meant."

"We thought it might be initials," Lena said.

"Right, but I couldn't find anyone with the initials of CC."

"Lots of other things—carbon copy, 'CC Rider'—none of them made much sense," Tina added.

"Because it turned out to be initials," I said.

"Huh? Thought you didn't find anyone wit' doze initials," Lena said.

"Nope. Not with those English initials. The Beatles video showed a Soviet rocket blasting off, painted with the initials CCCP, for the Soviet Union. In Cyrillic, an R looks like a P, and an S looks like a C. Guess whose initials are CC, or what looks like CC, in Cyrillic?"

It was quiet for a beat, until Tina blurted, "Sergei!"

"Sergei Strugatsky, right," I replied. "Look." I fetched my notebook from the coffee table and opened it to the last page. "Here's what his name looks like in Cyrillic." I had copied it from an ID I found that morning while looking through his locker in the maintenance department: Сергей Стругацкие.

"Sonovabitch!" Lena said.

"Yep. He is a son of a bitch. But his criminal days are over, at least at La Scala."

There was a knock at the door. "I'll get that," Bambi said.

"What was the deal with Misha?" Tina asked, then gasped and put her hand over her mouth.

"Just another student, a friend of Sergei's, I suppose."

"No, Beers," Tina said. "I just remembered. That was the name of the guy who sent the gift to Rosie. Remember? The dolls?"

Damnit. Not only had these two succeeded in causing mayhem at the store, they apparently had conspired to break up my relationship with Rosie. And it looks like they succeeded.

"Two sonsabitches," Lena mumbled.

Bambi walked up holding a gift bag. "There wasn't anyone at the door, but there was this," she said, handing it to me. Inside, wrapped in tissue, was a set of nesting dolls. Underneath them was a CD, *Bridge of Sighs* by Robin Trower. Opening the dolls revealed a slip of paper in the smallest one. It said simply "Goodbye."

"Hey, that looks like..." Tina started to say.

"It's from Rosie," I answered. "A kiss-off. I gave her this CD on her birthday." I stuffed everything back in the bag and set it on the counter next to the toaster.

"That's the who," Freddie said. "What's the why?"

Appropriately, my phone rang. It was Joe T. He had lots to tell me. I made notes so I wouldn't forget. When I hung up, I resumed my narrative.

"Remember you were telling me about the ethnic gangs, Freddie?" I said.

"Sure."

"Joe T just got some info out of Misha, who uses surprisingly good English when encouraged. Can hardly detect an accent. Joe T said after a few rounds of encouragement, Misha sang like David Werner." Puzzled looks. "Like…like Elton John." Now they got it.

"Joe T said Misha told them it was some sort of initiation for the Russian gang, Sacred Union. I suppose Misha was going through rush also. He's the one who followed me around, saw Rosie and me on campus, and he sent out all the threatening notes. He even called and threatened me once. He probably followed us all around and we didn't know who he was."

"Pete was also Russian, wasn't he?" Tina asked. "What ever happened to him?"

"Apparently scared off by Sergei," I explained. "Joe T said he must have figured out who was causing all the trouble and threatened to blow the whistle on him, unless Sergei gave him money to keep quiet. Misha got into the act and threatened him. He got scared and split. Probably went back to Russia. Joe T said they couldn't locate Pete.

"A few days ago, Pete disappeared. Walked off the job," I said. "Head of maintenance called me while we were drinking at The Crater, Freddie."

"When you ran out and left me with the tab, you jerk!"

"Yeah, sorry about that. Anyway, he found a pile of damaged clothes and a note written in Cyrillic, with CC on it. Said Pete up and quit. We found incriminating evidence in his locker.

"Joe T says Sergei fessed up. He made it look like Pete did the damage after he had already left."

"What did the note say?" Tina asked.

"It said 'eat me.' We thought it was a note from CC, but it was a note to CC from Pete. Sergei and Misha decided to fix Pete by incriminating him with the damaged clothes and markers in his locker."

"So dey goin' ta jail or what?" Lena asked.

I shrugged. "Or what. Joe T didn't tell me exactly how they got the information, or what was going to happen to them. He just said Sergei and his friend won't be a problem anymore. I wouldn't be surprised if they were wearing cement Brogans in Lake Minnetonka." I let the horrified looks build for a second, then said, "Just kidding. Actually, Joe T said they got the confessions on tape and turned them over to the district attorney. They're in the Hennepin County jail as we speak."

"So you saved Christmas, just like in 'Miracle on 34th Street,' " Tina said.

"More like 'Miracle on Ice,' " I deadpanned.

"Well, I guess things will get back to normal now, and your job gets a lot quieter," Freddie said. "More time for you to sneak out and meet me for lunch. Maybe knock back a few. Especially if you're single again." He wiggled his eyebrows.

"Maybe we gotta tighten up da security, Beers," Lena said.

"What do you mean?" I asked.

"Metal detectors. Guard at the front door. Keep out the crooks and dangerous looking folks," Tina suggested.

"Are you kidding?" Freddie asked. "That will never fly. Can you imagine people being X-rayed just to enter the building? That's absurd."

"I don't think we'll ever get to that point," I said. "Americans value their freedom. And you know Scalabrino doesn't like cameras or police in the store."

"I'm just sayin' we gotta keep out da riff-raff what's tryin' to blow up da place."

"This is an isolated incident, I'm sure. Things will get back to normal," I said.

"And that means you and me, Crater, three-martini lunches. Or beer, as the case may be."

"I don't know, Freddie."

"What? You did your job. Now you can coast."

"There's something else," I said. "I'm going away for a few days."

"What? Where?" Tina asked.

"Mr. Scalabrino—Johnny asked me to do a job for him." Freddie started laughing.

" 'Johnny,' ooooohhhh. You gonna whack someone? Maybe some more Russkies?"

"No, no whacking. But I have to go out of town. Las Vegas."

"Vegas?" Lena said. "No way!"

"Yep. Vegas. Scalabrino wants me to help him with a problem at the Vegas store."

"The one that's connected to the casino?" Tina asked.

"Yeah."

"What's the problem?"

"Not sure. He knows merchandise is walking out the door, but can't figure out who it is. They recently lost a solid jade bathtub, worth about 100 grand. Suspects it's an inside job."

"How do you lose a bathtub?" Freddie asked.

"They don't have detectives in Vegas?" Tina asked.

I shrugged. "He wanted me."

"When ya leave?" Lena asked.

"Right after the first." Lena and Tina looked at each other. Freddie looked crestfallen.

"Man, you get to go to Vegas, expenses paid no doubt, get out of the fricking freezing ass weather, and all you gotta do is get another lucky brainstorm to nab some crooked idiot," Freddie said.

I shrugged again. "Yeah. That pretty much sums it up."

"Damn," Tina said. "Gonna miss you, Beers. Wish we could go with. But I hope you have some fun."

"Give ya a quawtah ta play da slots," Lena said with a smile.

"Well. Don't give it to me yet," I said. "I'm negotiating to bring some assistants along with me. Don't want to split up the team, y'know." I smiled.

Lena and Tina looked at each other, then gave out a big whoop.

"It's not definite," I said. "So just chill. But Johnny seems to like me, so…"

"Beers, you bastard," Freddie said. "You know you need me to go with you."

"Sorry, Freddie. Sports fans wouldn't survive if they couldn't read your immaculate prose every day."

He snorted. "Better make that three sonsabitches," Freddie said, then lifted his bottle to me. "Cheers, Beers."

Someone had changed the music and I heard a new lyric embed itself in my brain:

Tonight I'm gonna party like it's nineteen ninety-nine…

♫

ACKNOWLEDGMENTS

THIS IS A WORK OF FICTION and in no respect should be considered an accurate account of real events occurring in the Twin Cities.

There is no way I can do justice to the brutality of Minnesota winters; you have to be there to understand. And don't go looking for La Scala because it only exists in my frozen cranium, although I understand it's a really nice store and you would enjoy shopping there.

No ethnicities were harmed in the making of this story. Information about ethnic gangs is entirely made up for purposes of moving the narration to what I hope is a logical conclusion.

Likewise, there is no such casino as the one depicted, or a bar called The Crater. I sure wish there was, though.

Thanks to my first editor, Nick Dimassis, for his excellent suggestions to turn my muddy prose into a somewhat presentable finished product. Much appreciation for the work of the Book Architects—Dorothy Molstad, Pat Morris and Linda Strommer—whose early encouragement launched me on this quest to turn my manuscript into a published novel.

Many thanks also to Aimée Bissonette, whose knowledge of book contracts was invaluable; that world frightens me. Laura LaRose, thank you for providing a crucial clue that I hadn't considered. Also kudos to Dana Davis for her mastery of the English language, which I tend to mangle at times.

I wouldn't have begun this project if not for the early inspiration of Brother Eldon Crifasi, whose guidance and sense of humor in high school English class spurred me to continue reading and writing in some fashion for a lifetime.

Finally, thanks to my wife, Jeanne Anne "Gigi" LaRose, who always entertains me and gives me the space to pursue my flights of fancy, and to all at Number 9.

Beers Detective Agency #1

Discover the roots of the Jim Biersovich story. *First Case of Beers*, the initial title in the series, introduces Beers, Lena, Tina, Freddie and the rest of the wacky crew trying to keep the ship of commerce La Scala afloat.

It's Christmas season at the turn of the Millennium. A vandal is causing mayhem in the department store where Beers is head of security.

Although he's not really qualified—his training was as a sportswriter—Beers is charged with finding out who is assaulting Johnny Scalabrino's business. A cryptic clue left at the scene of each incident baffles the amateur sleuth. In the end, his knowledge of classic rock music reveals the key to nabbing the culprits.

First Case of Beers, second edition, was published by Liquid Rabbit Publishing in 2020. It is available in paperback and e-book from Amazon and BarnesAndNoble.com.

Beers Detective Agency #2

Bet on Beers follows the crew to Las Vegas, where priceless artifacts, including a jade bathtub, have gone missing at the casino store owned by Johnny Scalabrino. Once again, Beers and company are called on to find the perpetrators while navigating the dangerous, high-stakes world of gambling.

This time, murder is on the agenda, and Beers suspects he is out of his league. The heists seem impossible, particularly the theft of the bathtub. A parallel assault on the casino's gambling operation complicates the investigation. Once again, a musical solution presents itself and Beers is able to answer the riddle of this baffling case.

Bet on Beers, second edition, was published by Liquid Rabbit Publishing in 2020. It is available in paperback and e-book from Amazon and BarnesAndNoble.com.

Beers Detective Agency #3

When the head of a sportswriter, a former co-worker at the Minnesota Herald, appears in the store, Beers discovers a long list of suspects. Everyone wanted Harry Devin dead, or so it seems.

Beers Ahead finds the brain trust enmeshed in a macabre investigation that lends an even creepier vibe to the Halloween season. Complications distract Beers from his task—mainly oversight of a construction project and a new honey to woo.

A mysterious stranger, a secret correspondent, a vintage chapeau and an unpublished manuscript are some of the elements the team encounters as the complex scheme unfolds. But Beers always has music to guide him down the right path.

Beers Ahead was released by Liquid Rabbit Publishing in 2018. It is available in paperback and e-book from Amazon and BarnesAndNoble.com.

Beers Detective Agency #4

Jim Biersovich is sent overseas on what figures to be an easy assignment: to scout locations in London for a future La Scala department store. But nothing is ever simple for our amateur detective, as he soon discovers in *Beers Abroad*.

With his unofficial assistant, Lena, along for research duties, Beers soon encounters issues with the preferred location. Not only is there trouble with the owners, but also with the security of the site, as murder soon comes into play. Repeatedly.

As the bodies pile up, Beers is dispatched to investigate the owners' reluctance to sell. The disappearance of one of the key figures complicates the negotiations. In the midst of the dilemma, Beers' reporter buddy Freddie arrives on a working junket, throwing more chaos into the mix. Beers once again is called on to muster his cunning and intuition, along with a bit of help from his friends and his music, to solve the case.

Beers Abroad was released by Liquid Rabbit Publishing in 2019. It is available in paperback and e-book from Amazon and BarnesAndNoble.com.

Beers Detective Agency #5

The tragedy of 9/11 turns the world upside down for department store security chief Jim Biersovich in **Beers Tapped Out**. In addition to a host of new safety considerations, Beers is confronted with a murder in store and assaults on the business from every angle. La Scala owner Johnny Scalabrino is forced to reassess both his lifestyle and store's policies to cope with the new reality. Hidden foes are attempting to sabotage his business, compelling him to pull out all stops in an effort to protect his livelihood.

A street project in front of the store creates ongoing mayhem. Caught in the center of the maelstrom, as usual, is Beers, who faces his own life when his girlfriend, Emmie, flees in fright. Is this the final straw for Beers, his exit strategy from La Scala?

Beers Tapped Out was released by Liquid Rabbit Publishing in 2020. It is available in paperback and e-book from Amazon and BarnesAndNoble.com.

Beers Detective Agency #6

Beers' world has been shattered by the events of the last case. Not only is he single again, but he also finds himself adrift in a new environment. No longer an employee of La Scala, Jim Biersovich finds a job in the music field, as a late-night deejay for a blues station in New Orleans, where his friend Lena now resides. In **Bayou Beers**, he strikes up a friendship with another deejay and part-time musician, Phineas Stoke.

When Phineas is murdered, Beers finds himself thrust into the middle of another investigation, this time fueled by his own desire to see justice done and assist the family. As he soon discovers, the process of playing detective is complex and exhausting, with roadblocks to navigate and more than a few viable suspects.

Beers enlists the aid of some trusted friends and hangs a shingle, formalizing what he had been doing for the past couple of years. Beers Detective Agency is born. Work starts flowing in, but the main job is learning the identity of his friend's killer.

Bayou Beers was released by Liquid Rabbit Publishing in 2021. It is available in paperback and e-book from Amazon and BarnesAndNoble.com.

Beers Detective Agency #7

The impossible happens. Freddie insists he's going to get married. Not only that, but it's a destination wedding to Iceland, of all places.

As his best bud and supposed best man, Jim "Beers" Biersovich goes along for the ride, thinking it's some massive prank. But hey, free trip to an exotic locale. Can't pass that up. Lena and Tina are also in on the festivities, along with Beers' former flame, Emmie Slayton. It promises to be an exciting ride, even if no wedding rings are exchanged at the end of the junket.

But the wedding is all too real, and so is the tragedy when a member of the wedding party turns up dead. Is it foul play or just an accident? And it's not the only death that infringes on the happy times in *Beers on Ice*.

With the whole Beers Detective Agency team in attendance, the trio is once again obliged to work out the solution and figure out whether a killer is in their midst.

Beers on Ice was released by Liquid Rabbit Publishing in 2022. It is available in paperback and e-book from Amazon and BarnesAndNoble.com.

Follow PM LaRose on Facebook. More information on Jim Biersovich can be discovered at the Beers Detective Agency on Facebook.

Made in the USA
Monee, IL
07 September 2022